Escape

From

Manhattan

By
Georgia Love

Table of Contents

Chapter 1

The television in the lounge was blaring away. No one was watching it as all the guests were busy talking to their partners or on their cells. Candy wanted to watch but her job didn't allow her the time. It was the Johnathon Show and he had an amazing panel today. Dr. Tim Bears-Den a Nuclear Physicist, who had just won this year's Nobel Peace Award, Grant Stallion, a Futurist who had written another book on his predictions and Aunt Amie Goldman, one of New York's most respected Psychics and a Russian Scientist.

My Aunt Amie is on this panel. "I sure wish I could listen to it. How exciting!" she whispered to herself

They were discussing the Russian's research of the Forth Dimension over the last one-hundred years. They had been able to develop this new science of scalar energetics in all areas of life. They were discussing terms. Energetics was the area that dealt with matter, They had created new super weapons. Bioenergetics dealt with living matter. Psycho-energetics dealt with the human brain and its interactions.

"Would I ever love to listen to that program today?" Candy sighed.

The show continued with Psychic, Aunt Amie Goldman adamantly stating ,"The reason the United States is so far behind the Russians, in this research was and is the religious right. They are afraid of the paranormal."

Grant Stallion seconded her. He agreed that America had not researched Nikola Tesla's ideas for over a hundred years. Russian scientists had eagerly studied all of Tesla's work. They eagerly researched Radiant Energy and the Forth Dimension. USA's Powerful Oil and Gas Companies had silenced Tesla's research. He had wanted to give free energy for every country. These companies did not want the American public to know about an infinite supply of free energy from what he called the Forth Dimension.

The Lounge's manager turned the station to sports so that was all Candy heard.

"Good evening Sir, My name is Candy. I will be your host for the evening. Can I take your order sir?" she asked. Candy was sexy with full breasts and auburn haired. She was dressed in a black mini skirt, black nylons, and three-inch high heels. She was a Goldie Hawn double for sure.

Candy looked at the disheveled balding man sitting in front of her. She wondered why he wasn't at home comfortable in front of his TV. Instead, he was at the most prestigious lounge in the city. The top brass of the Oil and Gas Industry used this as their refuge in Calgary, Canada. He was so out-of-place? Why was he here? She wondered. Why did he look familiar?

He gruffly responded with a "Yes, let me know when two middle aged women come in. Would you have a small board room for our meeting?"

Walter Brown had picked this exclusive social club, as it was more than a lounge and known for its famous Boardrooms that were noise insulated. One could talk privately on any subject. He had discovered this place through his years of law practice.

"Yes, Boardroom Discovery is available and perhaps you would like me to bring your menus, now so you can settle here for the evening?" asked Candy

From experience, he found women were always late. I wonder if these women will be on time.

"Ah, there they are now! We'll make great progress tonight." Walter Brown commented.

"Good evening! Was your trip pleasant? I have looked forward to this all day!" offered Walter

Joanne was a willowy brunette about fifty-five years old, wrinkles and gray hair at the temples. Her glasses rode down on her nose. She looked like a stereotype of an old librarian.

Susan was overweight with large breasts. She could have used an uplifting support bra. Her walk was Military. Had she just stepped out of a World War two movie? She was very rigid and her wrinkled face looked like it was chiseled in stone. An officious operating room Nurse, for the last thirty years showed in her manner.

"The flight in from Saskatoon was fine and we are all set to work out the details of our little Care Home." Susan stated

"Well, Walter I really must congratulate you on your attention to detail. Things were as you said. No one ever suspected a thing." Joanne chuckled

"I couldn't believe how easy it was?" She continued

"So everything is ready for our opening of our care home. We will have the place full within the month." whispered Susan eager with excitement at the prospect of their scheme realized.

They would have more money than they ever dreamed, when their efforts paid off. Foolproof! They had bought an old duplex in the poorer side of town; they didn't want any attention from anyone. They had taken out the center wall making it a six-bedroom care home. Result was a large living room and dining area, a working kitchen, an office and six bedrooms.

Upstairs was perfect! It was so low-keyed that no one would ever suspect what was really going on there. They could run their business without any concern at all.

Walter Brown, who had started this scheme confidently said, "I will be in court on Monday with our first client, I have convinced them that their mother will be comfortable and secure in our quiet, and discreet care home. With our security devices, no one will be able to reach her.

She has dementia and from New York. They are a wealthy family, who want to hide her. The embarrassment to the family is unthinkable. Marie Rothman is her name. Her daughters are ready to pay even $10,000 a month to hide her. New York Socialites who don't want her condition discovered. I think they wish to have her move in next week." Walter added

"Imagine starting our Care Home with three residents, especially with them willing to pay such large sums of money." exclaimed Joanne

Candy couldn't help but hear these last statements from Walter and Joanne while she was setting their table and immediately became concerned.

She had been best friends with Rachel and Sophie Rothman since kindergarten. Marie was their mother. They were sending her to Calgary to hide her condition. This did not make any sense at all. How could her daughters have changed that much? To hide their mother? Marie and her mother, Maureen were like sisters.

Candy remembered that she had her voice-activated tape recorder in her purse. To help her deal with the pending loss of her Mother, they had taped all of their conversations in the last three months of her life. It had helped Candy get through the lonely days after her death. Her mother was only sixty years old. She was too young to die.

Candy had to hear more so she quickly retrieved it and placed it where she would be able to tape their conversation.

Walter Brown continued with the second resident who would be arriving for the first week. The family had contacted him behind the scenes and compelled him to consider taking their Mother into their Care Home. He continued with his startling information.

"One of her sons is very high up in the 'The Dragons' an Organized Crime Syndicate and the family want to protect her from him as he wants custody of her. He wants his inheritance. The family has fought over her for years. Little do they realize that we can change her will and slide some of her money over to us? She is under our control to do with her as we please. They have given us 'Power of Attorney'! She is just one of many that will want our Private Care Home. Plus, do you know how many other families have the same need for a quick end to their parents, siblings, and who ever come into my Court Room?" He whispered, with the knowing that all is coming together.

"Well what are we going to call the Residence?" whispered Susan,

"Something simple, perhaps called after one of our children or our pet; something simple that would be easy for people to remember." suggested Joanne

Susan exhausted from the trip looked burned out. She slumped in her chair and stated, "Why I didn't do this long ago. I could have made so much money so easily, but I suppose this will work and in a few years we can retire."

Joanne chuckled and added, "You aren't the only one who is pleased with this, but it is only possible because we've met. We can see the ease of making a bundle now and for many years to come."

Joanne, Office Administrator of the Registrars' Office sheepishly grinned and chuckled. She whispered, "I have wanted to do this for so many years, but I had to wait until you two came along. I have six people scheduled for Court this coming week that need exactly what we have to offer. These families need a discreet place manned by simple care aids that would never suspect a thing. In addition, a Coordinator needed to manage the home.

We only need Susan to come in to look at the residents once a week and check their medications and time sheets for the care aids. What could be easier at $10,000? A month from each reside an average of $60,000 per month. No taxes on all of this. Of course, we will have to have the odd resident paying a normal amount of $3,000. Gravy train is here! Its' incredible!"

Joanne excused herself to go to the bathroom to freshen up. "Be back in a few minutes."

"How did you meet Joanne?" asked Walter as he leaned over the table and whispered to Susan.

"A conference last year; Joanne is Harry Hall's Aunt. He is the adopted son of one of our new arriving residents, Mrs. Ruth Smith-Schultz, a widow. She owns the south and west land area of the Saskatoon Airport. She is worth millions! According to Joanne, Harry will inherit all of this.

That huge piece of land is worth billions when developed. All that money will be ours! It will be easy to get rid of Harry once he has the land and is our business partner." Susan exclaimed

"Why would her son be willing to do away with his mother?" asked Walter quietly, who seemed shocked that a son would be so eager to have his own mother done away with.

She was already 83 years old; surely, he could be a little patient and wait for her to die on her own, which at this age would be not very long, anyway.

"Well it seems that she is not his real Mother and that Harry Hall has hated her for years for adopting him when he was a baby. Apparently, she had lost two sons with Cystic Fibrosis. They had both died within a six-month span. This devastated Ruth. She had no emotional support from her alcoholic husband. A friend suggested that she adopt an infant and since money was no problem, Ruth went ahead with the adoption. She hoped to have a son, who would love her and be a comfort to her in her old age.

Unfortunately, the alcoholic husband, Robert Jones took to beating him as a child and Ruth let it happen. She didn't protect him as she was so afraid of Robert. Harry left home at the age of sixteen and didn't have anything to do with her for many years. He didn't even come back into her life when she finally had the courage to divorce Robert Jones.

For a while, Ruth was alone and then she finally married a bachelor, Warner Schultz, a wealthy rancher, who owned acres of Northern Alberta land. Harry realized that he was her only son and he would inherit everything.

At that point, Harry decided to come back into her life under the pretense of a dutiful and loving son. Harry has done well for himself. He must have really hated his adopted mother, Ruth as he even went to the trouble of finding his biological mother and taking her last name of Hall. Harry is now determined to avenge his childhood and get even with her for his horrid childhood."

Walter stunned by all of this information questioned, "Wow that is a remarkable story."

Susan continued,"Harry Hall's natural mother, Marie Hall had married into money and had no problem sending him to University. He has climbed the ladder to a prestigious position in the government. He doesn't need the money. His salary is in the six digits. Harry has married well and now had three children of his own. No one would ever suspect him of being part of a scheme to murder his own adopted mother.

Joanne is very close to Harry and delighted to play this little game and can hardly wait to see all the money that will so easily be ours when Ruth is dead." Susan whispered

Just then, Joanne returned from the bathroom and she was humming a tune. "So what are we going to call this Care Home anyway? Susan why don't you name it after your daughter? Brenda's Care Home sounds nice and simple. I really do think that this is a good name for our little Care Home that will help so many people realize their financial dreams." Joanne suggested

Walter exclaimed, "My god, we will be so busy next week. Have you hired anyone yet to care for these people? Have you found a Coordinator? Have you received any resumes yet for this placement? Have you hired a nurse yet to train the Care Aids for Brenda's Care Home? Yes! Brenda's Care Home is the perfect name for it."

Susan offered a list of Philippine Care Aids that a friend of hers had lent her and stated," There are four young girls ready to start immediately. All are recent arrivals from the Philippines. Most of them can barely speak English. My friend brings them in as cheap labor promising them landed immigrant status if they work for three years for her."

"That's great! They won'tunderstand what is going on." Walter added and sighed with relief

"Even better there is one resume from a middle-aged woman, Judy Johnson, Licensed Practical Nurse, who has not nursed in many years. She has managed a few businesses. I think she can take charge of the place. She is ideal! She isn't connected to anyone here. She is from Ontario. She seems very naïve and has a pleasant manner. People like her when I phoned for her references.

I think she's just the right person to manage the place. She'll never understand what we are about as she has been away from Nursing for many years. She won't understand what we are doing. Plus she will be too busy managing the Care Aids to even consider for a minute anything else." added Susan

"My next person to admit to our Care Home is another woman, who the family is fighting over as she too is worth millions. Her name is Joyce Hillman, a cancer victim on oxygen. The family wants her in a Private Care Home, as her oldest son is Schizophrenic and has made one attempt on her life already. They have gone through enough media attention. They want a secure place, where she'll be safe from him and their names out of the newspapers." Walter stated

Yes, soon the place will be full and we'll have a waiting list. We don't even have to offer furniture as they want to supply their own furniture. It feels more like home to them. Ruth wants to bring her organ. Can you believe that? It just gets better and better." exclaimed Susan.

"March 26th, 2001 is the opening day of Brenda's Care Home. I'll finish the last of the legal proceedings tomorrow. I'll be making a numbered company to protect the home and only the necessary people will know the place by the name of Brenda's Care Home." Walter stated with his smug lawyer like flair.

Susan and Joanne hugged each other and toasted Walter. This would give them more money than they ever dreamed possible. Soon they would be living in luxury, without a care in the world. It seemed surreal that it could be this simple. The need was there for people to dispose of their unwanted family burdens. Parents with any of these ailments;

12

Dementia, Alzheimer, Heart Failure, Old Age, Comas, or Strokes needed care.

Walter and Joanne in their legal positions could choose the best clientele for Brenda's Care Home without anyone ever suspecting their intentions. Nurse Susan would never again have to work night shift or do all the menial tasks that nursing entailed. She was free to oversee their Care Home. The hardest work that she would do now is attending Walter's Court Room. She would be quick to introduce future clients to their wonderful Care Home. The turn over would be often. They could offer the best service to their real clientele.

The Home never suspected as the average time for most seniors, when put into a Care Home is six months. No questions! They would make sure to take only people who had a need for their facility.

Since it was only a six-bed facility, it didn't even have to go through the high standards of most Private Nursing Facilities. It was foolproof! Not a thing to worry about and the mercy killing could go on and on indefinitely.

They soon left and Candy ran to her tape deck. Had it recorded their conversation?

Thank God it had done the recording; all fifty-eight minutes of it. She had no time to listen to it now, but when she got home, she would certainly listen to it.

She had one more shift to do before she would be back in her Nursing Program. Had she heard that Walter would be coming back again tomorrow night to the lounge? Yes, he had booked the Discovery Boardroom.

Candy hurried home anxious to hear what was on that tape. She had some idea as the odd sentence here and there startled her so. She had gone into Nursing because she wanted to help people; not exploit them in any way. It was hard to think that some Nurses could be so cold and callous. Did she hear right? She was so busy with four tables to serve and that banquet room. Could she have misunderstood the conversation?

Her own mother had passed away last month with Ovarian Cancer

13

and she had dropped out of her Nursing Program to stay home and care for her mother. She had caught a few startling sentences the night before with the table in the Board Room. The words didn't make sense to her. Was she hearing right? A Care Home intended to quicken death for the residents. She could not have heard it correctly.

Walter had scheduled the same Board Room for tomorrow night to meet Harry Hall.

Candy was going to tape their conversation again. She would hear and see all that she could. Could there really be Care Homes like that profiting on seniors and deliberately and intentionally causing people to die quicker?

How awful! It was too soon after the harsh death of her beloved mother. It hit her hard! Was there anything that she could do about it?

Candy ran her tub climbed into it as she had done many nights before to listen to her Mother's voice on the tape deck. Tonight was different! She already knew that this would not be a comforting thing, but the opposite. Candy turned on the tape deck and after listening to the meeting for five minutes jumped out of the tub. What could she do about all of this? These people were wealthy and capable of anything. She steeled herself to listen to the entire tape recording.

The tears ran down her cheeks to think that Marie Rothman would die in this cold heartless place. How could her childhood friends be so cruel to their own mother? She finally went to sleep after swallowing Melatonin pills and chamomile tea. Candy woke before the alarm clock went off and quickly remembered the tape recording. This was her last night to work at this place. Candy arrived early for work and settled herself to handle tonight's venue.

Chapter 2

Walter Brown sat at the same table as the night before; hunched over scowling and anxiously waiting for Harry Hall to join him for drinks and supper.

Candy switched tables with her teammate and feigned eagerness as his server. She asked, "Good evening, glad to see you again. Do you wish to go to your Board Room now? Or do you wish to stay here for a while?"

Harry Hall swaggered in to the Boardroom. He was so proud of himself. He had just finished another difficult assignment. He was head of a task force, which was part of the Employees' Insurance. It was a secret job! He dealt with Government Workers, injured at work or related illnesses like Cancer that Fireman get when exposed to chemicals. It was his job to end some of their lives discreetly. In addition, he saved the Government money.

Vehicle accidents, drownings, or other various causes for his clients now paralyzed or so debilitated that their lives didn't have "quality of life" or so he thought. He was proud that he could help them end their tortured existence quickly. He was able to hasten the inevitable and he was proud of himself that he was saving the government money as it was expensive keeping them alive with hospital care and on machines like Respirators and Oxygen tanks etc.

All he had to do was burn their esophagus chemically and they would not be able to drink or eat again. They would just starve to death and in their fragile conditions; it was usually a fast end to their life. In addition, they couldn't talk to anyone about his actions as their throats didn't allow them to talk.

Walter was aware of this part of his work, as Harry's Aunt Joanne had told him about it. She had been there years ago, when he started this mercy killing. At first, he had found it hard and confided in her that he didn't know how he was going to do it.

Walter seemed eager to meet Harry Hall as he wanted to make sure that his plan to end Ruth Smith-Schultz' life quickly was definite. Walter was still amazed that Harry could wish to do this to his mother.

Harry Hall sat down, leaned forward, and stated, "I just wish to do, what I do for all of my clients; make a quick death for Ruth. Don't worry I'm committed. I've already contacted City Hall in Saskatoon and began the surveying of the land for the Mall. It will bear her name. I'm dealing with the Surveyors for the residential areas. Timing is critical. Although I have Power of Attorney, I need to move quickly. The infrastructure needs to be done before winter hits again and we are detained for another year."

Walter relaxed for the first time in weeks. He was on edge as his whole life and his future career depended on Harry's commitment. It was a done deal!

Harry breathed a relieved sigh and whispered," Glad you're on board; things will go smoothly and by next year at this time we will be on the Queen Sandra Cruise Ship relaxing in the sun."

Harry chuckled and continued, "You'll be part of an exciting cruise. You'll meet people that will change your life for ever there. Have you ever heard of the intangible elite group of our world known as the 1% who control our world?"

16

Walter replied, "That is just a farce, that group doesn't really exist. Its' all fabricated for magazines like the National Enquirer. Hype! Are you a conspiracy junky?"

Harry started to laugh, "You will be meeting with these people soon as they fill your Court Room. They are the people that make up 1% of the wealth in our world. They cannot afford to have their demented seniors in established Government Care Homes, where educated Nurses and Doctors work. In their senile ramblings, too much information will get out to the masses. They've wanted a place to dispose of their elderly discreetly, no matter what the cost. It would bring too much attention to them if they started dying off. There would be Police investigations, newspaper and scandal magazines exposing them."

Harry continued,"Our Care Home is their perfect solution. We can make millions of dollars providing this kind of privacy and security. I will prove this to you. Do you have any American money on you?"

Walter checked his wallet, "Since I have Credit Cards, I don't carry cash any more; let alone American money."

Harry called Candy over and asked, "Can you find us some American money. Here's a $100. Canadian. Don't worry about the change."

Candy intrigued now, "Why do they need American money?"

Harry loved showing off and so he decided to play a game with them. He couldn't resist the opportunity to show off what he had found out recently.

He proceeded to fold the American bills a certain way showing the Twin Towers in New York destroyed by two Jet planes and the second folded bill showed the White House damaged and on fire.

Candy looked in horror and amazement that someone would find this entertaining. She was an American citizen with a working visa. She loved her country and here was this strange man showing her this bizarre terrifying event.

Harry laughed, "Sept 11th 2001 this will happen, and the American people will believe it is terrorists from the Middle East that are behind it,

Candy left the room shaken to her core. Was her tape deck recording this information? She really hoped that she had set the machine properly as who would believe such a plan.

Walter leaned forward and whispered, "What does that have to do with our Care Home for heaven's sakes?"

Harry laughed a belly laugh, "From then on the 1% of the world's wealthy folk will be looking for our Care Home; a place to stash their unwanted seniors. Life will become very intense, as there will be another war, with the Middle East. The 1% of our world want to concentrate the wealth even more and this will do it. They wish to secure the money that their older relatives are keeping from them. Our Care Home will supply that need for them so discreetly."

Walter leaned back in his chair utterly amazed "Are you sure this will happen on Sept 11th ? That is only a few months away! How many people will die? This seems so bizarre! For God's sake can anyone stop this and why would this elite consider doing this. What purpose? It just does not make any sense!" exclaimed Walter

Harry smirked and repeated, "This is just the beginning so they can wage war on the Middle East, where there is so much Oil. It is important to control this supply of Oil and its' necessary to enrage the American People. A Terrorist Attack in New York! So many dead; they will demand justice and war will begin which will destroy their economy. The control of the people will tighten. They will once again increase their wealth as they supply ammunitions to the Armed Forces.

I found out about all of this two years ago, when I was on a cruise with my recent wife. It was the Queen Sandra Cruise Ship, which we will be on next year at this time. One of the elite joined me. As we discussed our work, he revealed to me his part of this supposed terrorism. He stated that he was originally from England, a Duke of something; I can't remember who exactly, but it was quite clear that he knew what he was talking about. I told him about my mercy killing and he thought that I should join him as they could use a mercenary like me."

Walter shook his head in disbelief, but as the minutes ticked on, he acknowledged that all Harry was saying made sense.

Candy wished she could check the voice-activated tape deck under their table. Was it recording their conversation? In addition, she had witnessed the money folding of the American bills. In fact, she now realized that this information was even more important than the tape she had listened to last night. Candy loved spy movies and intrigue but she never thought she would ever be involved in anything so bizarre.

Candy was horrified by the occasional parts of their conversation of Sept 11th, They were going to bomb the Twin Towers in New York? The White House? As their intentions came clearer and clearer in her mind, she determined to tell someone what was about to occur. Candy realized that she must not let them know that she was hearing them. She feigned a happy smile and even flirted with Harry. She must not let on what they were talking about shocked her. She joked that she was glad that she lived in Calgary.

She also realized that she was in danger being anywhere around these two men. They were the most dangerous type of criminal. Psychopaths! Her Nursing studies had involved researching Psychotic patients and other disorders. She recognized them for what they were.

Candy had spent many weekends with her beloved Grandmother, who had survived the Jewish Holocaust. She had listened intently to her Grandmother's stories of courage. There was one person she could confide in, Aunt Amie Goldman. She had been a baby, when their family had escaped Poland. Aunt Amie had Jewish connections in New York. Surely, they would listen to what she had just heard.

How she wished that her Grandmother, Hannah were still alive. She would know what to do with this information. Still shaking in her high heels, Candy reached under the table where she had positioned the tape recorder. Yes! It had taped their entire conversation.

Candy said goodbye to the other staff and her boss. She quickly filled out the last of her receipts, balanced her cash, and closed off her shift. She left work early and went home to pack and fly to New York. Thank God, this was her last night to work there.

She was able to catch the last plane leaving Calgary. She scheduled a taxi and before she knew it, she was boarding the plane. This information was too important to leave to a phone call or email. She had to speak personally with someone who would know what to do.

Rabbi Samuel had always been kind to her as a child and perhaps he would take her seriously and this event stopped. Candy was well aware that horrible things happened to innocent people; but this time she could do something or at least she could attempt to affect a different outcome.

On the plane, she gave a relieved sigh and settled into her seat. New York was not that far away. In a few hours, precious friends would pick her up.

Perhaps she could feel safe again. For now, she was going to have a few moments' sleep; but the scene of the pending crash for Sept 11th flashed into her mind. There was no way that she could sleep on a plane after seeing that tragic image.

Chapter 3

Candy had suffered with Dyslexia as a child and had developed a wonderful photographic memory. When she was on the plane, she reached into her bag for her note pad. A good artist, she specialized in sketching faces. She easily sketched both Harry and Walters's faces. She wanted to remember what they looked like.

She had taken the time to find out their names and their phone numbers. This information was in the Club's appointment book. She had made sure to write that information in a safe place.

She wanted to make sure of these important details. She needed them to back up what she would offer Rabbi Samuel. He was only thirty-three years old, but after listening to Jewish survivors, he would be able to handle this information. He would guard it until the right people told.

Why was she the one to get this information? Why her? All she wanted to do was get back into Nursing and get on with her life. It had been six months since she had been at University. Time was marching on. Now, this prevented her from getting back to a normal way of life. She would do the right thing as she always had. Even as a child; she did not play like the other children but wanted to do meaningful things.

When she thought about it, she was the perfect one to have this handed to her. She would not waste time feeling sorry for herself. She determined to make a difference. She arrived in New York and it hit her; the realization that those beautiful towers would soon be dust. The tears smacked her cheeks and the harsh March wind buffeted her.

What if! No one listened to what she had to say. What if! She could not stop these horrible people. Were they people? She had wondered who really was in charge of our Planet. since no one really seemed to care about the environment. Candy wanted answers to her zillion questions, but then she had always had so many questions.

An alcoholic had captained an Oil Freighter. Why? They knew the risks. He destroyed the coastline of Alaska when it crashed. That did not make any sense either!

The more she thought about how our Planet was managed; the more real the words were that she had heard from these men.

She had been the top student in High School even winning a Bursary to attend the Nursing Program at Calgary's University. She excelled at all she attempted. She looked like a movie star and with that kind of beauty it was hard for people to take her seriously. People wondered why she wanted to become a Nurse.

What would her mother think of this? How she wished she could go to her for advice. Candy looked through her address book and found her cousin, Heather.

She dialed the number and Heather answered the phone. Heather pleased to hear from her asked, "Why didn't you call me sooner, of course, I will come and get you."

Why had she come now? Many questions! Yes, she would be there in an hour and she was very happy that she had come. There was a family gathering that night and everyone would be happy to see her. Candy sat down to wait. She felt agitated. She scanned the Airport looking at all the people wondering which person would be the type that could hi-jack an Airplane.

Finally, her eyes spotted a paperback book abandoned on the seat across from her. In boredom, she reached out and picked it up. "Synchronicity!" Whatever did that mean? She opened the cover and found a message written that amazed her. "Everything happens for a reason; nothing is coincidence." This is exactly what she needed to see and she felt like someone had just given her a big hug. Her precious mother had always said that to her. Even as a child, she wondered what it meant. Of all things, here in this busy Airport was this book with maybe some answers.

Candy breathed a big sigh! She relaxed and continued to read story after story about unusual events that seemed offered by the Universe or by something bigger than what she had found lately. Ever since her Mother's death, she had longed for someone to talk with that understood spiritual stuff and now when she needed it the most; this little book forgotten by its owner was in her hands.

Maybe her Mother had found some way to give her this book. It seemed like a miracle to Candy. Totally lost in the book, Heather found her in a more relaxed state. Candy had always known that Heather was a chatterbox and today was no exception. She went on about this evening's event. A special occasion of the 50th wedding anniversary for one of Poland's surviving couples.

Maybe there would be people attending, who could help her understand those two wretched men's horrid conversation. They seemed to delight in people's death. She had to find someone who could help her understand this and she had to change things.

"Would Rabbi Samuel be there tonight?" questioned Candy but Heather didn't hear her as the blaring of a horn from a nearby taxi drowned out her voice.

Candy found herself lugging the suitcase and her overnight bag into the foyer of the Apartment. They were downtown New York as Heather was a dress designer and the fashion world thrived in the center of this.

She whispered to herself, "How do I get my family out of New York for Sept 11th? Will anyone listen to me, when I try to let them know what is coming?"

She struggled into the elevator and then down the long hall. Heather ran ahead and hurried back to help her with her suitcase. She questioned, "How long was she going to stay?"

Candy didn't know what to tell her. She did know that she would not leave until she had found a way to warn her family, friends and who ever would listen to her. More importantly, maybe, she could find a way to stop it. Could she get to the right perople. This was not the time to talk about any of this; she had to wait until the right time to tell her awful secret. She felt like the Jewish people in Germany before Hitler threw them into the Concentration Camps. The Ones that knew what was coming and no one would listen to them.

Yes, her Grandmother had told her that she had visions and dreams of Hitler's schemes and when she tried to warn her family, no one would listen to her. It had made her so sad that no matter how much she warned them; they just ignored her. Was this to be her fate? No way to warn her loved ones?

Candy vowed to find a way to wake up her loved ones. Would the Holocaust people be wiser and more receptive to warnings?

Heather asked, "Would you like me to run a bath for you and maybe some tea and toast?"

Candy nodded a weak yes and collapsed on the bed. She hadn't slept in more than twenty hours and exhausted she collapsed.

In the lounge, she was concerned that they might notice that she listened to them and that she had heard their conversation. It was a relief that she was far away from Calgary and safe at her cousins. They had no way of finding her here or how could she be sure of that. In her hurry to get away, she had not been careful to protect herself. She had bought her ticket with her Credit Card. If they had concern about her, they would know she was in New York.

Candy quickly corrected herself. She whispered to herself," I am just a cocktail waitress; they would never even consider for a moment that I could do anything. I am merely nothing more than a bug on the wall to them. No importance!"

Sleep over took her and the bath, tea and toast would just have to wait. They would not care about her; she was merely a barmaid. Nothing for them to worry about!

Candy slept for eight hours lost in dreams of younger days with her parents skiing. They were having such a great time. Heather called her name gently and let her know that she should get up now so she would have time to get ready for the Anniversary Party tonight. A light meal and a glass of wine were waiting for her. A comforting bubble bath poured. Aromatherapy was Heather's strong point. The place smelled like

24

spring; lilac time again!

Candy settled into the tub with her Tape Deck. She turned on the tape deck and listened. She forgot the time and that she had to get ready for this party.

The reality of the coming event for New York hit her; she was spellbound listening to the tape. Like a rabbit frozen in time, while the fox pounces.

Heather kept calling her and telling her to hurry. Time was passing and she wanted to do her hair for her just like the old days. Normal and happy with life, Heather bubbled about whom they would be seeing tonight. How excited all the family would be in seeing her.

She realized that Calgary's horrible cold weather had taken the joy of life out of her. After her mother's death, she was all alone there. She had worked long hours and had not noticed how alone she was. She had kept busy and the time passed quickly. Spring will come soon and it will be easier she kept telling herself.

March the 28th was today's date; less than six months before Sept 11th. That was not long at all. There was no time to lose if she was to help anyone. However, tonight she would enjoy herself. She would live in the moment!

Climbing out of the tub, Candy knew that she would make a difference. Somehow, she would meet the right people and explain what she had heard. With the back up of the two tapes, surely they would listen to her and not think that she was suffering from some mental problem like Histrionic Disorder. She had studied this disorder in the Psychology part of her Nursing Program.

After all, she had just lost her mother in her sudden death and one week later, her beloved Spaniel had died. Yes, she could see it now some Psychiatrist labeling her with "Histrionic Disorder."

Thank God, she had the tapes. Would they be enough? After all, she was in New York, and supported by her Jewish family who knew that horrible things could happen especially when good people sit back and did nothing. What had she done with the book that she had found? A book on Synchronicity! A miracle that she had found that book now.

"I will stay up tonight and read that book. There will be answers in it I know that will help me make sense of all of this." Candy promised herself.

Heather was calling from the dining room, "Hurry, Candy the food's getting cold."

"Coming, I'll have to dry my hair after supper!" Candy shouted.

Just then, the phone rang. The call was for Candy! Who knew that she was here so soon? Heather had been busy on the phone all afternoon. The family knew that she had arrived. Even her old boyfriend, Sam, was surprised to know that she was in the city. He was on the phone!

Candy thrilled to speak to him! Yes, he would be pick them up to take them to the Party. He could hardly wait to see her.

She wondered why she had ever left New York.. She had followed her Mother to Calgary. It just seemed like the thing to do. The Nursing Program at Calgary's University was highly recognized so she had left. New York.

She sat down to a delicious snack and tea. The sun was setting. In front of her was the glow of the sun on the Twin Towers. Candy was sitting at Heather's dining room table on the 20th floor of this High Rise. The fragility of the Twin Towers hit her hard, tears poured uncontrolled. Worse, she could not tell Heather what had set it off.

Heather, of course thought it was the loss of her Mother. Stroked her hand and comforted her; best that she knew how. Heather whispered, "Time would soften the pain she was feeling."

Candy simply nodded and took a big sigh determined to live in the moment. Hadn't she told so many of her patients the same message? It was her time now to get a grip on her feelings.

Candy asked," Will Rabbi Samuel be there tonight?" This time no taxi was blaring to drown out the sound of her answer. "Will Aunt Amie be there also?" questioned Candy

Heather handed her the list of the family that would be there tonight and their phone numbers. Candy thought to herself this is perfect. I can quietly talk with all of them in the next few weeks and perhaps they will have ideas how to prevent this attack. Yes, she was at the right place, at the right time with the right people. It seemed possible that she could create a difference. She would do the right thing; at the right time; in the right place and with the right people.

What was Synchronicity? Tonight she would read the rest of that book.

Chapter 4

March 27th, 2001, Susan, Joanne, and Walter survey Brenda's Care Home. It is a sunny morning and some of the birds are in the backyard chirping. Spring is definitely here!

Joanne commented, "Well, we've hired two of the four Philippine Care Aids and they start this afternoon. I'll make up their essential tax information. We don't want any problems. Are we ready to interview Judy? What is her last name again? "

Susan answered, "Johnson, she is from Belleville, Ontario. A quaint town settled by the United Empire Loyalists. She's Presbyterian. Wants Sunday mornings off so she can go to church. Between the Philippine Care Aids, devout RC;s and Judy's religious stuff; we'll have a church atmosphere. We can have church service here. We've Ruth's organ. I am sure someone can sing and lead the service."

Walter piped up, "Just today I had a request from one of the Reservations. They want a place foe one of their elders. He was their Spiritual Liaison. I think it would be very fitting to take him. We need a token male. He is full of jokes. Loves to play crib. It will look more normal with him here."

Joanne replied," Phone and have him come tomorrow. He can move in. Remind them to bring his furniture. Ruth is arriving in twenty minutes."

With that, they heard the slam of a car door and there she was at the door. Two movers hopped out anxious to deliver the small amount of furniture and her precious organ. Harry Hall and his wife, Linda helped Ruth up the wide wheel chair ramp.

Susan was glad that she had thought to wear her nurse's uniform. I must get uniforms for all the staff. We need to look professional.

Susan answered the door making sure that Harry, Linda, and Ruth were very aware of the Security device at the door.

Ruth smiled and introduced herself and her son, Harry and daughter-in-law, Linda

Ruth certainly was not suffering from Dementia. She was feeble, but very alert and seemed happy to be here. She had moved into a prestigious Assisted Living Home only a year ago with her late husband, Warner Schultz. They had been happy together, until his health went down a year ago with pneumonia, she realized that she was not strong enough to take care of him. It had seemed the right thing to sell their spacious home and move into that fancy hotel, which is what Warner used to call it.

They had been married for seven years at that time. It had been a wonderful seven years. He had been such a gentleman. He was always looking out for her. Always thoughtful! He had been so strong and we were sure his health was perfect.

It had been two years ago when Harry connected with Ruth. How grateful she was that he had come back into her life; when she needed him the most. He had seen her through so much in the last two years. The fire that had damaged the home.

The suite at Heaven's Harbor was beautiful. It was the only fancy suite there and saved for special rich folk like themselves. Every morning, the Minister from their Plenticost Church would come to visit and say prayers with them. Pastor James Bell! What a kind man and he always brought fresh flowers!

Of course, they would sign papers that would give him money for his church when the unfortunate time came that they would ascend to the

Pearly Gates. That was the only decent thing to do.

Ruth mentioned that her room looked a little small, but then she sighed, "Maybe it will feel cozy since I will live in it alone. Now that Warner is gone, I feel so alone. I wish though that I could see out of the window. I am so used to seeing the landscape at the ranch. This would have been hard for Warner. He would never have liked this room."

Harry brusquely commented, "Oh Mother, you are never satisfied are you? That is just you?"

Thinking, I have Power of Attorney over you. Nothing you can do about where I put you. Hell! I could put you in a one-room shack in a New York ghetto and no one could do a thing about it.

Linda seemed to read his mind and quickly changed the subject. She wanted to know if she could bring their children aged five and seven to visit her on Easter Sunday. She would bring the food. Could they have the dining room to themselves for a couple of hours?

This comment brightened Ruth's outlook immediately; delighted that her grandson and granddaughter would be coming for a visit in a matter of a few days. All of Ruth's furniture arranged, including the organ, the bed made and her clothes hung up in the closet.

Harry and Ruth had a short medical interview with Susan discussing her medications. Legal papers signed including the one that made sure there would be no resuscitation should Ruth have a heart attack. In fact, for any medical situation Harry was to be called immediately. Ruth seemed very happy about that. He was a good son. Her continuous comment was that she was glad that she had adopted him. He was the son that she had always wanted. He was healthy and wise!

A hairdresser would come once a week to do her hair and nails. He had thought of everything. Yes, he had thought of everything, especially, that no one but Linda, his two young children and himself allowed to visit her. Not even a phone call from any of her other relatives and friends. This order posted on the phone and at the front and back doors. Ruth isolated was at their mercy and secured for their future intentions. It was time for lunch. "Would Harry and Linda like to stay for lunch today?" questioned Susan.

Walter Brown and Joanne had left long ago. Now Harry and Linda had said their good byes.

It was now time for the last interview. Time to hire Judy Johnson. She was anxiously waiting to be hired. Walter and Linda passed Judy on the stairs coming in. Walter winked at Susan when he saw her.

"Yes, she will do nicely." he whispered to her.

Judy dressed in a white nursing uniform, white shoes and the hated white nylons. She definitely looked professional. Her face showed smile lines that proved that she had been a pleasant person in her lifetime. Harry guessed that she was probably fifty years old. This was a good job for her. He thought she will not make any waves even if she thinks something is not right. She'll keep her job.

Later that night, Harry phoned Susan and congratulated her on choosing Judy. Do you realize how much Judy looks like Sissy Spacek? She could pass for her twin for sure. Why not ask her if she would like to stay in the bedroom downstairs. That way she will always be on hand if an emergency occurs. Susan agreed. Judy now hired was happy to live there.

It was now three o'clock. The first of the Care Aids had arrived to meet Judy and Ruth. Susan introduced Cherry to Ruth and Judy and then she settled back to see the interaction.

Judy was also a great cook and liked to keep a clean home. This was good! Cherry seemed to relax right away. Her English was adequate. Ruth seemed indifferent towards Cherry but responded easily to Judy. It was as if they were old friends. It was not long before Ruth was telling Judy her life's story.

How she had lost her two sons in six months with pneumonia; as they had Cystic Fibrosis. How she had loved square dancing. How she had met Warner Schultz. What a kind and loving husband he had been. He had been so strong and capable like a man in his forties. How Harry had come into their lives just as Warner's health had started to fail.

Judy's ears picked up by that comment; but there was no way to continue their talk. It was then that Judy noticed the baby monitor by

Ruth's bed. Why was that there?

Susan came into the room. She was concerned that Ruth and Judy were getting along too well. She then dismissed the idea. There was too much age difference. They would have nothing in common. No need to worry; Judy was just a caring Nurse. At four-thirty, the doorbell rang again and their second resident had arrived.

It was Marie Rothman and her daughters, Rachel and Sophie. Both women dressed to the nines. Obviously very rich and they entered the humble home like movie stars playing a role. A chauffeur had just picked them up form the Airport.

Their flight had just come in from New York; their furniture had arrived yesterday and had been set up in the bedroom next to Ruth's room. Marie's clothes were already hanging in the closet. Now, Marie's legal papers signed; Power of Attorney and the" Do Not Resuscitate" document. Marie was theirs to do with as they pleased. Hell! They were all at their mercy!

Judy found this strange. Why didn't she do the medical exam and the paper work for these two residents? She was busy preparing supper for the two new residents to give it much thought. Marie was new to the home and seemed very disturbed by everything. She huddled in a corner of her room crying uncontrollably. In fact, she was wailing.

Surely, she had some drug that would calm her down. Judy thought that Maries was over whelmed by the flight in from New York. In addition, everything around her was new and strange.

Cherry was eager to help. She was attentive to both residents. Even Ruth seemed more cheerful around her. She was a gently soul and deeply religious. Cherry had come from the Philippines, a second time. The first time she had married a horrible man. It ended in divorce. However, while she had been in Canada she had made other Philippine friends and they had arranged for her to come back quickly.

Cherry said, "I love living in Calgary. All of my friends are here. Although I miss my family, it's more important for me to live here and make good money. I save many dollars and bring them here to join me."

Judy knew what she was going through, as she had to leave her family behind in Ontario. She knew what it was like to be alone. Perhaps we can be friends she thought. Supper served and to the horror of Ruth and Judy; Marie ate her food with her hands. She didn't want any help with her supper, but insisted that she feed herself.

Food slopped on the floor as Marie would not stay seated; instead, she kept getting up every few minutes to walk around. Marie was agitated and she cried uncontrollably.

Judy phoned Susan informing her of Marie's condition and requested a sedative that would calm her down. The answer; it would have to wait until tomorrow. Susan didn't have the time to get any medicine for her.

Marie's behavior was very upsetting to Ruth. Ruth retreated to her room without saying a word. Judy found Ruth on her bed sobbing, "Where am I? Why would my son put in me in such a place? Why does that woman act like that?"

Judy had no answers for her, but she was beginning to wonder what type of Care Home doesn't have sedatives for their patients or residents. Why was there so much security for a simple Care Home? Only special people are to see Ruth and Marie. Ruth is not allowed to use the phone. It was strange, as Ruth seemed totally rational and intelligent.

Cherry was leaving at eight. She would be all alone with these two women. How could was calm Marie down? How would Ruth be able to go to sleep?

Again, the doorbell rang; Joanne is there with another Care Aid for the Night shift.

Joanne introduced Kathy Brown to Judy. They were both in their fifties and perhaps they would become friends. Kathy was a large woman with muscles and a face that showed laughter and smile lines. Judy knew right away that she had a great sense of humor. Better yet, she worked nights, as she liked to bake food. That is a good thing; homemade bread, cakes, pies, soups etc thought Judy. At least the residents will eat good food.

Moreover, if she is baking food I know that she is awake and I will be able to get my sleep. I have been here now twelve hours and bed does sound very good.

Kathy reviewed the medication sheet for both women. She agreed to prepare porridge for seven- thirty in the morning. Her shift was eight at night to eight in the morning. Judy does the day shift. This is possible.

Judy offered,"Goodnight Kathy see you in the morning." Sleep blessed sleep. It has been a long day with lots of questions. Her bedroom is waiting in the basement. "Wow oh Wow." She could not believe her eyes! It was an executive suite like an expensive hotel. Deep wall to wall carpeting, the bedroom furniture cost a fortune and even the pictures on the wall were costly. The adjoining bathroom had a walk in whirlpool tub.

Outside the double French doors was a terraced garden like one sees in Home and Garden's Magazine. This was her bedroom! Another door in the bedroom opened into the exquisitely furnished Boardroom with leather swivel chairs and a real cherry wood Boardroom table. The cost of the furnishings in these two rooms would be worth more that the entire home.

She knew furniture as her deceased husband and his family had owned a furniture store in Belleville. They had been very successful with orders from South Carolina's manufacturing companies sending truckload after truckload to them.

"I think this furniture is from South Carolina. This set alone is worth $30,000." Judy whispered to herself.

Chapter 5

March 28th, 2001, all is well at Brenda's Care Home. It is nine in the morning. Marie and Ruth ate their breakfast and dressed for the day. Susan stopped for a sedative for Marie. Susan muttered to herself," Its' crazy! She can't behave like this. Its' too upsetting for the rest of the residents."

Judy relieved to see the prescription for Marie. I hope that it will work. From experience, Judy knows that many times it only made the condition worse.

Two more residents Joyce Hillman and Peter Fry will arrive. Susan phoned, "I'm on my way! I'll do the admitting." Joyce protected from the Organized Crime Syndicate, The Dragons. Peter Fry would be safe too, here.

Peter Fry had been a priest until he had gotten one of the young girls pregnant and the church had let him go. Elmer had been the result of that union. He had been a child on the reserve. As the years went by Elmer learned that his father had been a pedophile priest. Elmer didn't trust the care that his father would get from the local nursing home. There was still resentment towards his father's earlier indiscretions.

Four residents arriving in two days! This will be interesting thought Judy. Counting staff there are eight people sharing this space. All from different walks of life. For them to live in harmony will be an accomplishment. Judy thought to herself.

Joyce arrived at ten o'clock. Susan was there to do the interview, take the Medical Exam, set up her medication chart, and sign all the necessary documents.

"I wonder if she will have the "Do Not Resuscitate" document on her file, too." Judy muttered .Joyce's daughter Sylvia stated, "I work nights as a Head Nurse at Calgary's Intensive Care Unit and I have been the only one caring for Mom. I'm worn-out."

Joyce is on a portable oxygen tank. Its' obvious she would take a lot of care. Sylvia has seen the Care Homes. She knows the neglect that most patients receive. She has searched for a better alternative. Joyce liked the atmosphere and commented, "This is like a real home; I'll be happy here."

Sylvia replied, "I certainly hope so. I'm working non stop to make sure you are safe."

"Sylvia would you like a cup of tea or a bowl of soup? You do look so tired." Judy asked

"I do think this will be a better place for my Mom. I've been worried about her. Please let me know if any strange men or men appear around here. Poor Mom has two sons; one a serious criminal who has wanted her dead for many years. He wants his inheritance. The other is a schizophrenic. He sleeps in his car and you may find him parked outside here. He seems to think that he is protecting her. It is weird. Two crazy brothers! One normal brother would have been nice. Well, anyway, my daughter, Sue will be coming to visit Mom. She looks forward to seeing her." Sylvia sighed

Judy nodded her head and agreed," Family may be a blessing or a curse. It is hard to know why it is so, but it just is."

Ruth, Marie, Sylvia, and Joyce sat down for lunch of potato pancakes covered with heated apple pie filling and sour cream. A dusting of cinnamon and icing sugar topped it off.

A quick lunch but very delicious. The sedative for Marie had worked. She was letting Judy help her with her food. That's a blessing thought Judy; seeing as Sylvia has stayed for lunch. It is pleasant!

"I will play it for a while this afternoon." Ruth stated as she looked at her organ in the corner.

Lunch was over and Cherry has arrived to help Judy clean up and settle the residents for their afternoon nap. Cherry arrived late. "Sorry! I had an emergency!"

Judy replied, "Oh well, we made out fine. Complaining won't help anyway."

One o'clock, already, how time passes quickly. The doorbell rang again. Peter Fry and his son were at the door. Judy has been expecting them to arrive.

Judy asked, "Please wait on the veranda while I phone Susan to let her know that you are here."

Judy apologized," With so much security here, I just wanted to make sure who you were. Sir what is your name?"

Peter's son introduced himself as Elmer Fry, Chief of the Wolf Reserve near Bow Lake. He wanted his father to be safe and comfortable. They went into the office and waited for Susan.

Judy asked," Would you like a cup of tea or coffee while you wait? Would you like some lunch?"

They both responded quickly that they had not eaten yet and were hungry. Judy sat them at the dinning table and served them the Potato pancakes with all the trimmings.

Susan arrived just when they finished lunch. Peter settled into his new home. Susan interviewed Peter and Elmer Fry. The medical assessment done and all the legal documents signed, again, the "Do Not Resuscitate" document signed and the Power of Attorney handed over to his son.

Judy could not help but wonder why? Peter was normal and healthy. Why the patients treated the same way? What kind of Care Home is this? She had lived a curious life and questioning authority had always been something she did.

Peter came into his room in time to help put away his clothes. He seemed to be a quiet man with a quick sense of humor. He loved to play crib. A diabetic, very aware of his situation and when Judy questioned him about the "Do Not Resuscitate Document" he didn't seem to care.

He was at peace with his creator and stated often that he was ready to die at any time. The thought of dying no longer bothered him.

The day had passed quickly. It was time for Judy to make supper. Cherry had done a fine job caring for the residents. Everyone was content. Ruth played her beloved organ. The rest of the residents listened to the piano concert. Marie continued to walk around the center of the home. With the walls removed from the old duplex, a circular path existed for demented Marie to walk round and round.

The whole time that Marie did this she lamented, "9; 11 the planes; people dead" It was like a chant and made no sense. The sedative did not stop her behavior. This went on day in and day out; whenever, Marie was awake, she would frantically walk around the center of the Care Home and chanted, "9 11 planes, death, twin towers."

Judy suggested, "Susan can we get Marie decent shoes that would support her feet as she walks miles in a day. Can we get her a sedative that will work as this is upsetting everyone?"

As usual, Susan just ignored the request. It didn't make any sense to Judy. There was money to buy her a pair of supportive runners.

"Oh well, there is nothing that I can do about it" Judy whispered to herself.

It was Easter Sunday and Ruth was asking to go to Church. She had never missed going to Church before on Easter Sunday. Could she phone her nephew, David Smith, Pastor at the Plenticost Church in Calgary. He would want her to go to Church. She seemed adamant that it would be okay to call him. He was her nephew; Ruth sobbed, "I just want to go to church Easter Sunday; I have never missed a Sunday Service in my life."

Judy tried to contact Harry and his wife. No success! Then she tried Susan again no success! How was she to calm Ruth down? It seemed like such a harmless request. She wanted to talk to her nephew. Judy weakened and found the number in the phone book.

Ruth went into the office; phoned the Rectory. David Smith answered the phone. He was delighted to hear from his Aunt Ruth. He told her that of course he would pick her up; so she could go to Easter Service. He told her that he was happy to hear from her.

Judy helped her dress and Ruth beamed like a little girl at the thought of being with old friends and family again. Although she loved her son, she had lost touch with him 25 years ago. Even though he was very good to her and took care of her, "I need my family and friends. Why couldn't he understand that?" Ruth asked Judy.

Pastor David Smith showed up at the door in half an hour. Ruth was off to church and promised that she would be back at one o'clock. Harry, Linda, and her two grandchildren were arriving then to share Easter dinner.

"What a wonderful Easter!" Ruth exclaimed.

Ruth and her nephew were pulling out of the driveway as the phone rang. It was Harry! "What was going on? Why did she call him? Was she dead yet?" drilled Harry The eagerness in his voice when he asked was she dead yet put a chill through Judy's body. It was in such contrast to the love that she had just saw from Ruth's nephew. This desire for her to be dead shocked Judy to her core.

Who was this Harry? One thing for sure she knew that she was in big trouble for letting Ruth go to the Plenticost Church for their Easter Service. What possible harm could come to her for her going to Church with her nephew? It just didn't make a lick of sense.

Susan arrived in an angry mood. She called Judy stupid. Didn't she know that she was to protect Ruth? Their security was pointless if people could go out when they wished. Didn't she understand that people were here for their own safety? On and on Susan barked at Judy.

"Why doesn't she fire me? I know that I broke the rules." Judy whispered to herself. Finally, Judy stated, "Susan for heaven's sakes just fire me. It was not intentional, but I have broken the rules so please fire me. I deserve it!"

Susan huffed out of the room. Judy was glad that Cherry had not witnessed that entire emotional explosion for Susan's sake. What ever had gotten into her? Was she recovering from a hang over or what? What ever was all the fuss about? The woman had gone to Church for an hour and a half. This didn't make any sense at all!

Marie was the only one who had seen this emotional tirade. Thank God! Joyce had gone with her daughter to Easter breakfast and Peter was with his son at the Catholic Mass. The rest of the day, Judy wondered how long she would be working here. Her work schedule was five days on and two days off. She would start looking for another job. Maybe she could find a Private Nursing Position where she could live in and care for just one person. That sounded a lot better than this place if they had no respect for their employees. It seemed that there was no respect here for employees or residents. Judy decided to shake off all this negativity and pursued making a special Easter dinner with all the trimmings.

"Ham, pineapple, yams, scalloped potatoes a spicy sauce and lemon pudding made for supper. Maybe they'll get over their anger; if they can see what a great cook I am." She whispered to herself

Ruth returned at the same time that Harry, Linda and the grandchildren arrived. Harry scowled while Linda packed in Kentucky Fried Chicken.

Judy chuckled to herself another dame that cannot cook. Imagine this is Easter dinner. Well, I suppose the children like it more. They probably live on that type of food from how overweight they all are.

"Enjoy the dining room for the next three hours. I will need it at five o'clock to set the table for the other residents." Judy explained

Susan had called Harry downstairs to the Boardroom.

Judy feared that they would discuss firing her for letting Ruth go to church, although it seemed like such a trivial offense.

Then Cherry was called down stairs to the Boardroom. What ever was going on Judy wondered? Twenty minutes later, Cherry returned. A sheepish grin lit her face. Now there was a noticeable change in her attitude towards Judy. It was a condescending attitude. What words said in those twenty minutes produced that kind of change. Judy thought I have worked for years as a Nurse, but I have never seen anything like this.

Head Nurses screaming and swearing for nothing. So much secrecy! So much security! What is this place anyway, with all the residents having a "Do Not Resuscitate" document signed? When do these residents see a doctor? Are their prescriptions correct? It seems like twice the dose of blood thinner for Ruth. Does anyone check that? The dosage is for a 180-pound Woman. Ruth weights only 100 pounds. She would bleed out if she ever had a bad fall. All of these thoughts ran though Judy's head as she set the table for Easter dinner. Next Sunday, she muttered, "I will go to that church. Perhaps I will meet someone there that can help me understand what is going on here?"

Chapter 6

Back in New York, Candy dressed in a burgundy cocktail dress, which showed off her cleavage and again her favorite four-inch shiny black patent leather high heels. Heather was kind and lent her a 'one of a kind' fake fur shawl that clung to her throat and tailed down her back. She felt like a movie star.

Sam was in the lobby waiting for them. He hasn't seen her in seven years. She thought to herself. I wonder how much he has changed. Does he have a beer belly like the men from the Lounge? Life was moving so fast these days; she could barely keep up with it all. The elevator stopped and she took a deep breath. Candy whispered to herself," Would the old thrill still be there for them?"

Sam who looked like Nicholas Cage seemed even more handsome than what she had remembered. Say something for heaven's sake. He stuns girls. Don't be just another one of his bimbos. She told herself. Candy cleared her throat and concentrated on the last tape recording she had listened to in the tub. Phew that worked!

She could feel her blood flowing back into her head. She wondered if he had the same reaction to her as she had for him. If he had, he kept very cool.

Sam questioned, "Are you looking forward to seeing your family? You couldn't have picked a better day to return home. I won the bet you know. Your friends thought you would be going to Europe next; but I bet that you would first come home. Thanks to you, I now have an extra $375. Maybe you can help me spend some of it?"

Candy chuckled and said, "So you think you know me; oh, do you ever have a surprise coming. I've changed! You'll find out." She muttered," I don't even know who I am lately?"

Heather smiled and said, "You two look like movie stars; I knew you would get back together."

In unison, Candy and Sam chimed, "Hold the phone kiddo, not so fast!" With that, they burst into laughter.

They had arrived at the Hotel and the valet took the keys to park Sam's car. Each girl took an offered arm and strolled into the reception. Everyone turned and the clapping began. What a homecoming! So unexpected! Last night, she never would have thought this could be happening twenty-four hours later.

Candy caught her breath and the hugging began. She really loved them; and they her. They had truly missed her. Things here had not changed very much. Yes, Aunt Amie was here and Rabbi Samuel. Could she get them alone to talk with them or at least make a future appointment to see them.

Rabbi Samuel was the first to come over to see her. He had been so helpful when her father was dying. He had been kind and considerate. Even when her mother remarried out of the Jewish faith, he seemed to understand it. He agreed to see her tomorrow at noon at his office. She knew how important privacy would be. He seemed to grasp the visit was important and agreed to cancel all other engagements for tomorrow's afternoon.

Perhaps this would be easier than she thought. Candy then went over to her Aunt Amie, a double for Shirley MacLean. Now in her 60's she didn't look a day over forty. Candy wondered, How does she look so young and couldn't help but ask, "How do you stay so young Aunt Amie?"

Aunt Amie laughed and whispered, "Botox, plastic surgery, laughter and great food. When will you be coming to see me, I've tomorrow morning open for you. How about breakfast? Do you remember our quaint little breakfast nook that we went to every Saturday morning after services?"

Candy remembered how they had all laughed and ate so many knishes that she thought her stomach would burst. Aunt Amie must have read her mind and said, "I know we both can't eat like that anymore, but wasn't it fun when we could? I'll pick you up at nine; parking is horrid there so do be on time, dear."

Candy just knew in her heart that things would be okay with such a strong woman like her Aunt Amie helping her. Anything was possible! She'd enjoy tonight and put all that other business behind her. Tonight was her time to have fun. Eat, drink, and be happy. Life was good. Why oh why, had she ever-left New York? It was wonderful being home.

Just then, Sam quietly came up from behind her and caught her off guard with an enormous hug. Smiling and laughing said, "I am not going to let you go ever again!"

The time flew and soon just like Cinderella the clock struck midnight. If she were to get up tomorrow and accomplish all that she must do, she would have to leave now. It was important to have a clear head for breakfast tomorrow morning. Sam understood and gathered their coats. He was happy taking her home. He finally had her all to himself. He would tell her how he felt about her. Life was too damn short to wait any longer.

They glided by the Front Desk of the Hotel and he ushered her into his waiting car. The kiss was long and they both knew their romance had never stopped. Crazy in love! What a glorious feeling! Candy wanted so much to tell him what she had discovered, but this was definitely not the time. She was not going to spoil such a moment. It would have to wait until tomorrow.

Heather was waiting for them. Hot chocolate and desert waited on the coffee table. She hadn't wanted this evening to end. She had missed them, as they had all been close friends growing up. The nostalgia hit all of them hard that evening. The jokes, pranks, kidding and the old memories flooded back over them like a wave. One story led to another and before they realized it, the time was three in the morning. Bedtime now!

It was too late for Sam to go home. He would spend the night in the guest room. Thank goodness, there were two spare rooms in Heather's suite.

Candy didn't want to sleep with him tonight, but save their reunion for a more special evening. "Old friends first and plenty of time for us to be lovers again." she whispered

As Candy drifted off to sleep, her thoughts once more slid into the pending trouble for New York. Could she find a way to stop it?

"Mother, please look out for us as we sleep tonight" was her prayer, as she slid into a dream of peace and past times when the world was such a lovely place.

Heather had always been an early riser. This was especially true this morning. She had made the Coffee and yelled; "coffee services anyone" as she opened the door to Candy's room and then off to Sam's room. Coffee, orange juice and a bagel delivered to her bed. Candy exclaimed, "I could get used to this." Sam bounced on the bed seconds later.

Thank God! Its' only eight. She had an hour to be at the front of Heather's Apartment. She had promised Aunt Amie she would be waiting for her at nine. She would keep that promise.

Time to shower, get dressed, and put on her makeup. Sam was like a little kid talking excitedly non-stop and repeating how he had thought he had lost her. Sam repeatedly stated, "You are here!"

In a way, she wished that she could be as excited. With her head buzzing with pending 9/11, she wasn't able to show the same excitement. She hoped he wouldn't think she was disinterested. There simply wasn't any time to tell him what she had recently discovered. These ideas were still new to her. She needed time to reflect and come to grips with it.

They made a date for the evening; a special place where they had spent many hours as teenagers in love. At that time, they had no cares and the world was theirs to discover. Now things were much different. adult responsibilities hung over their heads whether they wanted to acknowledge them or not.

Being a Stock Broker in 2001 was no easy task. It had gotten harder in the last few years.

It was hard to predict which company would do well and which would fail. Many times, it made no sense at all. That didn't matter to him now. He had love back in his life. He was going to concentrate on that for a change and enjoy the flush that love can bring. Didn't someone say that being in love is as toxic as cocaine? The chemicals were endorphins in the brain. The brain responded as if one was doing drugs. He believed it!

Candy kept her promise and she was waiting for Aunt Amie at the front door. She hopped into the car and off they sped to their favorite breakfast nook. Aunt Amie, experienced Psychic knew immediately that something was wrong. Serious troubling was bothering Candy. It did not take long for Candy to tell her all the information. Ear microphones made it possible for Aunt Amie to hear the two tapes in privacy. Aunt Amie, when finished hearing all the conversations, shook her head and stated, "Candy I have known much of this information for a while now; I thought we'd have more time. I never thought they would stoop so low as to attack their own people in such a hideous way.

I am not surprised at all. It is the same group of people who created Hitler and World War Two. They organized all of that too. They have not changed over the years. I'm just sorry that you had to find out like this.

Then you are Jewish. I do think horrific events are in our blood stream. We keep going. No matter what! I do have people who I influence. They can do something about this recent information. I'll call them together and we'll discuss all of this tomorrow night for sure.

I'll need a day to organize them. Of course, they'll need some time to drop what they are doing to meet with us and discuss our defense to this attack.

"I saw you on television three days ago. You were on the Johnathon Show with that Soviet Scientist, and two other people. Can you tell them what I have just told you? What is the Forth Dimension?" asked Candy

"The Forth Dimension is where I get my Psychic information. Psychics call it the Akashi Records. Although some of our abilities do come directly from this Forth Dimension. You know that your grandmother, Hannah was Psychic and she helped many people get out of Poland before Hitler invaded. I still have contact to those families. Some live in Canada and Australia. In New York, they all know me. Money flows easily to me; as they trust my readings. They are respectful, influential people who depend on me. They'll trust our new information you have brought us. It'll still be hard to understand these people would do such a horrible thing."

"Do they understand these Forth Dimensional ideas? How many people are involved with this?" Candy asked, as she was concerned especially; when the Russian Scientist talked about super weapons of mass destruction on the television interview.

"My friends are aware of this research. They've worked with this science and won't be surprise my niece brings me this news. You've Psychic ability. In your life, you'll help many people and they'll depend on your abilities. " Aunt Amie continued

Candy then asked, "I found a book at the Airport, when I was waiting for Heather to pick me up on Synchronicity. Do you know about it?"

"Of course, that's how spirit works. When your Mother died, she knew that she'd be with you until your death; especially you're her only daughter. That bond is indestructible.

She'll be guiding your life with many coincidences, which I like to refer to as the force of Synchronicity. She simply had that person, who previously owned the book leave it behind for you.

When you're in Spirit world, you're very powerful; sometimes even more so if you have developed those gifts while alive. Your sweet

Mother had many spiritual abilities that she kept to herself. She'll now guide you to develop those same gifts that will make your life very successful. You'll help many people survive tragic events." Aunt Amie explained.

Candy shocked as she had no idea her mother had been Psychic. She had kept if from her. No wonder the phrase written in the inside cover, copied her Mother's Creed

"Everything happens for a reason; nothing is coincidence." Candy stated

Then she asked, "Does Synchronicity come from the Forth Dimension?"

Aunt Amie explained, "The conversation that she had heard in the lounge in Calgary was something her mother had arranged. Even dead, her mother had the power to make this happen. Even more incredulous, that Candy would have her tape deck with her so she could record it. This was just a small example of our loved one's power. In the Forth Dimension, they aid us in our lives every day. Small coincidences occur everyday. We just need be aware and grateful."

It was mind boggling.. She was Psychic. In her Nursing Program, she was told those types of people were Schizophrenic or whatever? They were not mentally healthy. No wonder her Mother had kept quiet about this. She didn't want to lose her only daughter's respect. "Oh Mother, I respected you too much to ever think poorly of you." whispered Candy.

"Aunt Amie, I was taught in Nursing that people who are psychic are crazy? How can that be when you are definitely not crazy? Why do they think that?" asked Candy

"My dear, I have had to deal with that my whole life. I do know that the Military have for some time now abducted children that are Psychic and that they've been training them to do this work for the Military. They now call it "Remote Viewing" but it is really the same thing." Aunt Amie answered

Aunt Amie held her while she sobbed. She had really needed to cry.

Candy hadn't allowed herself to cry. She was so afraid that if she started she would not be able to control it. She had seen what they did to people who had nervous breakdowns. She swore she wouldn't be doing that to herself. She would stay strong and survive. It was great to be in Aunt Amie's arms and let go of the pent up pain and recent fear.

Her Mother had guided her to Aunt Amie, the best person for her to confide in. The right people would escape this Terrorist Attack on New York and that is what she had to realize. Things did happen for a reason. Even the really sad and vicious events had a reason..

"Would you help me gain my Psychic abilities?" asked Candy

"I thought you would never ask and yes, my dear we will begin the study soon" replied Aunt Amie. The world seemed to shine again for Candy. Life did make sense. Spring in the air! An old sweetheart had come back into her life. He was still crazy about her! An Aunt loved her! Tomorrow she would move in with her and begin her life's study.

Chapter 7

Judy woke up with the birds chirping outside the double French doors. Blue Jays were singing their song; and a Robin hopped across the new spring lawn. March 29th 2001

Judy had arrived in Calgary on March 26th her birthday. Her fiancé had come earlier to Alberta to work for an Oil Company at Fort McMan. She had missed him. After his many requests, she had finally relented and had agreed to come. He'd be back in Calgary on March 30th and they would hunt for an apartment. It was a new start in the west.

Robert liked his job and the money was three times what he could make back in Southern Ontario. Yes, if they were to have anything to retire with they both had to make good money now, while they had their health and strength to do it. They had both gone through their life's savings dealing with their prospective partner's cancer ordeals.

They had met at Anderson's Funeral Parlor, when they were picking up the ashes from their partners. Judy's husband, Jack had died of Prostrate Cancer and Robert's wife, Bonnie had passed away with Stomach Cancer. They were both suffering and over whelmed by what they had endured. Watching their loved ones suffer and die had exhausted them financially and emotionally.

It hadn't been a great beginning for them, but as the days passed, they realized that they wanted the same things out of life. A quiet cottage by a lake; some serenity; peace and relaxation was their goal. Both of them came from healthy stock that lived into their nineties. They knew

50

that they needed to prepare for living that long.

Friendship grew into love and commitment. Alberta and the big money seemed the only way to get to their goals. Fifteen years of hard work by both of them would be enough for them to acquire the money for a comfortable old age. A simple life is all they were after. They'd both known money and living extravagant lives. Both had been born into money and rich life styles. Fancy cruises and Vegas holidays were a yearly occurrence. It never satisfied either of them. It was a quiet life enjoying sunrises and sunsets that brought them peace and happiness.

Just enough and no more was their motto. Health was what they wanted mentally, spiritually, emotionally and of course physically.

Judy recalled the people that she had nursed over the years and thanked her genetics and her ancestors for their healthy respect for their bodies. She'd never wanted to drink or smoke. She did all that she could to keep healthy. Live a balanced life! Would it be possible in this crazy world where people seemed so out of control?

Well, she must get up and start the day. Only four more days and she would be with Robert again. It had been two months since she had seen him.

Kathy was calling," Coffee's on and porridge made Come and get it hot!"

Judy ran up the stairs tripping over what she thought was a cell phone. She picked it up, pushed what she thought was the on button expecting to here a dial tone, but instead she heard Harry saying "She has to go we can't depend on her keeping people away from Ruth!" in a very angry voice.

It was Harry's tape deck and not a phone at all! Why was he so intent on keeping her friends and relatives away from her? This was so weird!

Judy sat down for Breakfast; gulped it down as fast as she could. She'd go downstairs and listen to this tape deck. What else was on this tape? Would there be some answers? She didn't have much time as Susan would arrive in twenty-five minutes. Kathy agreed to let her make some important phone calls and stayed a few minutes longer. Judy promised to make it up to her and give her some time off early the next morning in exchange for her help now.

Judy stepped out to the garden to listen to the tape recording. It was voice activated and had the sentences spoken in the kitchen and dining room. They were recording the conversations that had taken place in the last two days from the baby monitors that were all over the house. For God's sakes, why?

They had taped their own conversation with Cherry last night. No wonder Cherry had looked at her with such a smug look, when she came back upstairs. She would be the new manager. She'd have to wait for a couple of weeks for the status. She'd first have to prove her loyalty.

Ruth was not to use the phone again, not to see her relatives or friends. That she must make sure that Ruth would be isolated from everyone but them. If she did as they asked, she would be getting a reward when Ruth died. Did $10,000 seem like an amount that would interest her? Cherry excitedly answered, "Thank you Sir I'll do as you ask. Don't worry!"

Judy wondered what would they be asking and why did he sound so sure Ruth's death was so near. She didn't look sick to her. She was frail but then she was 83 years old. No time to wonder about that now, I've got to get this tape deck back into the Boardroom, on the floor, over by the window there. Hope he thinks that he dropped it there. Up the stairs she flew.

Judy thanked Kathy for her help. She had everyone at the Breakfast table when Cherry showed up at eight. When she answered the door, Judy feigned a good morning, never letting on for a moment that she realized what was happening.

Cherry seemed like her old self today. She helped the residents get dressed and wiped up the floor where Marie had dropped her food. What a mess! Again, this morning she was eating her food with her hands making a sloppy mess on the floor around her.

The other residents except Ruth, seemed to accept her weird behavior. Peter chided Ruth for showing contempt for Marie's behavior and it seemed to calm Ruth down. Peter gave one of his mini sermons," God loves us all; Ruth even when our brain no longer work like it should."

Ruth whispered, "I sure hope that I never get like that!"

Judy had heard that comment and later that morning assured Ruth that she would not be doing that in the future. Nothing for her to worry about! This would not be happening to her. Marie had a special kind of illness that affects some people in their old age. This would not happen to her. Ruth relaxed and told Judy all about the church service and meeting all her old friends. They were so glad to see her. Some had even thought that she was dead. Can you imagine that! This comment brought a tear to Judy's eye, "If she only knew how close she is to that event," thought Judy to herself. What can I do to prevent it? Is there anything that I can do to prevent this? She muttered under her breath.

Why do these people want her dead? She is just an old woman; she will be dead soon enough why wish her dead sooner?

She remembered how sad it was to see her loved grandmother die. No one in her family had wanted that to happen quickly. Everyone had taken turns caring for her. All the family members determined to keep her at home under their watchful care. Sure, she was very well off and everyone would receive something when she passed over, but no one wanted that to happen sooner.

These people were very strange for sure. Judy decided to contact the nephew. Maybe he could help straighten out this situation or at least give her some understanding of it.

That would have to wait for a while. She would have to get to a phone that would be private.

She'd have to find a way to use a phone that was not in this Care Home. When Kathy came at eight o'clock, tonight, she would need to take a taxi to a corner store or gas station. She'd phone. Thank God, she had found Harry's tape deck and that she had accidentally turned it on thinking it was a cell phone.

At least, she knew that she must be very careful how she talked and what she said from now on. Today two more residents were arriving and two more Philippine Care Aids would start work. Old friends of Cherry would join them. It was obvious that she wouldn't be employed here. Time was running out for her to help Ruth. How or what could she do? She had mentioned to Susan that Ruth's blood thinner was double the strength needed for her weight. Susan shrugged it off saying that Ruth's doctor was on holiday and would not be back until the middle of April. She could wait to see him.

How bizarre? An appointment that important had to wait three weeks. Was that how she would die so quickly? Bleed out from an injury when she fell. Ruth was not that steady on her feet. She wore high heels. Granted they were only two inches high, but that was not what she should wear.

She should have proper support shoes suitable for a woman in her eighty's.

This Susan was not much of a nurse. Judy finally concluded. On my days off, I'm going to get Ruth and Marie proper foot wear. Support shoes for both. If their families are too cheap to take care of them properly; well, I'll do it thought Judy to herself.

Southern Ontario seemed at times far away. Why were people in Alberta so different? No one would have behaved the way this nurse, Susan did. In all of her nursing days, back home she had never seen such negligent care of patients.

Another odd thing! Always, reprimanded for calling them patients! Well, how silly was that? Changing depends, dressing them and helping them eat; anywhere else, they would be patients!

"They were residents. Not Patients!" Susan would scream.

The doorbell rang! Joanne was at the door with two more residents. A tiny woman sat in a child's wheel chair. Anna was her name and she was 102 years old with degenerative bone disease. She weighed eighty-eight pounds and looked like a china doll.

Her daughter, Helen in her late sixties, by her side struggling with her cane came into the office. Susan once again would sign all the documents. The "Do Not Resuscitate" Well, this did make some sense. After all, she was 102 years old. Fragile and helpless! Helen's fall had left her no choice, but to put her mother into a Care Home. This was the first place that could take her right away. What a relief! Helen wanted the best care possible for her mother.

The other new resident was a man in ninety-nine years old. His name was Karl Adolph and his grandson, Ludwig with a strong German accent was anxious to admit him quickly. He had a flight to catch back to Germany. Karl could only talk German and Swedish. It had been a long journey for him. Karl went to bed immediately and the documentation filled out quickly by Ludwig Adolph

Joanne spoke fluent German. Even Susan locked out of the office for this special admittance. Karl would be there until he died.

Judy couldn't help but wonder if perhaps he was one of the Nazi officers who did so many horrible crimes against humanity during World War Two. He seemed to have that official air about him even at the age of ninety-nine. He was still a formidable person. He weighed 250 pounds and even hunched over, he was six feet tall. "Why are we taking residents from Europe? We've lots of people right here in Calgary that need a Care Home?" muttered Judy

Judy overheard Joanne say to Susan. "Would you believe it Ludwig is willing to pay us $15,000 a month. He's wanted by the Jews; for his part in the Holocaust! The family wants him dead and soon. He's a war criminal! Their concern was his recognition in Europe. They needed a safe place for him. They don't want international publicity!"

The doorbell rang again. The two new Care Aids were here. They could hardly speak a word of English. Cherry bustled to the door to greet them. One would do the laundry and the other would do housework. With six full-time residents, there was no way that Cherry or Judy could cope with the workload.

They both feigned friendliness towards Judy; but she knew that they would soon be under Cherry's supervision. Her days would be short as a Coordinator for Brenda's Care Home.

What a joke! It was really Brenda's Death Home. Who on the

outside would ever have guessed that fact?

Judy prepared supper and made sure that she would have time to go to the local store. She could get a cab to the Mall. She was going to buy her own voice-activated tape deck. She'd hear the conversations in the Boardroom. She'd record Walter, Harry, Joanne and Susan next meeting, Tuesday afternoon at two. She would be ready for that.

Supper went quicker than she thought it would. The extra Care Aids reduced the workload. The residents bathed and placed into bed before eight o'clock.

Judy would be ready to leave as soon as Kathy arrived. Cherry, Mary and Melody left.

Kathy arrived early which helped even more and Judy was wise enough to meet her outside on the veranda. Judy explained that she needed to get some melatonin to help her sleep. Kathy offered her car. Grateful Judy sped away to the mall. I will have time to talk for a few minutes hopefully with Pastor David Smith and buy a voice-activated tape deck.

Judy dialed the number to the Plenticost Rectory. It was Bible Study night and he was available. David answered the phone. He agreed to meet with her in fifteen minutes. Judy bought the voice-activated tape deck that could change things for Ruth. She then met with Pastor David Smith at Boston Pizza.

Would he believe what she would tell him? Maybe over the next few days her new tape deck would confirm her suspicions and she'd have tapes to prove what she was saying.

Pastor David Smith thanked Judy for her concern for his Aunt Ruth. He listened intently to what she experienced in the few short days that she had worked there. It had only been three days; but already a lot of weird stuff had occurred. Not her imagination! This was real. David sat there nodding as she spoke. When she finished, he agreed with her. He'd been in touch with the Plenticost Minister, Pastor James Bell from Saskatoon. He'd been concerned for Ruth. Warner Schultz had never trusted Ruth's son and had made that clear to Pastor Bell.

Warner believed that Harry had torched his ranch home. He believed that they were pressured into going to this fancy Assisted Living Home called "Heaven's Harbor" Warner said that he had never had trouble with his lungs. Pneumonia was not a thing that had ever worried him. Warner had been in perfect health until Harry came on the scene.

Warner had also talked with his brother, Arthur who still owned land south of his ranch. Arthur had gone to Pastor Bell with his concerns for his brother and Ruth. Pointing out that with Warner gone Ruth would own acres of land right next to the Saskatoon Airport. This land was worth millions! Worse, Harry would be the only relative to inherit all of this.

Judy blurted, "So that is why they want her dead so fast! How can we stop it?

Chapter 8

Back in New York, Candy arrived at Rabbi Samuel's home. He was waiting for her in his garden. He was pleasantly surprised that she had brought Aunt Amie with her. They settled in the dining room for a quiet conversation. His homemaker offered them various teas and cheese scones with jams and homemade conserves.

Aunt Amie complained about gaining weight. Candy laughed it off. "No worries. Auntie I'll have you so stressed over the next six months; you don't have to worry about gaining weight. She realized that she had made a joke out of such a horrendous pending event. Was it her nerves? How could she make a joke out of something so horrific? Was she loosing it?

Rabbi Samuel quietly assured, "Sometimes that is the way the brain will handle horror. Try to make it a joke. We, Jews have done that for centuries made fun of horrible events. It is our way of coping. Other cultures or people get angry while others break down with uncontrollable crying. They're all ways of coping. No one is right. It just is!" With that, Candy settled back in her chair and asked him to listen to the tapes she has brought him.

He listened intently and after just a few minutes asked to stop the tape for a moment. "May I record your tape recording as there are names, places, and times that I will not remember? I'll need this information to offer it to others who can change things or at least prepare for the inevitable." He stated.

They started Candy's recording from the beginning and again he listened intently. When they finished both tapes, he sat quietly shaking his head and then he finally spoke, "I have known about these American Bills being folded a certain way to show what is coming. One of my elders in the synagogue has the same information, but not as real as this is. I do research too. I have read the book, "Weather Wars Now" It does seem real that our weather and events are engineered," he continued

Candy asked, "Can we do anything?"

Aunt Amie added," I know that we are not alone in all of this, my dear, Spirit world is very much aware of our challenge. They are watching and listening! That is why prayer is so effective in any religion. Spirit knows no special religion. On that, side of the vale or the Forth Dimension there is only Spirit. That includes the spirits of all living things including birds, fish, and mammals that dwell on our Earth. We are not alone in this situation. Never forget that!"

Rabbi Samuel nodded his head in agreement, "Spirit world is very much alive; many times I have heard stories from my people where Spirit intervened to save their lives; I believe that no matter what; we are not alone. They help in many ways unseen; but always there."

Candy questioned, "I just found a book on Synchronicity. Aunt Amie has told me that is how our loved ones who pass over relate to us. They are in the Forth Dimension and they use unexpected coincidences that prove their existence every day. Is she right?" Rabbi Samuel nodded his head in agreement.

"The Forth Dimension exists and that is where we all eventually go. Our loved ones work from that energy zone. When we believe they can help us with our lives, it gives them the ability to do so. They will not interfere unless we ask. I have asked for their help for many years and they have never let me down." He confirmed.

At that moment, Rabbi Samuel's wife, Rose came home.

Candy suddenly remembered why she had first taken such an interest in the people in the lounge just a few nights ago. Candy related what had happened in the Calgary Lounge. When she had heard the two men mention Marie Rothman. Candy recalled the picnics that all of them had gone on just ten years earlier. She had been best friends with Marie's daughters.

Candy asked, "What happened to Rachel and Sophie? Why would they want to hide their mother? What had happened to Marie?" Marie Rothman had been such a dynamic intelligent woman who was proud of her work that she was doing in Alaska.

Rose stated, "Marie worked with resonance and vibrations. It also involved the Forth Dimension. At one point, she was working on a project called the "H.A.A.R.P. Program." Marie had given a speech three years ago on her research at the University. A means to control the weather, tornadoes, hurricanes and more"

Rose continued," Marie had researched electromagnetic energy, "Scalar Wave Energy." Marie had been so excited about it .She could see the world producing more food for people; hunger would be outdated; and people could live without fear of loosing everything because of a tornado or a hurricane. There was even a Newspaper article in one of her research papers. Here it was! Rose had saved the article."

The Good News!

"All diseases cured, physical or mental. Health restored! All ailments easily cured. It will be possible to reverse the aging process! Limbs re-grow and failed organs revitalized. This energy from the

Forth Dimension will heal spinal birth defects. Mental diseases will no longer exist. Life spans increased for all living creatures including our pets. Old age senility and degeneration eliminated. People enjoying full rich lives. Cancer, Leukemia, AID's and all hereditary diseases no longer exist. .Heaven on earth for all living creatures

The Newspaper article finished.

"Marie was very happy in her work. Imagine the shock for her daughters, when Marie came home nearly a vegetable. For months, she could not say anything but lay in the fetal position. Then she recovered somewhat with her frantic pacing and muttering "9 -11; planes; people dead". What had happened to their mother? She cried uncontrollably. Rachel and Sophie were beside themselves wondering what to do for her.

One of her co-workers, Mark came for a visit and explained that there had been an explosion up North where she was working. Marie had never been the same. They had sent her home to die. Mark had said that from that time on the place had changed hands. They fired him. Their research canceled. They were now using their scientific research for changing the weather patterns for the worse. The people in charge now were using their scientific research to harm the planet.

He didn't know what to do about it. He did want them to know that their mother might be in danger if she was repeating this "9-11 mantra. Mark had encouraged them to get their mother into an obscure place. A small Care Home in Calgary would be a safer place for her. Little did they know the people who owned this Care Home were part of this terrorist cell?

Rose contacted Marie's daughters immediately and asked them to come over as soon as possible. Marie had been very close to Candy's mother, Maureen. For many years, they were inseparable. Studying and sharing textbooks at the University together. This would be hard on them. Candy knew that they could not have changed that much.

They would only have done the right thing by their Mother. They would not have abandoned her in oblivion unless they felt it necessary for her safety. What ever would they think when they heard the tape, she thought.

She shuddered to think of more heartache coming their way. It was hard enough to deal with the death of her mother, Maureen but to know such vicious people were caring for their mother. That would be more than they would be able to bear.

They would be here at four. Tears streamed down Candy's face and not even her Aunt Amie could get them to stop this time.

Rabbi Samuel and his wife, Rose stood helpless until a Hummingbird tapped on the living room window. They all turned to look at it. Twice it came and tapped on the window. Aunt Amie quickly turned Candy around to show her the Hummingbird tapping on the window. Candy stopped crying. Yes, Spirit world was real after all. Her mother had used this hummingbird to let Candy know that she was there in their presence. She was making sure they knew Marie Rothman's danger. Even from the other side of the vale, Maureen did make a difference for all of them. Maureen had contacted them from the Forth Dimension through the hummingbird's tapping.

Candy realized how intricate Spirit world could be guiding those people to her section of the Oil and Gas Club in Calgary, their careless talking, their casual conversation and more. All this led to this moment. The truth revealed. Perhaps Marie was not as bad off as her Doctors had led them to believe; they just wanted to quiet her. Silence her! Powerful drugs used to make her look like she had dementia or worse. Perhaps with the right medical care she would heal. What a thought!

Tears turned to smiles. They decided to pray that the old Marie would return. She would come home within the next few days. Anything at this point seemed possible. The doorbell rang. Rachel and Sophie were at the door. Candy ran to hug them. It seemed like a dream. She hadn't seen them in seven years. They were so young! So vulnerable! The sadness showed on their faces. Too many nights of crying themselves to sleep had created black circles under their eyes.

It had not been an easy thing to watch their vibrant Mother return from the North a zombie. They couldn't leave their jobs to take care of her. Rachel was head of a magazine company, the family business. Sophie had realized her dream of dress design, with her own dress boutique. Yes, they had been successful, but not happy with their

Mother's unexpected illness. Seeing her like a zombie was worse than if she had died. It was strange as there was no family history of dementia or mental illness. It truly came as a shock!

They sat down while Candy explained why she had called them here. She explained the coincidence that had led her to tape the lounge conversation. Rachel and Sophie listened intently, tears streaming down their faces, makeup smearing as they carelessly wiped their tears away. They would have to rescue their mother and quickly. They would take her out for dinner and secretly bring her back to a safe hiding place here in New York. Careful that these people did not know where she was. Organizing this would take a couple of weeks. Could they get Marie out of there sooner?

Was there a way to heal Marie? Candy felt like she had accomplished something already in this bizarre mess. Rose cleared her throat and mentioned that she had an Aunt living in Calgary who might be able to help them. Gertrude, Department Head of Alberta's Registered Nursing Homes. She definitely had connections to people who would know what to do and how to do it.

She found her phone number in their Directory and left a message for her to call her as soon as possible. Although this Resident Care Home didn't come under her jurisdiction, surely something could be done to protect those people living at Brenda's Care Home. Candy still kept thinking what she could do next for the Twin Towers. September 11th 2001 was too close to be lax about finding a solution

She remembered that she had dated a Fireman in University. Would he believe her or her tapes? How could she reach him? It had been eight years since she had seen him.

Suddenly she remembered her date with Sam; he was to pick her up at seven o'clock. How awful, she had no time to change or freshen up. She phoned and asked, "Heather have you heard from Sam?" Do you have a phone number for him?"

Aunt Amie sped down the road taking short cuts. At least, she would be there at the door; if not ready for him. Whatever was he going to think of her for being late? He was so excited about their date with her and she wasn't even home. She prayed please let him be late, too.

Aunt Amie chuckled, "Do you recall your first date with him? You were late that time too. I wouldn't worry dear. He knows that you can't tell time. Relax and enjoy the time that you do have together. Life's short. Stop being such a worry hen."

With that, she slammed on her brakes. They skidded to a stop at the front door. Big hugs and Candy whispered, "How did I ever get an Aunt like you?"

Aunt Amie replied, "See you tomorrow. You're moving in!"

In the elevator, she reflected on how much had occurred in the last thirty-six hours. It was breath taking. It wouldn't take long for her to change her dress and apply fresh make up. She had already washed her face with all the tears shed in the last few hours. Maybe Sam was late too. Heather flung open the door with an amazed look on her face.

She asked, "Where were you, I tried all day to reach you? I was quite worried about you! Sam called and apologized as he is running late too. An emergency at work! He didn't have time to explain it."

Candy stripped down, poured a tub and climbed in she muttered, "Thank goodness I've time to relax in this tub and think about all that's happened today. I feel rested already as she sunk into the hot water. I'm going to enjoy myself tonight with Sam. I may even be good company. Certainly more relaxed tonight than I was last night, that's for sure."

In the hot tub, she dozed off for a few minutes. The bubbles tickled her toes. Life can be grand she thought to herself.

Heather called, "Better get out of the tub; Sam is on his way up on the elevator."

Chapter 9

Kathy was waiting for her. Judy had been two hours. It should have only taken half that time. Lucky for her, Kathy wasn't upset with her. She even believed her diarrhea story. She felt guilty for lying to her as lying was a behavior she really disliked. Her own mother had always told her, "The truth will always come out!" She'd believed her and had lived her life honestly. It did bother her to lie to Kathy.

All was well in the Care Home. Everyone was asleep but Marie of course. The sleeping pills didn't work for her. They seemed to agitate her even more. Ruth was asleep and snoring. Joyce was dozing off and on with the oxygen tank humming. Anna snuggled in her bed. Her breathing so shallow it was hard to see if she was still alive, Peter was playing solitaire. Karl was snoring.

All was quiet except for Marie who often called out "9 - 11, the Twin Towers, 9 - 11!"

Judy remembered back in her training days of a little girl, who had stepped on a nail. Her parents were alcoholic and had ignored her foot until gangrene set in. The foot and leg were cut off; that was bad enough, but the gangrene had gone to her brain, too. She had reverted to a six-month-old baby and for months, the infection took over her brain. It took three or four nurses to feed and change her. Her name was Nancy and all she did for three months was cry, "Ms. Jones hurt me!" this went on for nearly three months and then one day she started to recover. The infection in her brain subsided and slowly she regained her mind. Her brain recovered and although she had lost memory; she could think again.

Could this be happening to Marie? Could her brain be fighting some inflammation and one day she would be normal again? How she hoped that could occur! Judy said good night to Kathy and reminded her, "If you need me just call. It'll only take me a minute or two to get up here!"

She made her way to bed but not before, she took the time to put batteries into her tape deck and attach it to the ceiling fan above the table in the Boardroom. She was determined to hear what they were saying. She wanted the taped proof of these people and their plans. A hot soak in the enormous tub with the jets going was a blessed gift .Aches, pain and tension left her tired body. Crawling into clean sheets and saying a quick prayer for protection she expected to fall asleep, but instead she couldn't sleep. She wasn't able to stop thinking about the 1969 Red Ford Station wagon parked outside all day that had cardboard in all the windows. She had gone out to the car curious about it. Could that be Joyce's Schizophrenic son parked out there?

She had phoned the police, but they had just laughed it off. Officer Thomas stated, "Don't you know where you are? It's known as the old ghetto." Judy was too tired to remember if this son was the dangerous one, which had tried to kill Joyce. Sleep finally overcame Judy.

The next thing Judy heard is Kathy's scream "Help! Stop you bastard!" yelled Kathy.

Joyce's son had just escaped! Kathy could not stop him. He had climbed into the open window into Joyce's room and had tried to strangle her with the oxygen tubing from her machine. Kathy had come into the room and found Joyce lying on the floor with the oxygen machine turned off. She was gasping for air; her son standing over her. Kathy pushed him away from her and slugged him. He ran! Thank God! Kathy listened to the baby monitor and heard Anna call for help.

"Are you alright? How is Joyce? Is she breathing okay, now?" asked Judy

One thing for sure Judy was not going to get any sleep tonight! Kathy and Judy sat down and discussed how that must have happened. The window left open just a few inches. It was a warm night and Anna had wanted some fresh air. Kathy had not thought about it and opened it a few inches. They'd be more careful. Judy told Kathy about phoning the Police that afternoon. She only received scorn from the police officer for complaining about the parked car.

Was there any point in phoning about the attack? Would anyone at the Police Station care? Judy reached out and shut the baby monitor off. And stated," Kathy this is the weirdest place I have ever worked. I have been a nurse for over 30 years and this is by far the strangest. We haven't been open a week and this happens. We now know that we're on our own. We will have to protect these residents ourselves."

After she had blurted out this thought, Judy for a second worried that Kathy might be part of Susan's insidious team. A flood of questions raced through her mind.

Kathy breathed a sigh, "I've worked in a place like this before; it was in Winnipeg. I had to change my name after working there, as I was. concerned for my life. They'd been deliberately taking residents there that were at risk as these people here are. Wealth is not good for one's health in old age."

Kathy continued," I have noticed too that Nurse Susan isn't checking on the dosage that the residents are getting each day. Oh sure, they have us check the Bubble Packaging and the signing and all that; but the doses for Marie and Ruth are twice what they should get."

Judy relieved stated, "They all have the "Do Not Resuscitate" documents signed I think this place is like the one you worked in Winnipeg."

Kathy gave Judy a big hug and stated, "Thank God, you now know what I've thought for the last few days. I thought I was dealing with this by myself."

"You do know that every conversation that we have is taped down in their Boardroom as it is all connected to the baby monitors spread throughout the rooms?" asked Judy

They decided that they should turn back on the baby monitor in the kitchen, as it would look suspicious if it were not recording their conversation. Judy pretended to have just come back from the bathroom to cover the time that had lapsed. They got out pens and paper, wrote down a few more sentences, and compared thoughts. Daybreak was coming.

Kathy said, "Judy go to bed. Get at least and hour and a half of sleep. I'll wake you up in time. It has been a hell of a night for both of us."

Judy knew that the brain's sleeping patterns were an hour and a half. If one could get that sleep cycle, it was the same as having a full night's sleep. She had pulled many of those short night sleeps while working and caring for her dying husband. So here, she was doing it again. She could sleep sounder knowing now that Kathy was upstairs taking good care of the place and that she could be trusted. A smile crept across her face as she slept and dreamed about Robert.

The next thing she knew was Kathy at her bedside with a cup of coffee. "You didn't need to do that" Judy exclaimed. Kathy had let her sleep an extra sleep cycle so she had three hours of sleep. She had stayed an extra hour. Now, Judy knew that she had a real friend in this death house.

Kathy stated, "Cherry is upstairs dressing Marie. She will have her hands full for a while doing that chore. I told her that you had the stomach flu. Come with me. She thinks you are going to the Walk In Clinic. This will give you some time to photocopy Ruth's chart and prove that her medications are wrong. This could help us get her out of here." Kathy had made sure there was no baby monitor or tape deck in this room before she spoke.

Judy dressed within minutes and was ready to leave. "I will put my make up on later." She casually mentioned. Both women liked their spy and detective stories; it seemed like they were living a chapter. How strange in one week they had developed a strong bond. They were friends, real friends! Memories of their teen years when they had that type of friendship came up for both of them. Marriage and children had stolen the closeness from that type of friendship.

Only now, there with so much at stake; it wasn't for fun, but for survival. Loyalty and decency was the glue for this friendship. They had breakfast in a small coffee shop in the Mall after they photocopied Ruth's medical chart. Kathy could then fax it to an undercover police officer that had closed down the Care Home in Winnipeg.

Her courage had exposed that Care Home which Kathy referred to as the Death House. She had changed her name easily after that event. Since, she had a clean police record; she had simply gone back to her first ex husband's name. It was very simple to do and took only a few minutes at the Government Agent's Office.

"Oh well, I guess it is a good thing that I was married twice as I will need to go back to my maiden name this time." explained Kathy.

Judy chuckled, "Well I guess Robert will have to marry me now! We've put off the date, as we wanted to have a honeymoon. We had to save the money, but now our plans will have to change. Thanks for the rides Kathy. I'll see you tonight. Be careful."

Judy closed the car door and hurried inside Brenda's Care Home. Cherry was upset, as Marie had been very difficult to dress this morning.

Frustrated Cherry exclaimed, "I sure hope you don't give your stomach flu to these people. Can you imagine how that would be?

Judy smiling said, "Doctor thinks it is just something that I ate. Don't worry its' not contagious. But we'd better label all the food in the fridge with the right date. Make sure, no one else eats outdated food"

With that Judy went through the fridge throwing out anything that could be suspect.. Ruth still needed her bath because she had refused to let Cherry do it. She'd demanded that Judy help her dress.

Ruth stated, "I want Judy to take care of me and only Judy." Cherry was very angry about Ruth's attitude as she felt it was a racial thing. She couldn't help being Philippine. She was a hard worker and very dedicated.

Cherry angrily stated, "This place will be better when you are gone, old lady."

Judy heard that comment and determined to make sure that she was going to get Ruth out of there. Maybe, she could not close down the place, but she was going to do all that she could to get Ruth out of there. That was a promise!

Ruth smiled when she saw Judy coming down the hall. Ruth had been in the bathroom brushing her teeth when she had heard them arguing. Ruth knew that she was in safe hands with Judy. They had become more than resident and staff. She considered Judy a friend. Was it because she took the time to really talk with her and not treat her like an old unwanted piece of furniture, which is how so many nurses did in these Care Homes.

That is why she had decided to leave Heaven's Harbor after the death of Warner. Ruth was delighted at the prospect of having her own apartment. The live in nurse was her granddaughter, Lana. She was Harry's oldest child, from his first marriage. She was such a lovely girl, pretty with golden hair and the bluest of eyes. In a way, she was her oldest granddaughter. She was just 21. In fact, she looked a lot like Harry when he was young. Her name suited her "Lana Hall" She wanted the vocation of a Nurse and this was to a trial to see if she would really like that career or not?

Everything was going beautifully until she had the fall and broke her hip. Poor Lana devastated. The damn rug in the bathroom had caused it. Lana blamed herself. She loved Ruth. Lana hadn't wanted any rugs in the apartment, but her father had insisted that it would be better for Ruth to have a warm rug to step onto after her bath. Lana had explained that was the cause of so many old people falling and breaking their hips. He ignored her. Lana knew what she was talking about; she worked as a "Candy Striper" for the last three years and had heard the stories of the patients during that time.

She was at Ruth's bedside for weeks, nursing her back to health.

Harry told her that Ruth was going to put into a Private Care Home. Both Ruth and Lana were heart-broken. They had grown very fond of each other. Harry had won like usual. He would not listen to her and closed the apartment.

Lana swore at her father, "How can you be so cruel to both of us! We haven't done anything wrong! Falls happen! Why are you separating us? Why can't I work in the Care Home, where you are putting her?"

Harry maintained his cold decision and refused to let Lana know where he was putting Ruth. When asked he would shrug his shoulders and mutter, "none of your business!" Lana infuriated finally screamed, "I do not want to see you ever again!"

Lana took the first plane to England to join her Mother. She now understood why her Mother had left her Father. She sputtered. "What a nasty piece of work he is; he has no real love for anyone but himself."

Ruth asked, "Judy, can we go for a walk in the garden out back? I want fresh air. Can I please have a few minutes in the sun today?"

Judy readily agreed knowing that there were no baby monitors out there. They could finally talk privately and she would be able to get information from Ruth.

"Information that Kathy and I can use to help her leave." whispered Judy to herself.

Judy asked, "Ruth do you have any people who you'd like to see?"

Ruth responded with the story of her Granddaughter, Lana. How she missed her. She asked, "Can you find Lana as I would love to see her. I don't understand why she never comes to see me?" Where was she now? She didn't even know that! Harry always changed the subject every time she asked him about her. How she did miss her! Why couldn't she go back to her apartment? Why couldn't her friends come to visit her? So many questions that Judy could not answer.

Chapter 10

It was lunchtime; Judy hurried to the kitchen and heated the fresh homemade soup that Kathy had made last night. It really smelled good. The smell penetrated the home!

This was the trick to getting the residents to eat well; have food cooking on the stove or in the oven so their taste buds, saliva glands. and stomach would be ready for their next meal. Homemade bread had just finished baking and the home smelled wonderful.

Even Marie was sitting at the table waiting for lunch. She had stopped her frantic pacing around the circular hallway.

"Take a look even, Marie is sitting at the dinner table waiting for lunch." mentioned Judy

Cherry nodded in agreement and replied, "She seems quieter, lately."

"How is Joyce this morning after her ordeal last night?" asked Judy

Cherry responded, "She's scared and she's still shaking you know!

Judy stated, "Heaven only knows how much abuse she had already suffered from him. I think it has brought a lot of memories back for her. Her daughter will be here at one thirty. To talk with Joanne, Susan and Walter about her attack last night. I hope the Police will take a better look at what we have here and start protecting us. It's a good thing that Kathy is a large woman. Did you know she is an ex army nurse with martial arts training? She's a strong capable woman."

Sylvia Hillman was at the door. She arrived a few minutes early.

Judy asked, "Would you like some soup; it's fresh, and home-made bread?"

Sylvia had been crying and the tears had ruined her makeup.

Sylvia asked, "I'd like to freshen up first and yes, some lunch would be great. Didn't stop for breakfast. At the Police station this morning. I got a restraining order for Joseph. He isn't allowed to park outside or come within five miles. I should've done that earlier. I feel responsible for what happened last night. "

Judy nodded in agreement and responded, "I phoned them yesterday afternoon and told them that there was a station wagon parked out front, but they just laughed me off They weren't the least bit concerned even though I told them that this was a Care Home. Their response had been didn't I know what neighborhood that I was in?"

Sylvia shook her head and muttered, "I wonder why we pay taxes! They know the cruelty Joseph has done to Mom. What is wrong with them?"

Sylvia sat next to her Mom and eagerly ate her lunch. Joyce calmed down too as she was beside her daughter. Her hand holding Sylvia's left hand through the lunch.

It was sad to see Joyce so frightened; Sylvia added, "If the Police would have just done their job."

Susan, Walter, Joanne, and Harry were here at the door. Surprised to see Sylvia and agreed to talk with her in the Boardroom downstairs.

Judy had made sure earlier that the voice activated tape recorder hidden behind the ceiling fan was recording properly.

"I am going to find out what these people are all about and I'll have the taped evidence to convict them. She was glad that Kathy had dealt with this before. How they made the ordinary car hijacker seem like Santa Clause. The real criminals were this type; the white-collar gang." she whispered to herself.

"It was strange. In all the Hospitals where she had worked for many years, there was always a group meeting to clear the air. These meetings made sure all the Care Givers were doing a good job. There were discussions of the patients oops residents. Everyone needed to know how to take care of them." She stated to Sylvia

Sylvia raised her right eyebrow just as she headed down the stairs and nodded, "Yes" in agreement.

In the meantime, Judy settled the residents for their afternoon nap. It always pleased her to care for her china doll, Anna. What a brave little soul she was. Even at the age of 102, she determined to use the pole to help her get in and out of bed. She was a proud little one! Her bones were so fragile and she never knew when she would break another one. The calcium didn't stay in her bones anymore; Supplements really didn't work.

"Anna! Thank you, for calling out for help last night! That was a brave thing for you to do!" praised Judy

"I wish that I was strong like when I was young. I'd have finished him off!" she whispered. Anna didn't want to upset Joyce again.

"How did he get into the room?" asked Anna, as she had been asleep until Joyce had fallen on the floor.

Judy responded, "He crawled in the window. We had it open a few inches so that we could have fresh air. You know how warm it was last night."

"I so like the window open! Will that mean that we can't have the window open at night?" Anna asked.

"We will have to see! This isn't a safe neighborhood! " responded Judy

Well maybe things around here can straighten out. It is fun to have a house full of people to care for. They are so appreciative.

"A small Care Home is a better way to go than the institutional care. How I wish this was what this home pretends to be." Judy thought to herself.

Sylvia had finished her talk with the "gang" and had come back into the kitchen just as Judy was taking apple pies from the oven.

"Would you like some tea and a piece of apple pie?" asked Judy

Sylvia looked at the pie. One piece wouldn't hurt and she needed a reward for confronting those cold people downstairs. They didn't understand why she was upset. It was beyond her! She had paid for the month and she would need time to find another place for her Mother.

Sylvia and Judy sat down and had their afternoon tea. Both ate in silence lost in their thoughts. The day zoomed along. Judy was busy preparing supper when the Board meeting was over.

The "gang" came upstairs to the smell of frying onions and freshly baked apple pie.

"Well, Judy you are doing a fine job of keeping the residents fed and happy." stated Joanne

"Any one visiting couldn't help but see that." Joanne muttered to Susan.

Walter stated, "Keep up the good work! It does smell good here!"

Supper served and Marie even let Judy help her eat. She was eating her food normally. No food dropped all over the dinning room floor.

"Roast pork and all the trimmings for supper tonight." shouted Judy into Karl's ear.

Ruth asked, "I used to love to cook for the ranch in the fall. We'd have twelve people sitting around the table. I have my recipe book here with me, would you like some of my recipes for your collection, Judy?"

Joyce and Anna chimed in, "I want to give you some recipes, too."

"There are some I really miss, that I wish you would make for us; I get a craving for my cherry cream cheese desert that I use to make for church socials." offered Ruth.

It all seemed so natural for a real Care Home. A tear slipped down Judy's cheek.

"Yes, I'll take all of your recipes tomorrow morning. We'll make a small cook book that will stay here in your home." Judy stated

This was Thursday and tomorrow the hairdresser would be coming to fix Ruth's hair and nails. Ruth played her organ after supper and the place really did feel like a home. Everyone settled for the night; all the windows secured. Judy had time to run downstairs and get the tape deck. They would have time to listen to it outside when Kathy got there. They would both hear what secrets were on it.

What would be on this tape? Kathy would know who should receive it. Judy thought.

Kathy arrived and they checked on all the residents. Making simple conversation so the baby monitors would pick up the humdrum comments that they should hear. They then zoomed out to the terraced garden in the back of the home. Both women were intent on hearing the conversation that afternoon in the Boardroom. I hope the tape recording has real information.

The meeting had gone on for three and a half hours. They wouldn't get all the conversation as the tape would not hold it all. I hope that there would be something worthwhile on it. It begins with Susan backing up her decision to hire Judy.

Susan stated," She is handling the residents and the Care Aids better than I thought she would have."

Harry butted in and argued, "She cares too much for Ruth! She's too caring! What's going to happen when Ruth is dying? How will she react to that situation?"

Joanne added, "She seems to calm Marie down too. I've noticed that she eats at the table when Judy is there. She even lets Judy feed her!"

Walter suggested, "We should give her another week or two to see how she handles the place I think it is too soon to dismiss her. Her clean scrubbed look and professionalism is good for our Care Home. If anyone comes snooping she is just the right person to show the place. People respond well to her. Even Karl seemed to tolerate her. They love her cooking and they are eating like they're years younger."

So at least, Judy knew she had a job for a little longer. Kathy relieved said, "I don't want to be here alone caring for these residents. I don't trust Cherry with her smug attitude. She handles the residents as if they are sacks of flour. She would do anything they told her to do without question; as long as there was money for her she would do anything." Kathy exclaimed

The tape played on Joanne referring to the already many inquires for a place in the home. Where would they be putting these people?

Joanne mentioned," I have another German man who is a Nazi War Criminal. His family wants him here as soon as possible, I have asked for $15,000. A month for his residency and they agreed to the amount."

Susan exclaimed, "We'll have to move Peter in with Karl. We then have room for him. If we have him as a temporary guest, it is possible. We can get away with having the seventh resident; besides if a government official checks on us a bribe will work. No worries."

Harry smiled and stated," Who'd ever have thought that our little care home would be so popular. I guess it's who you know that makes a business successful."

Walter chimed, "Well, that is more than any of us could have dreamed possible. It sure is a good thing to have you with us, Harry."

Kathy and Judy looked at each other incredulously. What had they ever have gotten themselves into here at Brenda's Care Home.

Susan stated, "Cherry can handle the other Care Aids, but she could never cope with the patients. It'll be hard to replace Judy, so we have to handle her carefully. I know she shouldn't have let Ruth go to church with her nephew, David Smith. It would have even looked worse if she had not gone. This way we can see and hear her visits with this Minister and know what Ruth is thinking."

Harry angrily voiced, "But she can now connect with her relatives and friends. What happens when her nephew questions his inheritance? When he finds out that he's not in the will; but instead all the money is coming to me. He'll be angry enough to hire his own lawyer to fight this will. Pastor James Bell from Saskatoon might be upset. When money Warner promised him isn't in the will? This could all be a big problem for us!"

Walter attempted to calm him down with, "One day at a time, we will have the answers when that time comes. We will figure it out don't worrrrrrrrrrrr"

The tape ended. They know they haven't heard everything that would prove their case against these people. It wasn't enough.

Judy headed to bed. Tonight she would sleep as three hours the night before wasn't enough to keep her going for twelve hours. Besides tomorrow, she would be with Robert for the next two days and she would be able to tell him all about her new job. What would he think of it? Was it even safe for her to work here? Yes, she should look for a new job and not return. Safety was her first priority for herself and Kathy. They still had a lot of living to do.

Chapter 11

Candy hugged Sam. Tonight she would be all his. Undivided attention; no dire thoughts would change this celebration. He had taken time to buy her the most beautiful spring bouquet of flowers. Sam concerned, as she seemed so distracted the night before. He was hoping that she was not trying to get over some love affair that had gone sour in Calgary. Some jerk who had betrayed her.

Oh well, she was here now and it was his ambition to make her his tonight. He was going to sweep her off her feet. He didn't have any trouble doing that with the many women that he had courted in the last seven years. He felt confident that he would be able to do it again; even though he realized that she wasn't like any of the other women he dated.

She was special! She was the one! That was a scary thought. She knew him; really knew him. They headed out the door and into the elevator.

"What do you think about me moving in with my Aunt Amie?" asked Candy

He looked at her quizzically and questioned, "Why are you moving over there; you know that I had hoped you would move in with me?"

She gasped, "It's way too soon for me to drop that on you! I want some time to date you. I want a courtship! I want you sure that I am what you want. Plus, I want to know that you haven't changed and become some horrible monster since I have been gone."

"Oh really, you think I am a vampire, maybe? Alternatively, I have underworld connections. Maybe, I have another wife. Perhaps, I'm a bigamist looking for a second wife?" Sam questioned

By this point, he had her laughing. "No, I just don't want to rush things. I want time to enjoy this. I need a courtship!" she giggled

I need time to work out this terrorist threat and to do whatever I can to stop 9 -11 from happening. Would he even understand what was at stake here?

Should she let him hear the tape when she got it back from Rabbi Samuel? Questions! She just wanted to have fun tonight!

"What did you do today? Why were you late?" Asked Candy she tried to turn the conversation away from commitments. She wasn't ready for serious conversation tonight. Arriving at the posh New York Steak House that they had frequented often in their teens, she gasped with delight. Their seat reserved. The band was starting up and their favorite song was playing,

"Always" How romantic?" She whispered in his ear.

He immediately whisked her to the dance floor and they twirled around until she got dizzy and had to sit down. Sam had not changed; still a romantic man; much more romantic than she was that's for sure. She had changed; her concern about terrorists and his concerns about music, food and dancing. How would they ever get along? Sam wanted to stay a kid forever and she was this serious old person.

Her mother's death had taken her ability to relax and have fun. How was she ever to get that back. Part of her wanted to go back to being a big kid, too; but when she thought back to her teens, even then she had trouble being a kid. She had concluded that she had always been serious.

"What ever do you see in me? I'm a wet blanket. Is it the challenge to make me laugh and enjoy myself that makes you so interested in me?" Candy asked boldly

Sam didn't answer; he just gave a sigh and stated, "That's it!"

Whatever, that first glass of wine hit the spot? They were ordering their meal! No hesitation there! At least, she knew what she wanted. Taste buds were still normal thank goodness. The garlic from the Caesar Salad and the freshness of the crisp Romaine leaves tickled her tongue. The chef was flipping their stake over the grill in front of them. Yes, it was triple A AA Beef from Alberta. She had to admit that when it came to stake Alberta knew what it was doing.

The main course was over. They would dance for a while and then have some desert. A camera girl came around and took a Polaroid of them. It would be a nice memory to cherish. It hit her hard this restaurant was on the main floor of one of the Twin Towers. Yes, this would be a memorable picture for sure. She had to trust Sam with her knowledge or they would never have a real relationship. He would have to listen to the tapes and care as much as she did.

They would have to do something to stop it. He was a stockbroker. He knew influential people. Maybe he knew just the right person to help stop this attack. She had to give him a chance at least to help. Not tonight!

Rabbi Samuel said that he would give her tape back tomorrow. She trusted him. He had wanted to keep it to make copies. Especially for his friend, who had written the book, "Weather Wars Now?"

Candy was eager to meet this man, too. Perhaps the author of this book might even come and talk with all of them. What was his name? Sam seemed to know when she drifted off and he had caught her daydreaming again.

He asked, "Candy, what's keeping you tied up in knots?"

Candy shrugged it off and commented, "There is just so much to take in. I hadn't realized how much I had missed you and everything when I was away in Calgary."

Sam seemed satisfied with this answer. He got her back out on the dance floor again and they were dancing to "Blue Swede Shoes" an Elvis impressionist was actually doing the old song some justice. They gave it all they could and exhausted returned to their table.

Sam stated, "Another wine and some desert and then I'm whisking you off to my place for the night."

Candy taunted, "I may fall asleep and disappoint you! "

Sam retorted, "You couldn't have aged that fast. You're still the hot girl I know; stop teasing me!"

They danced another two fast beet songs and then a slow one. It had been their favorite song through high school. They had both loved this theme song, Laura from the movie, Dr. Zhivago.

They had always believed their love for each other was comparable. Now, they looked at each other with all the old memories coming back and the love bloomed once again for them. Maybe tonight Candy could leave her troubles behind and just go with the flow. Sam was really a wonderful man and she had to let him know that. Tomorrow, they would listen to the tapes at Rabbi Samuel's home, but not now.

It had been seven years, since Candy had made love; no wonder she was so hesitant. She had only ever loved him and when the relationship ended, she was so crushed that she didn't have the courage to get involved again.

Her mother was her companion and that was enough for her. Her mother's death was so much more devastating as she had not only lost her mother, but her best friend. She had been her only friend. Arriving in Calgary at the age of twenty-five, she was too old to have the opportunity to make any close friends. Close friendships happened when you were going to high school or university.

She wanted to get her Nurses training finished as quickly as possible so she could take her mother and her on vacation trips around the world. They had such plans for the future. All that stopped abruptly when the verdict of cancer struck her mother. The battle to save her life took all of her energy as she tried to stay in University and take care of her mother.

Six months, from the time the time her mother's diagnosis to the time she died. Not long enough to adjust to the idea that she was gone. The following month, she worked two jobs to get the money to go back to University and now this event with these horrible men. It was hard for her to relax and enjoy being a woman. It was strange and so far from her thoughts.

Would she ever be normal again? Women her age thought of nothing else, but having lovers and such. For Candy to think of this stuff was like being on another planet. Somehow, she would be normal again.

Sam poured her a hot tub, lit candles, put on her old favorite mood music, and poured her another glass of wine, and then he went to the bedroom to undress.. He had thought to buy her the prettiest ruby negligee, which hung on the towel rack beside her. Gardenia scented bubble bath. What more could a girl ask for?

"Would you like you're back washed?" He gently whispered in her ear.

Candy felt like a princess and responded, "I think that would be acceptable! You have to join me in this girly perfume."

Candy's body took over and she was once again a sexy woman. She could feel again! He had been her only lover, but she was not going to let him know that. She had read enough girly love stories in her past. She could play the part of a ravenous woman. She let her imagination guide her body and he did the rest. After they lay exhausted.

Candy decided to confess, "Do you know that you have been my only lover? I haven't been with anyone else in all these years. So I have been quite hesitant in having sex with you as I am so out of practice."

Sam amazed, "You haven't dated other men in all these years?"

"I'll make sure that we catch up. I'm amazed! Why in heaven's name wouldn't you have gone out on dates and had love affairs?" questioned Sam

"I was too busy going to University, taking care of my Mother especially, when the Cancer hit, and then after wards so devastated with her death that I threw myself into working two jobs. I told myself that I just didn't have time for frivolous stuff," answered Candy

"Being a woman and enjoying yourself isn't frivolous!" scolded Sam

"What have you been doing with yourself in the last seven years? Being a playboy no doubt? Chasing all the skirts you could?" teased Candy

"Actually no I haven't had that much time either, There was the odd girlfriend. None of them measured up to you, so the affairs didn't last very long. Besides learning all the tricks of a stockbroker is more than a full-time job. I work an average of a fifty-five hour week. That doesn't leave much time for romance." Sam replied

"So I guess maybe our relationship is destiny and that we are together until death parts us. Scary thought don't you think?" She suggested

"Are you proposing to me? Did I hear right?" Quizzed Sam

Candy defiantly answered, "Heavens no! Just wondering what is going on in the Universe. Weird and wonderful things are happening to me. I can't help but wonder what is going to happen next."

With this, they fall asleep in each other's arms. Contentment and happiness took over. They have breakfast together in the sun porch. It was simple; toast, fruit and coffee.

Candy asked, "Would you be able to meet me today at five tonight at Rabbi Samuel's home?"

Sam breaking up with laughter, asked, "So you are setting the date already for a wedding; that is fast isn't it even by your standards of being impatient?"

She realized how that must have sounded and laughed back.

She answered, "No, that isn't why. It is a meeting of very important people from all walks of life that will be there to discuss a coming terrorist attempt."

Sam collapsed onto the bed. "What are you talking about? What terrorist activity are you talking about?" quizzed Sam

Finally, she revealed her part in the secret meeting. The Calgary Lounge's tapes were important evidence! Many powerful people would listen to these tapes. She wanted him there. He needed to understand how committed she was to protecting their beloved New York.

Sam amazed agreed instantly! He breathed, "You're amazing. No wonder I couldn't get over you!"

He dropped her off at Aunt Amie's home. A real kiss this time! She felt relieved. She could kiss him again. "Wow! That's the kiss I remembered." he chuckled as he took off to work.

Chapter 12

Friday morning came early and Judy needed no alarm clock this morning. The blue jays outside her window had awakened her

Today, she would be seeing Robert and they would be going home hunting. The breeze was blowing the curtain and she felt it touch her cheek. She would be ready by four. He'd be picking her up.

A quick shower, even quicker getting dressed and up the stairs, she flew. Oatmeal, raisins, and walnuts were her favorite breakfast. A delight! The coffee smelt especially good this morning too. She hadn't seen Robert for many weeks. Had he been taking care of himself? She would soon know!

Kathy joined her for breakfast. Ruth was dressed and eating her breakfast. Ruth was all excited too. She was getting her hair and nails done today. Judy looked in the mirror and realized that she needed to do something with her hair, too.

"Kathy would you mind picking up some hair dye when you get the meds?" asked Judy

"What color should I get? A dark golden blonde? Might look good?" Kathy asked.

"Time for me to go blonde? Robert won't know what hit him if I show up strawberry blonde. It might do him good!" Judy answered

Judy planned the meals for when she would be gone. Simple meals that Kathy could help prepare on the night shift. This would make it easier for Cherry. She only knew how to cook Philippine dishes. This wouldn't have made the residents happy. The residents liked good old-fashioned Canadian food..

"I hope Ruth will be okay while I am gone." Judy thought to herself.

I've done all that I could do. I will have to trust that God will take care of her. She realized how fragile Ruth's situation was, but there was nothing more that she could do for her. She would leave the tape deck under the boardroom table, as it would be safer there. Kathy would take care of the taping while she was away.

"What would Robert think? Would he even let her come back?" she whispered.

Kathy arrived back from the Drug Store. They said goodbye. They exchanged phone numbers. The day wore on slowly; the clock was definitely slow today. Lunch came and went. The hairdresser showed up at one, in the afternoon.

Delighted to see her; Ruth even at her age of 83 liked to look as good as she could. The hairdresser was about forty-three years old; bleached straw blonde hair covered in a mask of makeup. She seemed anything but a hairdresser. Very unkempt! I wonder where they found her. Judy wondered.

Oh well, I guess it isn't easy to get hairdressers to come to Care Homes and work on the elderly. They are part of the fashion parade and this is probably what they think is one-step above doing the dead in funeral parlors. She reasoned.

She asked, "Do you also do hair for folk in the Funeral Parlors? "

Her name was Wendy. She responded," Oh yes, I enjoy working on the dead. They are much easier to please." With this, she gave a hearty laugh.

Judy got chills from that comment. No doubt, she was a close friend of Harry's. Perhaps at Halloween she can come here dressed as Dracula or an ugly witch. It would be much more her style. Oh well, Ruth did not seem to mind her so why should she. It was just something about the woman Judy didn't like. Did she smell drugs on her? Booze? At the time, she just didn't like her. This was very unusual because Judy liked everyone.

I must hurry to make supper and have the residents all ready so I can leave early she thought to herself. She smeared the color on her hair and returned to her food prep. Marie was frantic again walking around and around wailing "9 -11 the planes"

It would be good to have a break from that scene and yes; she would take the time to get shoes for Marie and Ruth.

Finally, three thirty, time for her to wash out my color and dry my hair. I need to get changed and ready to leave. Cherry could do the rest for supper. She had done all she could.

Cherry came into the kitchen and asked, "You'll be gone until Tuesday morning?"

Judy smiling said, "Yes, I will return Tuesday at eight. I hope that you have a good weekend. Kathy will make supper during the night and all you will have to do is reheat it at supper time."

Cherry gave a sigh, "That's good! I don't know much about Canadian cooking."

The doorbell rings! Robert is at the door. Judy handed him her suitcase and asked him to wait in the van.

"I have to say goodbye to the folks; it'll only take me a minute or two, okay?" she asked.

She gave Ruth, Marie, Joyce and Anna hugs. They watched her go out the door. You could tell that they didn't want to part with her; especially Ruth A tear slipped down her cheek as Judy left the home. "How would they make out in the next three days?" Judy whispered

Robert looked as handsome as ever. He looked so much like her favorite movie star, Kevin Costner. He gave her a big hug and a kiss that left her melting. How did he do that to her? She was too old for him to affect her like this.

As they drove along, Judy noticed a hotel that would be nice for them. They had a smorgasbord; all you can eat! That sounded good to her. There was a swimming pool and a hot tub!

Judy asked, "How about that place for tonight? Tomorrow we can find somewhere else."

Robert tired from driving over 500 hundred miles on back Oil Patch roads agreed. Did she read his mind or what? He certainly didn't want to spend much time looking for a place tonight.

"Thanks Hon, I need to lay down and the sooner the better!" he replied.

They checked in and soon found themselves lying on the bed. "It's been so long since we cuddled." Judy added

"Do you still snore?" asked Robert

They snuggled up and before long; they had both dozed off. a few hours later, Robert nudged her awake. "Are we ever getting old?" he chuckled

"Supper is waiting for us in the banquet room; let's get to it!" exclaimed Robert

She stretched and explained, "I haven't been able to sleep well for the last week! I'll tell you why over supper." They filled their plates with

Prime Rib and Baked Potatoes. Guilty reminding each other, "Watch it; we're on diets remember." They whispered

Over supper, Judy told him all that had happened at Brenda's Care Home.

Ruth and her adopted son, Harry Hall

Marie from New York and her condition

Joyce and her schizophrenic son's attack

Karl from Germany who is likely a Nazi War Criminal

Peter the ex-priest whose son wanted him safe

Anna the 102 year old; as fragile as a china doll

Then she explained Harry, Walter, Nurse Susan and the Administrator, Joanne Hall. Psychopaths or sociopaths? Which insanity, she hadn't figured out yet.

She included the tape recording that she had found on the stairs dropped by Harry Hall. The bribe of $10,000 offered to Cherry if she proved her loyalty what ever that meant. The phone security was extreme. People restricted from the residents. The baby monitors in all of the rooms recording downstairs on their very elaborate tape recording device. Why was there such an expensive Boardroom and Bedroom Suite? This was not an ordinary Care Home. Something very different was going on there,

Robert shook his head amazed!

He whispered, "You can't go back there. Its' too dangerous! It sounds like a Death House not a Care Home to me. Thousands of dollars will flow into this care home. They'd think nothing of killing you if they thought you would endanger their scheme. Think about it! You have heard them say on the tape that Karl Rudolph is paying $15,000 a month. Ruth and Marie are paying $10,000 a month. This is just the start of things to come. Six residents each pay them $10,000 a month! Total of $60,000 per month or $720,000 a year untaxed.

They aren't going to let anyone get in the way of that kind of tax-free money. You can bet that they will have on paper an amount of $18,000 a month with the going rate of $3,000 per month for each resident. You are not going back there! That is definite!"

Judy blurted, "I have to Kathy is all alone there. She is depending on me and so is fragile Ruth. I can't abandon them."

"We can't talk about this anymore here!" warned Robert

Judy with tears in her eyes muttered, "You have to understand!"

"When we're in the van, we'll talk about this some more; I understand how you feel; hell I feel the same way. I just don't want to lose you. These people are psychopaths and killing is a pleasure to them."

They finished their supper in silence. Thank goodness, they're the only ones out on the deck eating. No one had heard their argument. It was seven-thirty, and back in the van, Robert told her that he had looked at a Motor home. He had found one for sale that needed a little mechanical work, which he could repair easily. He had wanted to buy it but had to see how she felt about it.

"Can we go see it now?" questioned Judy as she felt that in it she would feel safe.

Robert pleased that she liked the idea responded, "I was hoping that you would want to do that; I have already set up an appointment to take it for a test run tonight. They're expecting us at eight this evening."

"Yes, I want to go to Fort McMan with you and find work there. You are right; its' not possible for me to work as a Nurse now. If Kathy and I have, our plans go through with exposing Brenda's Care Home I'll need to do something different. I may have to marry you just so I have another sir name. These people are powerful! Do you still want to marry me?" asked Judy

"Are you proposing?" asked Robert with a hearty chuckle.

"Yes, the honeymoon will have to wait; besides we can always do our honeymoon with this Motor home. We'll park at Jasper or Banff. That sounds like a great honeymoon to me.," replied Judy

91

They have arrived at the R.V lot and there it is, their escape home. "We can park that on our acreage when we find where we want to settle. It'll be more than enough to live in while we build our cottage. In the meantime, we can live in it while we work either in an oil camp or construction site. There is a lot of road building going on too. How would you feel about working summers and taking the winters off in Arizona?" questioned Robert

"How can we afford it?" asked Judy

"Price is $15,000 including the tax. What a great deal! Shit it costs that much to rent a hotel room in Fort McMan for a month. Aren't you glad I lived in the van for those first two months? It was very cold; but it was worth it. Now you know why I saved the money. I can pay cash for it now! Maybe I can get him to fill the gas tanks and some winter tires. "Added Robert

Sold! The Motor home was theirs. The deal finished!

Robert asked, "How'd you like to cancel the hotel room, drive to Banff, spend the night in our new little home?"

Judy couldn't believe her ears. Robert drove the Motor home and Judy followed behind him with the van. They stopped at the hotel just long enough to grab their suitcases. They parked their van in the Hotel Parking lot so it would be there when they got back. Now, they were on their way to Banff just like that.

They would drive for a couple of hours and park in one of those pull offs. It would face the morning sun. Waking up to a sunrise in the Canadian Rockies was a marvelous way to start the day. They were having the holiday, they had dreamed about all these months. Judy kept pinching herself; could this really be happening she wondered.

Overhead, the sky was alive with the Aurora Borealis. This was the first time that Judy had ever seen this glorious sight and she was amazed.

Robert stated, The Northern Lights or Aurora Borealis are quite common here in Northern Alberta. It is truly beautiful. Can you believe it; scientists are taking something as beautiful as this and using it to create billion watts of laser energy. They have been playing with this incredible beauty that God has given us and are using it to destroy our planet. I'll tell you more later, when I am not so tired.

Aurora Grandeur

Chapter 13

Aunt Amie ran to the door to help Candy with her luggage. She had waited years for Candy to live with her. She had never had children and had always thought of Candy as her own daughter. Especially, when her sister died leaving Candy all alone. Now it would be her turn to teach her what she knew. Aunt Amie was wise enough to know she could never take the place of her real Mother but she'd be a close second.

Her home was an authentic heritage building erected in 1899 by the Mayor at that time and built with exquisite artisanship. Carved cherry doors, stained glass windows, marble floors, ceramic tiles and she had kept the old world flair.

Candy asked, "How did she afford such a grand home?"

Aunt Amie replied, "Through my work with Numerology, I have bought and sold homes with the right numbers and at the right times so that I have been able to make a lot of money on Real Estate. In fact, many of my richest clients come to me for Real Estate advice, as the word is out that I make good Real Estate investments. Yes, what I do is not hocus pocus but a real science. Never mind that the so-called scientists laugh at my work, as they do not understand what I do. I really could not care less. I know it works well for my clients. My home here has helped me to provide the impression that I needed to do my psychic work.."

Her Jewish friends and relatives came too. Sometimes a movie star when visiting New York would here about her and drop by for a reading. She never knew what each day would bring. Life was never boring! She had wanted earlier to teach Candy some of her art but her mother had not wanted that; instead she had hoped Candy would have a professional career in Nursing.

There were many things that Aunt Amie offered which included Astrology, Numerology, Dowsing, Tarot and Angel Card readings. She even did Hypnosis with a specialty in Past Life readings. Once a year, she would be on Radio and Television as a celebrity in her own right.

Candy knew all about it and had often wanted to know about some of these metaphysical ideas; but her mother frowned so much on it that she obeyed her Mother and didn't pursue it. Now years later, she could delve into all of this mysterious knowledge.

In fact it was her intention to learn as much as possible and as quickly as she could. She had always thought she had talent in this area, as she knew when people would call her, or even when the phone was going to ring, or what the weather would be like the next day, when a letter would come in the mail, better yet, whom the letter would be from, and much more. Now it was time to take this ability to a higher level. This was exciting!

Up the stairs, Candy followed her Aunt Amie to her waiting bedroom. She remembered how pretty it was when she was a child. Wallpaper with pink roses and butterflies on a white silk background. Pink satin bedspread with curtains to match created the prettiest little girl's room. Would it be the same? Aunt Amie had renovated the room. Now the wallpaper was vertical stripes in three different shades of rose, modern cellular pleated shades hung in the windows so she could see outside, but no one could see in. Valances covered with soft rose and side panels to match framed the windows.

A large damask rose comforter with matching pillow shams and dust ruffle anointed the bed, An Indian rug hugged the floor. A collectors Chandelier hung above the bed. Fresh flowers were on the dresser. How very elegant! "How did you know what my favorite color was? Oh of course how silly of me, you're psychic!" exclaimed Candy

"Do I have to continue calling you Auntie? Would it be okay if I just called you Aunt Amie? You seem more like a friend than an Aunt?" asked Judy

Aunt Amie gave her a big hug and replied," You bet, I was hoping that you would feel that way!"

The two of them put away her clothes and the small amount of stuff she had fit into her suitcase in her hurry to leave Calgary. Time for lunch, Aunt Amie had earlier prepared a lovely jellied salmon mold and it took only minutes to dish it out and they were eating. Jasmine tea, croissants, and homemade jam finished it off. How Candy had hated eating alone and now, she would have Aunt Amie to share her meals with her.

More importantly share ideas! Life was getting better and better. Maybe it did have something to do with the Mantra that she had said for months now. The Mantra she had promised her mother to say every day.

"I am in the right place, at the right time, with the right people doing and saying the right thing for my success and happiness now and in the future," She stated.

Aunt Amie looked pleased with that statement. And stated," You know a lot more than I thought you would by making that a philosophy to live by. You are years ahead of most people in understanding how the Universe works"

With that, Aunt Amie went to her office and brought back books that continued with the Power of Positive Thought. How everything contained a frequency or its vibration. This began her first lessons in Numerology. She learned that the pain of loosing her Mother had brought down her vibration level so that she unknowingly was in the space of those people planning that wretched Care Home and of more how she would be in the space of these two men that could so easily discuss the terrorist act planned for 9 - 11 in New York.

Aunt Amie continued on explaining how the Spirit of her Mother had intervened and had acted on her behalf to get her out of Calgary. That she was on the right path and that it wouldn't take long for her vibration energy to shift and she would return to the young woman she once was. The cares and pain would lift off her shoulders as a winter's coat comes off in the spring.

Sam had phoned to say that he would again be a bit late to pick them up for the visit to Rabbi Samuel's home.

Both of them were fine with this as there was so much to discuss. The doorbell rang and Aunt Amie answered it to find a delivery van from the local florist. Sam had sent flowers to her. He had remembered her favorite flowers were Gardenias.

Candy was still having cultural shock. The harshness of Calgary compared to the genteelness of New York. Was she even on the same planet; she wondered?

Her first lessons in Numerology were fun. The ancient science based on frequencies each person's name added up to a different number. Each letter in the alphabet had an assigned number.

A, B, C, D, E, F, G, H, I was 1, 2, 3, 4, 5, 6, 7, 8, 9 respectively.

J, K, L, M, N, O, P, Q, R was 1, 2, 3, 4, 5, 6, 7, 8, 9 again

S, T, U, V, W, X, Y, Z   was 1, 2, 3, 4, 5, 6, 7, 8 respectively

This seemed very simple, but as she played with the names of people that she knew their frequencies did add up to what their names were. She learned that Numerology based on the Kabala and old Jewish belief system used and still used for thousands of years.

Her name Candy for instance worked out like this C – 3; A – 1; N – 5; D – 4; Y – 7 when added up equaled "eleven". She read what it meant to be an eleven vibration and realized that she had the energy of a Master Number. Whatever did that mean?

"What is a Master Number?" she asked Aunt Amie

It means that you were born with Psychic abilities. You could use these gifts to teach others and do spiritual readings. You can easily channel passed over loved ones. When you are ready, you will see and hear dead people. A recent Movie, "The Sixth Sense" deals with a six-year-old boy's ability to see dead people and talk with them. You will become a recognized Psychic or Metaphysical Lecturer.

Numerology when applied to the name Aunt Amie worked out like A – 1, M – 4, I – 9, E – 5 added up to the number 19. When further added together became the number "1" a Spiritual Teacher, Leader or Guide. Candy found this fascinating. Out came all the textbooks on Numerology. This was interesting but as she glanced at the many books on Numerology, she realized that it was very complicated and would take many tedious hours to learn. However, it would be interesting and rewarding work.

Two hours went by so fast that neither of them even noticed that it was already four o'clock in the afternoon and they had a mere hour to get ready before Sam would be there to pick them up to go to Rabbi Samuel's home.

"Oh that's right, he did phone to tell us he would be a little late. Thank God." sighed Aunt Amie.

"It's going to take me many months to learn Numerology alone; never mind all the other stuff that is in this office for me to understand, study and know so one day I will be a Psychic too. I will learn all of this." Judy promised.

What an amazing Aunt she had! How very lucky she was to be able to learn and what an unbelievable future lay before her! She thought to herself. She wanted to stay here with her and study. There would be plenty of time to get married In the future; but for now, she wanted to study these ancient arts.

"Why didn't my mother want her to do this?" Candy asked

"It scared her when she got messages from the other side of some one's pending death. She found it very frightening and I suppose she didn't want you to have to deal with it. I think she knew that you were very gifted in this area. She was concerned that it might consume you as she thought it had done with me. She blamed my gifts for me not ever marrying and having a family.

It was so interesting that I just had no time to play boyfriend and love games and such. I was far more interested in how the subconscious, conscious, and super conscious mind worked in harmony! Reincarnation and Astral Traveling were my specialties. I never had time to get married as so many people wanted readings." Aunt Amie continued

Candy could see how her mother had meant to protect her and she wished that they had spent more time talking about all of this. They could have had so much fun. It was four-thirty and Sam was ringing the doorbell.

"We are off to the wonderful world of Oz!" he chuckled not knowing the seriousness of the coming meeting. He had simply forgotten about the tapes that Candy had mentioned earlier as his day had been so hectic.

"By the way, where are we going to have supper tonight? I haven't made any reservations.. Where would you two like to eat? Aunt Amie, do you have a favorite restaurant nearby? Any great restaurants?" babbled Sam so full of excitement.

I wonder if its' too late now to plan a June wedding? That is only two months away! Oh well, we do have plenty of time to get married I would be just as happy with a fall wedding maybe in September or October, when all the maple trees are in their glorious autumn colors. I must have patience or I will have a run away bride. She is good at running away. I must go slowly! He thought to himself.

They arrived and he was amazed to see so many cars parked in the street. What ever was the occasion? Was it a funeral and no one had told him about it? He turned to Candy and asked, "Why are there so many people here? "

Candy shook her head "Have you forgotten what I told you this morning before you left for work The tape recordings that I have brought from Calgary which hold such important information. I thought you would remember the terrorist's plan to attack New York. So much has happened. Maybe I didn't make myself clear this morning. It's not your fault that you didn't remember as such shocking news is hard to accept." Candy replied

The group welcomed Aunt Amie, Candy, and Sam into the large living room. Everyone was eager to hear the tapes. Telephones had been very busy for the last two days organizing this meeting. Rabbi Samuel's congregation was waiting to hear the tapes. Meetings happened here regularly. They came to hear guest speakers on many subjects.

Last month, he had Scientist Tim Bears-Den talk with them on his research in Energetics what the Russians called "Scalar Longitudinal Waves" from the Forth Dimension. They now could tap into "free-energy" with the use of this science. How the Russians had researched Nikola Tesla's Research for more than a hundred years.

In fact, Rabbi Samuel had tried to have Futurist, Grant Stallion come to this meeting; but unfortunately, he was in Canada doing some more research. When Rabbi Samuel told his parishioners that he had shocking news that they had to hear and keep secret; they knew it was important. They were waiting for the information. His intent was to calmly stop this coming attack.

Quietly manage this terrorist crisis in a calm way. Limit the damage as much as possible.

Rabbi Samuel cleared his throat and stated, "I have brought you

100

here to listen to this important taped conversation. This tape was done in Calgary last week. Do not be over come with fear, as that is what these terrorists want to have happen. We must keep cool heads and deal with this carefully. There will be no gossip about it. Many lives, including our way of life depends on secrecy. After listening to this, we must plan our action not reaction.

This is the time for control. The Jewish people have always had harsh events that have hurt our people. Fear is not what we want at this time but calm decisive action."

Everyone listened to the tapes that Candy had brought from Calgary. Silence followed!

Rabbi Samuel thanked Candy for having the insight to tape the two conversations. Those that knew Marie Rothman were sad to find her in such a horrible place and talk began with how to get her back home safely to New York. Some of the distinguished men gathered stood up and promised their friends that they would be doing all that they could to search down these terrorists and prevent the coming attack.

They cautioned that they would have to do much of this in secrecy. They could not afford to trigger chaos in New York. This privileged information must not get into the hands of the wrong people as it could speed up the attack. Worse, the attack could happen in another city. Caution and secrecy had to go together.

A silent moment honored!

Sam hugged Candy. Relieved he stated, "No wonder you've seemed so distant and far away!"

Chapter 14

Robert pulled off the highway and turned the Motor home around so it faced the East. He wanted the first rays of sun to hit their faces. Just as they were going to sleep, the Aurora Borealis flickered in the sky above. "How beautiful!" Judy exclaimed

"Judy, the sun is going to shine on your pretty little face in the morning.," he stated.

Robert had planned this trip for months. It was a holiday; but it had to include research to see where they would buy their acreage and settle down. Over the small table in the tiny nook, he showed Judy that they would stop at Banff. Then take the highway to Jasper. His co-workers told him there were scenic, good priced properties near a village called Alberta Beach.

His friend, Mike was expecting him to stop by for supper Sunday night. They lived on acreage at Lake Isle.

Robert asked, "We'll see a lot of Alberta in the next two days."

He continued," It was important to stay close to Edmonton so he would be within calling range of the Oil Company that he worked for called Hellcana. The people joked about the name as it was like Hell in a can to work there at times. He didn't want to buy any property near Fort McMan as it was too expensive and even colder than the rest of Alberta. "Better to have our cottage near a city and yet have the beauty of the country." He added

They climbed into bed too tired to make love. Just as Robert had said, the sun beamed on their faces and the light breeze off the lake caressed their cheeks. They had nothing to eat or drink in their hurry to escape the city,

"Oh well, let's get going; we'll find a truckers stop down the road a few miles. Will you be okay till then?" asked Robert

"You bet I have a chocolate granola bar in my purse. Would you like half?" she asked

In a few minutes, they would be having breakfast in Canmore. The thought of coffee, crisp bacon and eggs quickened the miles. Sitting down at the busy truck stop, it seemed surreal. They had persevered through hard times and now look at them. A week ago, Judy would never have thought anything like this was possible. Robert was good at keeping secrets.

"I think I am going to enjoy being married to you," she whispered.

Now they were on Highway 1 heading to Banff. "We'll stop for a while and take some pictures. We have to do some touristy things, don't we?" he asked

"I hate getting my picture taken these days; it's hard to remember when I actually took a nice picture. I guess I just haven't come to terms with getting old." Judy sighed

"You'll do old girl!" he laughed

"You're not very romantic are you?" replied Judy

"That's for sissies; I'm a real man don't you know? You're going to need that so you don't freckle." He shouted as he threw a baseball hat at her.

It was March 31st. The place was quiet; the tourist season hadn't started yet. The area was pleasant. They were all alone on the beach and this seemed just fine to them.

"I checked on the property around Lake Isle. The prices are reasonable. Maybe I can even find a mechanic's job in one of the nearby towns. If we are both working and living in our Motor home it won't take long for us to safe the money to build a cottage." he stated.

Judy liked his confidence and replied, "I know that I won't stay very long at that Care Home. I don't feel safe there. You're right about my safety. Do you think that you could take a couple of weeks off and park this Motor home in Calgary close to Brenda's Care Home? You can keep watch over me. I'd like to spend another two weeks there. I need to keep my promise to Kathy and I wouldn't feel right abandoning Ruth. I know that you want to get back to work, but I have to stay there for a little longer." Judy added

"Let me think about it for a while. It's a sudden change of plans for me; but maybe I can research cottage packages and other work around Edmonton. I'd feel better if you weren't in that house while you're asleep. Hell! Anything could happen to you! We'll see just let me think on it for a bit." he replied.

"Time for lunch and a little nap." he stated as he gave her a wink. A big smile spreads across his face as he reached over and squeezed her thigh.

"It's been a while; I am out of practice you know. Four months now!" he chuckled

With that, they pulled into Lake Louise. "We're going to dress up a bit and eat in this fancy place with all the rich folk." He stated.

Judy looked at him as he changed his shirt and pants. "So, I might as well do likewise! You want to be one of the rich folk?" she asked with a smirk

It was a beautiful view of the lake. The snow had melted and the lake was unfrozen. Seagulls soared and the breeze tickled their faces as they walked to the restaurant.

"Just think maybe six months from now we'll be sitting in our own dining room looking out over our own lake. You're just as good a cook as these highbrow chefs. I'm a steak and potatoes guy. I'm an old-fashioned guy." he grinned.

Two in the afternoon! They needed to hurry up if they were to get to Jasper by supper. They needed to find a quiet place to park. "We better get going!" they both spoke at the same time.

Highway 1A turned into the Ice Fields Parkway. The scenery was awesome. Coming from southern Ontario, Judy, amazed by the grandeur of the Canadian Rockies continued to whisper, "How beautiful!" There was plenty of wild life. The pastures and fields of southern Ontario full of domestic animals couldn't compare.

Robert had been in Alberta long enough that he now took it for granted. He really wasn't a hunter. He felt the precious wild life left on the planet should be protected not killed. A camera was his choice; not bullets to capture their beauty. He had seen so many beautiful places since he had arrived here. He wanted to live here. He knew there was nothing but sad memories back east. He wanted a fresh start. He knew how lucky he was to have such a great friend and partner.

She was "down to earth" and funny. Not that hard on the eyes either even though age was taking its toll on her and for that matter on him too. I'll always like looking into her eyes. Green what an unusual color. It

105

contrasted her golden reddish blonde hair that brushed her cheek. He knew that she died her hair and he was glad as it made him feel younger too. Time would turn them into white haired old folk.

Both had experienced their dead loved ones visiting them. At first, it had really startled them. Actually, that is what had started their relationship; Robert had joked in the elevator at the Funeral Parlor. He turned around to find Judy behind him.

He said," Stop kidding around Bonnie that hurts; it's my sore shoulder you know better!" Judy looked at him and responded, "I haven't touched you! What's the problem?"

They both realized what was going on as she had experienced the same thing only more so. She could even hear Jack, her dead husband speaking to her, especially as she dozed off to sleep.

"Honey Jean, don't worry I am sending someone to take care of you soon." Jack stated. "What ever" she whispered and drifted off to sleep.

"Guess you're the one! Bonnie said that she would introduce me to a good woman. You look like a pretty good lady to me." Robert joked.

"Funny she always thought I liked red heads. We would get into silly quarrels, when she thought I was looking at a redhead and now she brings you my way. Strange how women think! Anyway, I always did what she asked when she was alive; so I might as well follow through on this too." He continued with a chuckle.

They went for coffee after they picked up their past mate's ashes.

"Even this coincidence is incredible; imagine the timing on this for us to both be here to meet each other. This is incredible. Who'd ever believe us? The other side of the veil; some call it the Forth Dimension did you know that?" Judy asked

They both shook their heads in awe that their loved ones could order such a coincidence, from the other side of the veil of death.

"They really do intend on taking care of us! No one would believe us; so don't go telling anyone this." whispered Robert.

As they traveled through the ice fields, they saw a mother bear and her cub; a mother elk with her baby; some mountain goats and a few big horned rams with of course sheep. This country was much different from Southern Ontario where community after community dotted the countryside. Alberta bound. She had fallen in love with all the nature here. They traveled the miles and arrived before supper at Jasper.

All of the RV Parks were full. They had not thought about all the people skiing up in the mountains as the snow was still there for this last weekend.

"All the R V Parks are full." Robert stated coming back from the office.

"Let's fill the fridge and cupboards with some food enough to make breakfast and tonight's supper. I want to make a nice dinner for you anyway. I can't wait to cook you a meal." Offered Judy and they kept moving along.

They drove past Hinton and Edson. It was six o'clock and they had forgotten the time as the miles flew by.

"Let's stop at the next truck stop so we can have some coffee? I'm running out of energy?" Judy asked.

"You read my mind again, Honey Jean I think we can stop at Alberta Junction. They've told me about a strange map that hangs on the wall in the diner there. I had nearly forgotten about it. You know we're not very far from Mike's place. If we ate supper there, we could probably park at his place tonight. I'll phone him from there. I'll get directions and let them know we will be getting there tonight." Robert stated

Judy had got used to Robert calling her "Honey Jean" At first, it bugged her, but after a while, it just sounded very natural. In a way, it was like having her dead husband, say a quick "Hi" and then he was gone. Her own father had called her "Honey Jean" too. Maybe he was taking care of her too.

What ever it was a comforting nick name. They sat down to supper and before the server came, she noticed the map on the wall. It was eight feet wide and six feet high. No one could miss it. The map was very upsetting. A man named Grant Stallion created the "New Earth Map"

Half the Continents were missing!

Robert explained, "The men I work with have read Grant Stallion's books and know what that map means. The ordinary person wouldn't understand it. The coastline off the Pacific for the States and Canada is missing; Parts of Ontario including Belleville are gone too. Areas of Europe are gone including most of Britain, Ireland, Scotland and more. Iceland is huge and areas in the ocean that long ago had vanished into the oceans resurfaced. Lemuria and Atlantis are visible land masses."

"How does this happen?" Judy asked

"We don't have time to talk about this now; I'll be explaining it and more as soon as we have a free afternoon. There's so much to learn. I've a large book collection by this author. Some that explain what is coming and sooner than we all think." he replied

Life was getting more interesting, but more frightening. What did that map mean and why was Alberta still there when so much of Canada was missing? A thousand questions flooded Judy's brain.

"Does Mike have a wife? Did you reach him on the phone when you called him earlier?" she asked,

"Yes he does have a nice wife about your age. You'll have someone to talk with, when Mike and I go off to his garage. He's worked on an engine that uses magnets. He's very excited about it. He thinks that soon, he'll not have to use hydro or gas. He intends to use this machine to run his truck and Motor home.

He's an intelligent man who reads a lot of science magazines and books. He talks incessantly about a scientist and inventor named Tim Bears-Den. Mike has studied Nikola Tesla's Research since he was a child. His wife likes metaphysics and is a traveling psychic; well known in New York, Seattle, and Los Angeles. Would you believe it she has movie stars phoning her for advice." He replied

Chapter 15

Mike looked like Mel Gibson. He met them with his German shepherd, Beau. Rosemarie joined them a few minutes later. Yes, she missed her own dog, Sparky who had died a few weeks after her husband's death; It had been a double blow. Beau came right up to her and licked her hand. He seemed to know she was missing Sparky. I wonder if dogs can see the Forth Dimension or spirit world. I bet he sees

Sparky beside me here. I feel his soft presence often.

Robert introduced her to Mike and Rosemarie.

"Would you like some home-made desert and tea?" asked Rosemarie

"I would love a cup of tea?" Judy asked thinking to herself how much Rosemarie looked like Sandra Bullock.

Tea poured and blueberry pie served Judy felt very comfortable with her new acquaintance. Rosemarie was studying homeopathy and natural healing. She's a recognized Psychic and still had time for all of this. Judy thought to herself.

Judy asked," How do you find the time to study all of this and do your Psychic work too?"

"I plan it; in the winter I do my studying and research; once spring comes I do my Psychic work all over B.C and Alberta." replied Rosemarie

"Are you tired; it is a long way to travel from Calgary?" Rosemarie asked

"We did that trip last summer and it was beautiful but exhausting. They will be in the garage until midnight. You know how they are with gadgets?" she continued with a laugh.

As the conversation changed from subject to subject, it eventually landed on the Map Judy had just seen at the old-fashioned truck stop at Alberta Junction.

"That Alberta Junction truck stop could be out of the fifties; the decor has chrome chairs and plastic red checkered table clothes. Yet, it had this map on the wall. What do you know about this "New Earth Map and Robert talked about a man named Grant Stallion? Who is he?" asked Judy

"Mike and I have looked deeply into this map; I was as shocked as you were the first time I saw it. I've spent hour's researching Grant Stallion. He's very interesting and I can't wait for his next book to come out. I saved this from one of his last interviews. Would you like to hear it?" Rosemarie asked

Judy responded, "Yes, I'd like to hear anything that would make sense of this map. As right now it seems very weird. I would love to hear it!"

Rosemarie turned on her tape deck and they both listened intently to the radio show.

Futurist, Grant Stallion is here tonight on our show to talk about his visions of dramatic Earth Changes, including the rise of Atlantis and Lemuria and the loss of large areas of land on the Pacific and Atlantic Coasts.

Grant Stallion begins, "We're moving towards great changes soon on Earth. People will become more aware. It will be an "intuitive society" where people will be more group-oriented. The "Me" generation is ending. My visions of the Past when Atlantis existed lead me to believe that there is an infinite energy supply waiting for us to use. We will tap into Atlantis' wireless power source. Huge gigantic crystals inside their Pyramids harnessed the power of the Sun. Energy from the sun provided all Atlantis' energy needs. This energy will replace all our present energy. Nuclear power plants and fossil fuels are nearly over. Our vehicles and buildings will be using this new power soon.

Pyramid power returns. The beings who built the large Pyramids; created them knowing that they would stand through time and lead us into the future. Our space brothers and sisters will be returning to Earth soon. Some believe after Dec 21· 2012's, you will hear the doom and gloom predictions and yes, some of this will happen including loosing a lot of people and land. However, when these spirits realize how it happened; they will be a reckoning force.

Spirit world has the power to fight back. It will be very interesting how the dead change things. "The Intuitive Society" A new world will evolve overnight. A new Earth!. A brave free new world is coming. The old political structures replaced by a New Vision of the World. The power mongers that are here now will be gone. Could the movie, Water World be real? The elite's time is

nearly over. And although, they will try to destroy the entire planet; they won't succeed."

Rosemarie stopped the tape deck as she realized that Judy would want to discuss this amazing information.

"Is that what Mike and Robert are talking about when they said that they were working on a "Free-Energy" generator? Does it have something to do with this Pyramid energy that he just talked about?" asked Judy

"Yes, some of the guys at Fort McMan are working on this new science or rather this very old science that man has lost. Electromagnetism! They are using what they call "Scalar Longitudinal Wave Energy." I'm no scientist; I just repeat what I have heard. It is very exciting! A new world begins. No one goes hungry! Everyone shares in the wealth. This new energy has replaced fossil fuels." Rosemarie replied

"I don't think the rich of this world will ever let that happen. Where I work, I'm witnessing it daily. The wealthy seniors who I care for are in danger of dying quickly; so their relatives can have their money. One dear resident, who owns the property around Saskatoon's Airport, is at risk. She experienced a broken hip a month ago. She has just recovered. I have this eerie feeling that somehow she will have another broken hip soon. This time it will be her death. Pneumonia will take her life. I'm witnessing this and I'm powerless to prevent it." Judy sighed

"Hinton, a little town a few miles away had the same type of home where the wealthy farmers were quietly and quickly dying at the hands of their relatives. One of the Night Nurses caught on to what the management was doing and the place closed. I forget the name but it was something like Sharon's Care Home.

They only had six residents in their home. They wouldn't be investigated as they were to small. The Police Reports proved that Sharon watched the senior's Custody Court Cases. Sharon approached the winner of the Custody fight to place their senior into her Care Home. The term "Ambulance chaser." takes on a new meaning." Stated Rosemarie

"I knew one of the people who were there. He is dead now. His son wanted the farm so he could do a large Marijuana Operation and his father wouldn't agree to it. They went on a holiday to Florida where the father had a heart attack. His son didn't admit him into a local hospital there, but drove for thirty-six hours and brought him back here to this Care Home.

He died there! That is what started the Police Investigation. He was a ladies' man so I think I know how he had a heart attack; but then that is only my speculation." Rosemarie continued

"Did you say the woman's name was Sharon? The Nurse that manages the Care Home where I am now is Susan. Do you suppose she is the same person? " questioned Judy

Rosemarie shrugged her shoulders doubtfully and added, "I think she would still be in prison."

It was midnight, and they joined them. "A glass of beer and munchies?" Rosemarie asked

"Tonight, we got the machine to work. Then for no reason it quit. It is a perpetual motion machine and runs on magnets. I can't believe that it is not on the market. Imagine our world without nuclear power plants, hydro, gas, oil, or coal. Our planet would heal. I want to make these machines and sell them! We'd be rich beyond our wildest dreams." Mike exclaimed,

Robert added, "I'll look for steel and magnets when I am in Calgary on Monday. We have to return for Judy's job. It looks like I am going to stay there for a week or two just till she gets her paycheck and she looks after some of the residents,"

Judy looked at him and smiled so he is going to let her finish helping Ruth, after all. What a relief! She couldn't bear to abandon Ruth, the dear old soul. She needed someone she could trust. Even Marie needed her, as she would only eat properly with her help.

By midnight, Robert and Judy cuddled in their own bed in their Motor home. They had decided to call it a name, Belleville after their Southern Ontario town. They would never be home sick. Yes, the place needed a name. They were two eccentric old folk and that was okay with them. What a day! It seemed like every couple of hours there was yet another surprise.

"Judy, I haven't told you yet; but I've found a piece of property close to here. Mike helped me find it. A small acreage close to here is for sale. I hope you'll consider looking at it tomorrow, as the people who own it are anxious to sell it and are leaving the area. It's a once in a lifetime chance. It's half priced. Would you be willing to look at it?" Robert asked

Judy amazed asked, "What did the property look like? Did it face the west so they could enjoy the sunsets at night?"

"In the past, it had a railway track running through it which is why it's going so much cheaper as the owners are concerned that the train's noise would be annoying. It's a private sale and I can probably put half down and the rest in payments. This is a better way to buy it." He added

"I love the sound of a train. I always have." Judy stated

"We'll build as far as possible away from the track and I can barter my mechanic skills in exchange for the work of a back hoe. A large berm will protect the home; so we won't ever hear the noise of the train at all." He continued

"Don't have to go to all that bother on my behalf; I really do love the sound of the train, especially, at night." Judy repeated

As they discussed this, they felt certain that they would be able to buy this land.

"Tomorrow will be exciting!" exclaimed Robert.

They would survey their new project. They didn't need to set the alarm clock to wake up. They had their Belleville home turned so the sun would shine on their faces. A lovely sunrise would be all they would need to wake up.

"Loving in the morning? Honey Jean?" Robert whispered

Judy didn't hear a thing. She was old cold. Sleep had won again! Morning came early with the sun beaming on their faces. The soft lapping of the lake's waves nudged them awake. Blue Jays were calling

114

and the odd sound of a Raven. A dog howled in the distance, but the noise didn't bother them as it was too far away. They looked out the window and there on Lake Isle were men fishing in their small boats.

"Imagine us going out and catching our breakfast? " Judy asked

"We'd be hungry; sitting out there a couple of hours fishing." Robert replied

"Well for now, be happy with bacon and eggs, coffee, Sir?" she stated as she poured his coffee.

Mike and Rosemarie came to take them to their proposed acreage. They were excited to see the property too. Around the corner, Mr. and Mrs. Barns were waiting for them. They wanted to move to the Okanagan. Their friends had moved there and they were lonely. They thought the winters would be milder there. They were eager to sell.

"Yes, I am willing to take two lump sums; one now and the rest in three months." Mr. Barns agreed.

"This does make it possible as I have $25,000. To give you now and I will give you the rest in three months." Robert promised

They shook on it and Robert picked up Judy and swung her around. He was soooo happy. "Honey Jean we have our new home.!" He shouted.

"I'll see you in Stony Plain tomorrow morning to finish the paper work at Lawyer Gerald Howe's office." Robert stated

Mr. Barns responded, "Ten sounds good to me! His office is across the street from the CIBC Bank you can't miss it."

With that, the Barns drove away leaving Robert, Judy, Mike, and Rosemarie with the legal drawings of the ten acres. They all climbed back into the SUV 4X4 and headed in that direction. They needed to see how the railway train tracks would affect their property.

Mike piped up, "I have a friend with a back hoe and he'll build a berm for you; he'll be happy to barter with you."

Robert stated, "I had a feeling I'd be able to do some bartering. The berm in place and a road put in. The property value will double. I'll be able to find a lender that will give me the rest of the money. Our motor home, Belleville will be a fine home until the end of October. Seven months is enough time to build our home. Double Garage Packages are under $20,000 for the materials and framing. By Christmas, we'll have a small finished cottage just right for two old folk." Robert continued

"Dimensions of 30' wide by 24' deep give 720 sq ft. A good size cottage! In addition, a 12/12 Pitch roof gives a main bedroom looking over the living room. Their home supported on steel I-Beams. They would pay taxes on the property. Buying a garage package is a small loan. It isn't a mortgage. At our age, we don't want the burden of a mortgage." Robert continued

"This is an amazing surprise; I didn't know we would be able to do this so soon. How do you keep these secrets?" asked Judy delighted with the aspect of having her own home again.

"I can't wait to design the inside. We'llreplace the garage doors with two bay windows and a double door in the front. I would like an energy wood stove on the north side of the home. Two bedrooms and bathroom in between will be perfect. The bedroom in the loft, overlooking the living area gives a feeling of spaciousness. My sister used a garage package to build her cottage in Barrie and she loved it. Using a high-pitched roof will make it even better. No shoveling snow off the roof in the winter." Judy added

Robert smiled and stated, "By Christmas, we'll be "snug as a bug"; that is a sure thing. Maybe we can invite someone for Christmas. They all think we are crazy for leaving Ontario. This will show them another way to look at life."

Judy pinched herself! It just seemed so surreal! This had all happened in less than a weekend. Time was flying by so fast. She suddenly realized that she wouldn't get back to Calgary for work. Instead, tomorrow morning, they would be at the Lawyer's Office at ten o'clock to sign the legal papers for the land. She would have to phone them now and let them know that she would not be able to make it until Tuesday morning. I have to do this immediately.

116

"I don't want them to know where I am as things are going to get nasty there soon. Can we go to Stony Plain to phone them?" Judy asked

Excitedly, they agreed and off to Stony Plain to make the call. They celebrated with brunch in a restaurant, renovated from an old railway station. It certainly had the feeling of the early railway days. Even the menus looked old. Better yet the food was homemade and scrumptious.

The phone call to Brenda's Care Home gave Judy a surprise. Cherry hadn't answered; but some one new. They had hired another Care Aid to do the Sunday shift. A woman with a brusque confident German accent stated, "Brenda's Care Home, Elke speaking, how can I help you?"

Judy responded," My name is Judy and I'll be held up here for another day. I'll return Tuesday morning. Please pass the message to Susan for me. Is everything okay?"

"All is fine here. I'll do another shift. Yes, I'll let Susan know you'll be back on Tuesday." replied Elke

"I will be coming in on Tuesday." Judy answered Pleased that she would have another day with Robert and their new friends. There seemed an edge to that woman's voice. "I think something is wrong at the Care Home; something isn't right I can feel it." Judy sighed.

On their return to Lake Isle, Mike and Rosemarie invited them to spend the afternoon and offered supper. The guys went back out to the garage. Tinkering away with machines seemed their escape from the world.

"Thank goodness, they aren't sport's nuts; I couldn't handle listening for hours to football or hockey." stated Rosemarie

Judy agreed," Can you imagine what some poor women have to put up with; hours of noise from those boring games. Robert played University Hockey and you would think he would be watching it; but he says after all his games he can't stand watching it. He still wants to play. It is just too frustrating for him. Is there an old man's hockey club here?" asked Judy

"I think there is a club in Stony Plain." She answered

They sat down for a cup of tea. Judy noticed a deck of Angel Cards. She asked, "Rosemarie do you mind doing a reading for me; especially with a focus on the Care Home where I work?" Judy asked

"Certainly, I was about to ask you if you would like a reading as I have received images about the residents there. I am clairvoyant and claire audient. I have done predictive readings since I was four years old. My grandmother was happy about it, but my mother hated it. She was religious. I shut down after the age of six. The minister of our church made me feel so ashamed. They called me Satan's daughter. I didn't get my gifts back until I was twenty years old. I have studied for the last twenty years to regain my abilities. I never miss an opportunity to do a reading. I would love to do one for you." Rosemarie exclaimed

She further explained, "I think I am spiritually connected because I was the twin that survived. My twin sister died at birth. That is why I have a double name Rose and Marie. My mother had wanted to call me Rose and my sister, if she had lived Marie, but when she died, I got both names.

I think that my twin sister was and still is connected to me and her messages are like a telephone receptionist to the Spirit world. I have studied for the last twenty years to prove my psychic abilities are real. If people remove their fear of death and spirit world, they can start to live life more joyously. Fear does horrible things to people. Although, it hasn't been fun having this gift as I see so much pain long before it happens, I am still grateful that I do have these abilities. The Fourth Dimension is very beautiful, but at the same time very sad. I've accepted it and I use my gifts to help as many people as possible." Rosemarie added.

Judy looks at her in amazement. Had she found a soul sister?

Judy whispered, "I have always had this ability too; but even more now since my husband died. Now, I've stronger abilities. I have shared this with Robert as he's getting the same abilities as his dead wife is communicating with him. Visions from my late husband have helped me lately. Robert also gets visions from his wife. I am no longer afraid of death. We are protected by our past over loved ones. I know there is definitely something past death. As a child, I too had clairvoyance, until the Plenticost Minister of my mother's church shamed me out of it. The elders of the church put their hands on me and pretended to cast out the evil spirits. I shut down for many years too. I finally, came back to my gifts through dreams when I turned thirty."

Rosemarie gave her a big hug and answered, "I'm so glad to have found a soul sister, one that is alive and that I can share with."

As the Angel Cards are laid down, it became clear that Judy would not be working at the Care Home again. She would help Robert with their new home.

This would keep them busy for a week in Edmonton.

"This Reading has helped me know what to do. I didn't want to abandon Ruth, Kathy. or Marie." Judy sighed

"What about Ruth? How is she doing? She continued

Rosemarie shuffled the cards again and laid them once more. "She isn't at the Care Home; but is in Calgary's West Hospital. She has broken her hip again. She is in a lot of pain." Rosemarie stated.

Chapter 16

Rabbi Samuel thanked Candy for bringing the two tapes. He then introduced Cindy Mayes a metaphysical practitioner who lectured all over the states.

Cindy began her talk with asking the listeners **"Does anyone here know about the One Hundredth Monkey Syndrome?"**

No one had heard of it and all were eagerly waiting for an explanation.

Cindy spoke about how important thought is. **"Our thoughts control our lives."** She added

Cindy continued, **"After the Second World War, the social scientists wanted to know why people who were as educated, intelligent, hard working and sensitive as the German people could have ever fallen for Hitler's scheme. There was a lot of research going on in the scientific community. One group of scientists went to the Cayman Islands and taught all the monkeys on one of the Islands to wash their sweet potato before eating it. Once all the monkeys on one Island washed their sweet potatoes. Guess what happened?"** she asked No one had any answers

She continued, **"All the other monkeys on all the other Islands automatically washed their sweet potatoes. It is "The Flash Point." You see it in candy making; in the Beetles phenomena; Elvis Presley hysteria, Hula Hoop and Hitler and more.**

The People behind World War One and Two knew what they were doing when they established Hitler. They were already using Mind Control. They worked on crowd hysteria. It could happen anywhere at anytime. People can reverse this. If enough people want peace, that concentrated thought brings it. If we want our world to stop, using fossil fuels and use "free-energy, we have to think it into being. Nikola Tesla and Tim Bears-Den talk about infinite energy from the Forth Dimension to fuel our energy needs. Our concentrated thoughts around the world can make it happen.

It is up to us to spread the word that there is a viable alternative to our energy needs and that it is free without any side effects. **The idea of fossil fuels is obsolete! This idea spread via the Internet or Cell phone conversations changes our world. We can collectively stop our planet's destruction. We concentrate on an alternate safe energy source."**

Rabbi Samuel said, "I have had in the past as you all know different guest speakers that have come to our meetings to discuss "Free-Energy" .Tim Bears-Den last month was explaining it to us. We are aware of the government sector who is keeping us from educating people. This infinite supply of energy is available all over the world. Candy's tapes give us more info. The 1% elite group is determined to destroy our world."

121

Cindy responded, **"There is a new computer world coming as I have seen it in my visions where people connect with each other continuously; instant communication all over the world Through this new device and new social websites people will change. We can change our world, you can use this to educate and inform people. It is a matter of putting into the mass consciousness the idea that fossil fuels are obsolete and that "Free-Energy is the only energy needed. There will be struggle; but it is possible. The mass consciousness has to "think" the world that we want to live in."**

"I have listened to Tim Bears-Den lectures and I know he is a remarkable scientist and the research that Nikola Tesla did a century ago

is still valid. He was a remarkable scientist and engineer. Don't forget he created the generator that still gives us our electricity from Niagara Falls as we speak. This whole room heated and lighted by the very energy system that he put into being more than 100 years ago.

I think Nikola Tesla and the research done by the Russian Scientists can change our world over night. At least Tim Bears-Den seems to think so. His experiments use "Longwave Electromagnetic Energy". I will be bringing him back again to talk with us next week." Rabbi Samuel continued.

Cindy Mayes asked**, "Do you think we can bring together a group of new age thinkers and scientists to work on this project to avert the 9 - 11 attack?"**

The group gathered look at each other with hope and a determination to succeed.

"I will call Grant Stallion and see if he will take part in this. He has written many books and has even drawn a "New Earth Map" which is both astounding and frightening. I know he really cares about what is happening to our planet. He seems so certain that half the world as we know it; will be gone in the coming years. He is one of the doomsday teachers that say there is no way to avert it. Maybe, we can change his mind. If we control our world by our thought then we can alter the coming events." Aunt Amie Goldman asked.

Cindy replied, **"Yes, I would like to have Grant Stallion join us. I think people like Tim Bears-Den can change his mind about world destruction. Mass mind can see and bring into reality a new world.**

The 1% elite group want to destroy. Then they'll have a smaller population to control. They have wanted for years to destroy 80% of the population. In fact, their goal is to bring the world's population down to 5 hundred million by the year 2012. With scare tactics and terrorist attacks like this one planned for Sept 11th, 2001 it is possible for them to carry out this reality."

Mr. Richard Silverman, a distinguished older man in the back of the room stated, "We are aware that the 1% engineered World War One and Two, Vietnam, Korea and Eastern Wars to concentrate the wealth into their own hands. Their goal was and is to kill off our finest youth on the battlefields and to put fear into so many countries. This has been going on for centuries.

They get richer with each war as they are the arms manufacturers. People need to know that they were playing golf when Germany was bombing Britain. They didn't bomb the German Factories that were producing these bombs. They were getting rich from these factories. They owned them! British Banks put money into Hitler's war efforts.

It has to stop and we are the ones who will bring that about. I was part of the Jewish underground during World War Two. I promised myself that I would make the world a better place. I survived and yes, I have become prosperous. I'm willing to back the concept of "Free - Energy" A world with abundance for all! Tim Bears-Den's "Free-Energy" is reality; if I can help make it happen!"

Rabbi Samuel offered," Let us take a break and have a snack and then I will play my recent interview of Grant Stallion that I've taped. I want you to leave tonight inspired."

All listened eagerly, the room went silent. The tape began.

Jack McKey, the radio interviewer hosted Grant Stallion, the Futurist.

"I have researched your illness and your intuitive ability. I still

don't understand why this would have caused you to suddenly have this talent. Can you explain this?"

Grant Stallion responded," During our lifetimes we have crisis points. We take stock of our lives. Our intuitive part sometimes assists us in re-evaluating our lives. It opens a door to our super Conscious mind; which we all have and brings in new information. We access our infinite intelligence. We've all lived many lives and our collective unconscious that Carl Jung spoke about is everywhere.

The Forth Dimension Energy tapped into holds the Akashi Records. The thoughts and intentions of everyone exist there. We've all lived many lives and played out many dramas through the eons of time. Everyone is capable of accessing this knowledge. I have taken the time to develop this ability as it fascinates me. Some are born with these talents depending on what they did in their past lives. You only take to your next life your thoughts and knowledge. So yes, some are born with this gift just like some are born with the ability to play the piano without any lessons."

JM: "Do you think that we cause events whether; physical or emotional that will cause us to heighten our intuition? Why would our intuitive self, subconscious mind or soul create these crises?"

GS: "We all have experienced past lives. Many times the past has been fraught with pain full experiences. Our subconscious mind has conveniently forgotten those times so we can start fresh in this new life. At times, we meet people who trigger those memories. Should we have died a tragic painful death previously, we may bring that injury or illness into this one. That way we can deal with it and cleanse it. Rise above that past event. Doing this can often bring the awareness of that lifetime. The subconscious or intuitive mind then opens at that level.

You have had many other life times, which ended peacefully and in harmony. Some lifetimes you could have been a saint; others a monster. The physical and emotional body reveals many lifetimes. Trigger points occur throughout your life. Subconscious planned it that way."

124

JM: "Does synchronicity exist? Does Spiritual Channeling exist?"

GS: "Synchronicity is spiritual forces in action. Nothing happens by accident. All our meetings are planned destiny. Nothing is by chance! We astral travel in the sleep state. During the day, we act out our dream state. The Hawaiian metaphysics teaches that the dream state is the reality and that when awake we are merely following our dreams. We set up our meetings when we are on our astral plane. Our meetings with others and events in the physical world are planned. Synchronicity is an example of this. Forth Dimension is part of this.

Whereas, Spiritual Channeling occurs when one surrenders their physical body to a sleep or trance state examples are Edgar Cayce, Einstein, and Nikola Tesla. All three men took naps to receive their knowledge from this Forth Dimension or the Infinite Universe. In the dream state, they found answers and solutions to problems. Blueprints for inventions! Our altered states of consciousness include our dreams and sleeping states. A great library of knowledge exists there. Infinite Mind or the Akashi Records are part of the Forth Dimension."

JM: "What do you think about predestination, Edgar Cayce and the Akashi records?"

GS: "Although a life may follow a set pattern that one has chosen before coming back to Earth, it is always open to re-negotiating their contract while in the present incarnation. However, the soul's whole intent is to improve and grow with each lifetime. Thus, it inherently chooses events that will cause it to grow. Today's souls are free in comparison to what has gone in the past and have even more chance to rise above birth expectations. The Akashi records are redefining it as civilization develops at a faster rate than in the past. These records include all thoughts and deeds. Like a large computer's hard drive. This Main Computer exists in the metaphysical world.

Psychics can receive information about a client through this means. They know their history from past lifetimes. People born with Clair Audience, Clairvoyance, and Psychic abilities access these records. Some need an altered state of mind while others do it as easily as reading the breakfast cereal box. Our next generation of children the Crystal and Indigo Children access this information as easily as sneezing. The Intuitive age is at hand."

JM: "Is that why the 1% is so intent on destroying 80% of the population as they know these Indigo and Crystal children will see through their feeble attempts to control them?"

GS: "I do believe that is why they are intent on this destruction. At present, they are using the H.A.A.R.P. energy to destroy our world. They are using it to access the hidden gas deposits deep in the earth. Plus using it to create weather wars over the continents

All the time pretending that no such energy source exists. What they are doing now and plan to do in the near future is the largest Crime against Humanity that has ever existed."

JM: "Do you believe then that there is an unlimited supply of energy accessible. It is capable of producing all the energy ever needed?"

GS: "Yes, I do believe it not only exists but that it is already being used to destroy much of our planet. There is a deliberate attempt to destroy the ecosystem of this planet. Could an alien or alien like beings be altering our planet to their needs? Perhaps, human beings are an endangered species."

JM: "That is an alarming statement!"

GS: "I do believe that there are forces at work here that would boggle the human mind if it should ever come out. You see the children being born today are already recognizing them. They can't hide from them. I think the Harry Potter books show already that these children are able to see into the Forth Dimension. That is why this book is so popular."

JM: "Do you believe in Karma? Could there be a collective karma for a nation? Could there be karmic consequences for the 1% who engineered the world wars? Could there be Karma for the

126

people who tortured the Jews during World War Two?"

GS:"I believe that people do answer for their past good and bad deeds. Every thought whether acted upon or not; records in the Akashi records. Thoughts or actions recorded. It is important to watch what you put into your mind! Movies based on terrorism, criminal behaviors, fighting and wars build thought forms that eventually produce chaos. Responsible thought! Fear is not something we can afford as instant Karma is building as we speak. Destructive thoughts build in psychic strength and eventually manifest into the physical dimension."

The tape ended here.

It was a lot to absorb and as they looked at each other, they realized how important this message had been. Our thoughts control our life. These thoughts control whether there would even be life on earth in the future.

The meeting adjourned and the intent was to have Tim Bears-Den speak to them as soon as possible.

Candy, Aunt Amie, and Sam left the meeting not hungry as their minds were reeling from all the information. As they passed, the Lobster House they decided to have a late night snack and discuss what they had heard. Realizing that they could not discuss anything in public; they decided to keep quiet.

"I knew that Rabbi Samuel had these meetings every week but I had no idea that they were as interesting and as frightening as what we have just experienced." Aunt Amie said quietly as they sat down.

"A bowl of clam chowder, hot cheese biscuits and some sherry wine." they ordered in unison.

That would be just what they needed to fill their tummies and help them go to sleep.

"I think that we need to spend some time talking tonight as there is no way that I can still my mind to go to sleep easily, after that meeting." stated Sam.

Chapter 17

Back at Aunt Amie's home, in the living room, they comfortably settled beside an old-fashioned fireplace. Sam fed the fire until it filled the room with heat. They began their review of tonight's discussion at Rabbi Samuel's home.

Candy had taken some notes as some of the terms and ideas were foreign to her. Aunt Amie knew what some of the information meant; she understood the terms Indigo and Crystal Children as she had done some research of her own on these ideas.

"I have researched both the Indigo and Crystal children for some time now and yes, he was right when he said that these children are different." Aunt Amie stated

"The Indigo children have been born in the last 60 years with many coming in after 1945, they were not afraid to speak out against injustice and many gifted with Psychic abilities. Many of these children are now in their 50's. They were the baby boomers; earlier known as the "hippy" generation. There are now Indigo people in their late 30's, 40's, and 50's who will be leaders. They bring advanced technology and have little patience with the old-line political ideologies. They will stand up to the 1% that is trying to control the world with the agenda of a One World Government.

Steven Spielberg is an example as he creates movies that wake people up. Another one is Bill Gates who brought the commercial computer into our homes which gave a person instant availability to knowledge and communication. There are many more Indigos that are creating infinite change in how people think and what they expect from life." Aunt Amie continued.

In fact, she had written a book about the early Indigo People, as they are no longer children. "Have you heard of my book, "Indigo People Are Here Now?" She asked

"No I haven't heard of your book; but I have heard of the Indigo people; but I thought they were from some country. Are they an actual type of human being who would be my age and older?" Candy questioned

"The term "Indigo" was given to this group of children as it described their aura color and energy. Indigo children have a lot of indigo blue in their auras.

This is the color of the "Third Eye Chakra." The energy center inside the head located between the two eyebrows. The Pineal Gland is part of this Chakra, which regulates clairvoyance, or the ability to see energy, visions, astral travel, and the spirit world. Many of the Indigo children are clairvoyant." Aunt Amie continued

Candy asked, "Could I be one of them as I have some of these abilities? Do you remember when I was three years old? I told Mom that Uncle Harry was dead on the side of the road with his car upside down. Within hours, the telephone rang confirming that fact. Do you remember how upset she was with me? I stopped saying anything after that; but to this day, I still get those weird visions when something horrible has happened to one of our family. I saw when our school bus had its accident and my soccer team was so badly hurt. I couldn't go that day as I had the stomach flu. I told you about the vision.

Do you remember me telling you and I felt like I might have caused it. You assured me that I had not done anything to create it; but I would probably get visions all my life and not fear them."

"Well, I have often wondered whether you were an Indigo as you have the warrior presence. You are ready to protect New York from this pending attack of 9 - 11without any concern for your own safety. You have acted since a child in a brave manner. The Indigo's purpose is to destroy the old systems. They have come to rebuild educational, government and legal systems that are corrupt. They need to fight and display their anger with fierce determination.

Even as a child you could sense dishonesty, like a dog can sense fear. You knew when they patronized, manipulated, or lied. You often acted up! Remember the fight you had with that horrible teacher in Grade 8." continued Aunt Amie

Candy asked, "Is that why I have had so many jobs; where I notice that things aren't right and I have to leave or fight as I don't want to lie or steal?"

"I think you are right as you can't dissociate from your feelings and pretend like everything's okay. You remember when your mother wanted to put you on pills to calm you down. Remember when I told her to take you to the homeopathy doctor instead. He realized who you were. Thank god or else you may have gone the way that so many Indigo people do. No wonder so many addicted to drugs!" Aunt Amie sighed.

"Unfortunately, the Indigo People misdiagnosed with labels like ADD or ADHD are put on medications to control their behavior. There are still those who are getting their goals accomplished as you have done and are doing now. You and the other Indigos are a force that the 1% will have to reckon with!" chuckled Aunt Amie.

"She sure is a force; I haven't been able to forget how she fought off that purse snatcher when she was 16 years old. I am curious about the term Crystal Children. I have never heard that term before. What do you know about these Crystal Children?" asked Sam

"Now, the Crystal Children are starting to arrive with some coming in around 1995. With psychic gifts and they are here to help us evolve. They will show us a new world order. They will help us acquire this brave and free New World. They will show us that we are powerful and that we are divine. They will bring in new spiritual understanding that will overthrow the Old Religions. The idea of sin and eternal hell fire or eating cream cheese with an angel on a cloud will be outdated. These Religious concepts will be gone forever as they remake their world. Their ability to see through pretense and deceit will be the decline of the present religious dogmas.

Concerned for the welfare of the earth; they work as a group, They live by the code of "The Law of One" also known as "Oneness Consciousness." They bring world peace and love for all on our planet." Aunt Amie continued

Sam asked, "I have a niece, Crystal that is a joy. She was born in 1995 and although she is only five; she calms every one down. She was late in talking and her parents were very worried about her. Child Psychologists told them that she was autistic. They demanded that she take medications. Could she be a Crystal Child?"

"Sad to say; many of these children misdiagnosed as Autistic. Teachers and Speech Therapists do not understand that these children are not abnormal in their speech. Crystal children aren't indifferent to others; just the opposite. They are slow to talk as they are using mental telepathy to understand each other. From what you have just told me she is a Crystal Child. I have done a lot of research on them and a Metaphysical teacher by the name of Dorothy Valentine has written a book on these children. Have you heard of the book, "Our New Children; Angel or Human?" asked Aunt Amie

Candy asked, "Do these children have large penetrating eyes. Do they hypnotize you with their penetrating gaze?"

"It can seem like that for sure. I have experienced that too as their gaze is so compelling. Does she have those eyes?" asked Aunt Amie

Sam replied, "She does have some of those qualities and yes her gaze is unnerving. She thinks it is funny. At three years of age, she loved to out stare you. She made it a game!"

"When she gazes at you, does it feel like she is seeing your whole life and everything about you? Asked Aunt Amie

"That is exactly how I feel; but she isn't judging me. It is more that she finds me amusing. She is so curious. I tease her about this by calling her the "WHY Kid" instead of her name and she breaks up into uncontrollable laughter when I do that." replied Sam

"From my research, Crystal children are very curious and they have asked me questions like why is the grass-green? Why is the sky blue? Why can't we fly? It is like they have lived in another world much different from ours and need to know why it is this way on Earth. It is unsettling the questions that they ask!

They are our new healers; they are unlike any other generation. They will lead us into a New World. The Crystal Children are gentle and calm. Occasionally, they have temper tantrums but they last for a moment. They are very loving, forgiving, and happy. The Crystals are the generation who gently bring in a safer and more peaceful New World.," stated Aunt Amie

Sam added, "She is very much like that already. She brings home stray cats and dogs to the worry of her parents. She is always asking how I am. Do I have any pain? Many times, she knows without me telling her where I hurt. It is like she knows when my back is acting up."

"Is she confident, joyful, and understanding beyond her years? I am sure that if you could see auras that you would see her with an aura that is opalescent and a rainbow in pastel hues. Does she show a fascination for crystals and rocks? Does she show you how to make them work? Does she have trouble at play school with other kid's?" questioned Aunt Amie.

"Their natural talent of spiritual abilities often will lead to misunderstandings even at her age. Their telepathic skills slow down their talking early as they can read people's minds. Parents of the Crystal Children are developing mental telepathy as they communicate with their little wonders. These parents transfused with telepathic talent from their children." She continued

"Maybe she is one of them. I have found them as the most connected, communicative, cuddly, and caring of any generation. Gifted with psychic abilities and compassion, they are considerate and always thinking of others. They are sensitive to the needs of others. Kindness is in their every thought. They hug and laugh easily and are always ready to help if there is a need with either an animal or a human.

Autistic children do not do any of the above as they isolate themselves from their world mentally and emotionally. Crystal Children are the opposite of these children in that they are forever putting the needs of others before themselves. They do not need medication of any kind. These children are "awe some" We should be in awe of them. They are our world's future." Aunt Amie continued

Sam added," Yes, she is very much like that and she was slow to talk. We worried about her for a while. But when she did start talking it was in full complete sentences and the quality was that of a child twice her age."

"I would love to meet her. Would you arrange a meeting with your family for me? These children in their infancy are quietly but steadily working evolutionary change on our planet. Their expanding abilities are angel like. Just their touch is capable of healing us. Their minds use telepathy to know what we are really thinking. It is impossible to lie to them." Aunt Amie added

She continued," As time speeds up, we will become more aware of our own intuitive abilities. We will assess the body language of the person talking. We will become aware of their actions and see the expressions on their faces. Communication will be faster, more direct, and more honest. I have seen in my visions small phones that people use like mini typewriters. They send messages constantly. to each other. With so much communication, mental telepathy will take over. Our world is evolving. Movies like "Ghosts" with Patrick Swaze and Demi Moore bring the idea of Spirit World to everyone. Shows like this will be commonplace. "

Candy gave a sigh, "You make me want to become a mother so I can have a child like that. I will have to get married and bring one of these Crystal children into my world."

Sam's eyes lit up and he reached over to her. He pulled her on his lap, he asked, "Did you say get married and have children?"

Aunt Amie chuckled and stated, "Well kids, it is finally time to go to bed and dream of a new world that is full of love and happiness. It is possible. We will discuss the rest of tonight's lecture and tape recording tomorrow. I am exhausted and ready for bed."

Sam asked, "Is it okay if I stay the night as I feel too tired to drive across town?"

Aunt Amie responded," I thought you knew already; your bed has been waiting for you since we got home. I even put a heating pad in the bed so it would be warm for you! You know I hope you don't mind but I prefer that you sleep in your own bed until your wedding in June."

Sam looked at Candy and asked, "Did you tell her that I wanted a June wedding?" Immediately Candy whispered, "Did you tell her that we were planning a June wedding?"

Sam winked at her and replied, "I guess she is Psychic after all."

Chapter 18

Judy had to check what she was happening at Brenda's Care Home. It looked like they had replaced her already. Well that was a relief.

"Well, according to Rosemarie's spiritual reading poor Ruth has had another accident and within three months she has broken her hip twice. Of course it is the same hip and that much harder to heal. I checked earlier and she is in Calgary's West Hospital. I wonder if I can go visit her?" she asked

Robert looked relieved and responded, "We can try! I know she means a lot to you. I guess it's because you were a children's nurse and saw so many parents dealing with sick children. You're a caring person. I am sure grateful that Bonnie saw that in you and made sure to poke my shoulder that day. Do you remember that day?"

It was ten o'clock and they were in Lawyer's office. Mr. and Mrs. Barns greeted them with a warm handshake. The signing of the legal documents took a few minutes. They were such a friendly couple. Too bad, they were leaving the area. Judy thought to herself.

Judy asked, "If you are ever in the area please stop by and visit us. Do you suppose you'll ever come back this way?"

Mr. Barns replied, "Yes, I would like that very much as I'm curious how you'll fix up the land and how you'll build your home. I know that for now you are living in a Motor home. Many years ago, that is what we did, when we came to this area. We built our home and saved a lot of money by living in our Motor home too. It was far more convenient as we were right there on site to do all the work. I hope everything goes well for you two."

"Let's go for a coffee before we start back to Calgary. You know we might stop for a few days in Edmonton and view those Garage Packages at Devon's Home Center. That is only a few miles out of Edmonton and we could enjoy the countryside on the way. It is so pretty this time of year." Robert asked

"I love the big sky country! Yes, let's stop at the next truck stop and have some lunch. I'd like to see those garage packages too. I'll buy some drafting paper so I can plan our new home. I designed and drew the house plans for the home that Jack and I built at Miracle Beach on Vancouver Island in 1989." She continued.

With lunch over, they decided to take some private time in their Belleville, Motor home.

"Do you realize how much we have done in the last three days?" Judy exclaimed

"Well, I'd hoped to do all of this, but I didn't want to get your hopes up. I had to figured this out. I know that I trust Mike to help us. We've been through some hard times on the Oil Patch. You get to know a person when you have to work so many long hours and under stress. I think we both would like to build these "Free-Energy" Generators and

136

sell them. We've nearly figured them out. I can't believe how cheap they are to make." He continued

"Our cottage built before you know it. They frame it at the factory and then send it out on a semi nearly all finished. Of course, we then have to put in the insulation, electrical and plumbing. It saves time and money." He explained

"I know as I built my home in Barrie that way. It was a house package of 1640 square feet. It went up in a day; so a 900 square feet cottage will be even easier to do." She replied

An hour and a half later and the sun moved in the sky to shine directly on their faces. A raven screeched in the sky. They jolted awake. They had not meant to sleep that long; but I guess they were not in a hurry any more. We can sleep and eat when ever. We are not on a schedule.

"But don't forget our Van is in the parking lot. We only paid until Monday. Can we go there tonight and get it?" She asked.

"Yes, we have to pick up the Van. We'll stay on this Highway and be in Calgary by supper time." He replied

The miles sped by and their conversation drifted over to the New Earth Map. Mike had told him about it. According to Grant Stallion, because of the continuous use of fossil fuels we are depleting our ice at both the North and South Poles. Ice is melting and increasing the depth of the ocean. This also causes the planet to shift on its' axis. Our planet will change as the oceans rise.

A man named Edgar Cayce back in the 30's prophesied this event. Grant Stallion is giving us more predictions about this coming event and explaining why it may occur.

"We saw how the Ice fields had melted away when we drove past them on Saturday. They are quickly disappearing. Our world is in serious trouble. My guys at Fort McMan worry about it. A lot of them are very knowledgeable scientists and engineers.

We have been researching a new science called H.A.A.R.P. an acronym for High Frequency Active Aurora Research Program. We believe they are using this science with its' billion watts of laser energy to create giant icebergs. These scientists are using this energy to create an open ocean, shipping route, year round about Northern Canada. That is why our weather all over the world has been so bizarre. Could this be the cause of the extreme Manitoba floods? Could this science affect the breadbasket of the USA?" Robert continued

"I have visions all the time of Vancouver Island sinking into the ocean. For many years when I lived there with Jack, I would wake up terrified. I took the time to see where the coalmines are on Vancouver Island. The whole Island is honeycombed with these coalmines; some of them are still active, that is they have fires burning in them. One for heaven's sake sits under one of the largest hospitals on Vancouver Island. The city if Nanaimo even makes you research your property before you can build a home on it as they don't know where all the mineshafts are? Can you imagine what will happen if an earthquake hits there?

I couldn't wait to move back to Ontario and solid ground. People do not realize it but the Island's under structure is like Swiss cheese full of holes. I thought we would be okay if we built a cottage at Miracle Beach up the island between Courtenay and Campbell River. I was wrong as the land there is nothing but gravel. We dug out a basement to put the house on and found that we had continuous deep water in the basement.

Even eight feet down, it was still gravel. I was glad to sell and leave there. If there is ever an earthquake or a tsunami the area will just disappear into the ocean. My dreams were probably a lot more than dreams but warnings." Judy exclaimed

"It is solid ground that we just bought, Honey Jean! Just so you know that you don't need to have those dreams again." He added

"I feel that we are doing this just in the nick of time. I feel urgency to it. I know it feels like we have lots of time; but there is still a gut feeling that we need to hurry." She sighed

"Dealing with Jack's illness and death has overwhelmed me. The extreme effort; caring for him and all the bills have exhausted me. Maybe I am stuck in this mode of non stop pressure." Judy continued

Robert looked over at her and shook his head in agreement, "I think you're right as I haven't had time yet to really grieve. Neither have you as we both lost all of our savings dealing with all of it. Work has had to come first. I'm glad that I've been able to make so much money. I was able to save over $45,000 in the last four months." Robert stated

"We're better off than I realized! Maybe we can take it easy for a while. I never thought that this could be so possible in such a short time!" Judy added with a chuckle

"Where would you like to go for supper?" He asked as they arrived in Calgary

"They advertise all the time on T.V. What do you think of the restaurant, "Chicken Time" They offer pork ribs and chicken in their house sauce? Kathy had said that she liked that place and that we should go there. Oh, no! I forgot to call Kathy. Can we stop at the next truck stop? I need to call her. I have to phone her." She asked

It was six o'clock and Kathy awakened when the phone rang. She was glad to hear Judy's voice.

"Where have you been? I couldn't reach you at that phone number that you gave me. I was worried about you. They hired Elke, a nurse from Germany. Where have you been?" asked Kathy

"You'll never believe it; I can hardly believe it myself. I have just got back from Jasper. Would you like to go to supper with us? You know the Chicken place that you told me to go to when I left on Friday?" asked Judy

"Hey, that sounds like a great idea! Give me a few minutes to shower and I'll be ready. I live at 3437 Ruby Crescent just off." Kathy stated.

Robert wanted to meet Kathy. He needed to know what type of person she was in case Judy insisted on going back to take care of Ruth.

At least, Ruth probably was safer there than in that dreadful death house, a mere pretense for a care home. He was going to make sure that they were self-sufficient and wise to those types of people. Maybe it is a good thing that we'll never be rich.

The address was easier to find than he had thought it would be. He always found Calgary a hard place to find addresses. No place to park the Motor home! Four blocks away they parked Belleville. After walking to her door, they rang the doorbell.

Kathy hugged Judy and stated, "I was worried about you especially when you never answered your phone."

I wasn't at my friend's place; instead, we bought a Motor home and took off for a holiday. We've done so much in the last three days that I completely forgot that you might be worried about me." Judy exclaimed.

"Well then what have you been doing? I can tell you're just dying to tell me all about it!" asked Kathy.

They found a booth in the "Chicken Time" Restaurant. Their order placed.

"For God's Sakes! Get a cell phone so that I don't have to worry like that again! You could have given me a heart attack!" Kathy warned

"Yes, we'll need one and tomorrow first thing I will buy one!" Robert promised

He immediately liked her honesty and straight forwardness. She was a woman who you could count on. She reminded him of his Aunt Mary who had died last year. She'd been such a help to him when Bonnie was dying. He knew Judy was safe if Kathy was part of the Care Home. He thought to himself.

"So now tell me all about It.? What happened to Ruth? How did she fall again?" asked Judy

"Remember when you told me that Cherry would be getting a reward of $10,000 if she showed her loyalty to Brenda's Care Home. Well, I think she will be getting that money. I didn't trust her; remember me telling you that, the first night that I worked there. I was right! She wouldn't take the time to feed Marie her food; so Marie was feeding herself with her hands; and walking around while she was eating. Not even Peter's warnings that it was unsafe for the rest of them. She was dropping food on the floor. Peter concerned about falling and breaking a hip, too. There were two Care Aids on Friday night, when it happened.

There was enough staff to feed Marie. There was no excuse for her walking around and dropping food on the floor. It was an accident in the making."

Ruth had just had her hair done and decided to dress up and look pretty. She put on those damn three-inch high heels that are ridiculous for a woman in her eighties to wear. According to Peter, she seemed drunk as she started dancing around the table. She was singing and dancing around. Ruth fell and an awful scream followed. The ambulance came and off to the Emergency ward she went. I got the full details from Anna when I got there at eight o'clock that night." Kathy explained.

Robert and Judy sat there shaking their heads.

"These people are really clever. Just the right type of residents to make sure that this would happen. It really was only a matter of time. Poor Ruth! Do you suppose that we could get in to see her?" asked Judy

"Well, I have tried; I even wore my Nurse's Uniform thinking that might help me get in to see her. No such luck so far." answered Kathy

"Maybe if we casually both go in at the same time dressed in our uniforms, we might be able to get one of us to her. She'll be so frightened! I wonder what ever made her act that way. She is usually so reserved. Dancing around the table! In three-inch high heels! Where did they come from? I checked her clothes. That is the first thing I do when I enter a resident into care. She didn't have shoes like that. I would have thrown the shoes out." Judy exclaimed

"I asked Peter had anyone come to visit her that afternoon and he said that her son, Harry had dropped by bringing her a present. It was wrapped; so he couldn't see what it was. It was the three-inch high heels." Kathy thoughtfully said.

"I would bet a thousand dollars that is exactly what happened; she had her hair and nails done and then he shows up with those three-inch high heels. She had loved square dancing. Harry or that horrible hairdresser slipped her a happy drug. The next thing you know she has fallen again." Judy agreed

Robert angry by now and concerned; realized that this place was unsafe for either of them.

He stated firmly, "I'm going to the Police with this information. I wouldn't do it in Calgary as he probably has them on his payroll; but I do have some City Police in Fort McMan that would be interested in this information. I want you two out of there and yesterday."

"We have to wait until I've some more taped conversations. Kathy did you change the tape deck in their Boardroom on Saturday?" asked Judy

"Sure the heck did! We might have the proof on those tapes that could close that place down. I'll check it tonight as soon as it is safe to do so!" promised Kathy.

Chapter 19

Spring, finally! Candy stretched and climbed out of bed. She had gone to sleep dreaming of wedding gowns, cakes, bridal showers and on and on. Yes, there had been a marriage proposal of sorts the night before; if you can consider your own Aunt doing the proposing.

"My life is just too strange, weird, and wonderful!" she exclaimed in front of Sam.

She thought to herself "I would never have thought that I would be getting married in a few months. Last week, at this time I hadn't even thought of any of you as I kept struggling to keep going in Calgary. It was so bitterly cold there. The weather seemed so much colder and harsher there than here in New York.

Aunt Amie had served her coffee and a cut up grapefruit, followed with scrambled eggs and toast. Yes, she was hungry!

Sam had already left for work.

"Would you like to go downtown and look for your wedding dress? I had always hoped to have a daughter to do that with and you my dear will do nicely?" asked Aunt Amie

Candy couldn't believe her ears. "Yes, I would love to; but are you sure that Sam is really thinking of marrying me in June? That is very sudden isn't it?" She questioned

"He is going to join us at one o'clock this afternoon at Goldman's Boutique. My cousin owns this dress shop and I know I can get a good price from her. I have helped her out many times in the past and I know she would love to do this." Aunt Amie replied

"You two are ganging up on me but I am happy that you are. It certainly has changed my mood being around the two of you. So much excitement! I can't remember this much excitement since my graduation days. Mother would be so happy to see me getting on with my life and she always did like Sam. How I wish she were alive to share all of this! " Candy responded.

"How do you know that she isn't already seeing all of this? I feel her presence continuously! Her presence is definitely here. She will come back as your little girl. What do you think about that?" asked Aunt Amie

"That seems impossible; but you know she often in the last few days' mention that she was going now; but she would not be gone for long. She loved going to the toy stores and looking at the great toys.

She even wanted me to take her to the Baby Shops to check out the cribs, bassinets, and toys. Convinced that she was coming back soon and she wanted to know what was out there for babies and children. In fact, last night when you were talking about the Indigo and Crystal children; I seemed to feel her presence. Do you suppose she has brought Sam back into my life? She always did want me to marry him. She thought he would make a great father." Candy whispered as if the idea would vanish if she said it aloud.

"I do so many readings where the Mother has died with breast cancer and they seem to know that they are cutting their lives short so that they can come back as their daughter's baby. This has been going on for my Psychic readings for over forty years.

A few months after their death, I will get a call to do a reading for the daughter and she wants me to assure her that she is marrying the right man. The cards lay out that she will be having a baby girl within the year. I can't help but think that reincarnation is real. When the child's personality matches the deceased Mother, it makes one think. The child likes the same food and clothes. A few years later, a replica of the past on Mother shows up at my door for a reading. It has happened too often for me not to believe.

It is to me concrete proof that we all reincarnate and faster than we first thought. After all the Chinese have believed that for a thousands years. The Roman Catholic Church removed the concept of Reincarnation only five hundred years ago. The Jewish Faith removed the concept a hundred years ago. The Druids believed in it also. It is a concept that holds strength in all cultures. Including today's Modern Wicca." Aunt Amie stated

"Oh how I pray that you are right!" Candy exclaimed

"I can even prove it to you through the use of Modern Astrology which I have researched for over forty years." Aunt Amie stated

"This I want to see! You can't mean that junk in the newspaper next to the comics can tell me that my Mother will be reborn to me. That is impossible!" Candy exclaimed

"I know what you are thinking and I agree totally. I hate that stupid newspaper astrology crap just as much as you do. It makes it so hard. Intelligent people discard Astrology because of the Newspaper crap. They never realize that there is something to Real Astrology, which I refer to as Modern Astrology. I have spent hours researching this ancient science. I have even written a book called, "Modern Astrology." Most Astrologers have made it seem so complicated with their jargon that only a few have any interest in it. I have simplified it. This modern approach

145

works well for doing all kinds of research. I can even do predictive work; which is impossible with the old methods.

In addition, my simple method makes it easy for anyone to learn it; not just the mathematicians and intellectuals. This science is for the humanitarians, spiritualists, and social scientists. My research has led me to believe that energy from the Forth Dimension affects us every milli second of the day. It is from our Divine Infinite Source. We take on this energy at the time of our birth. The stars' placement in our solar system makes the Birth Chart.

Aunt Amie Goldman's Modern Astrology Chart

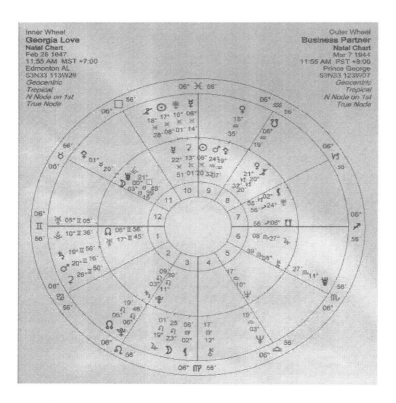

Stars have no occult properties, but similar to satellite stations

146

that receive the energy from Space and direct that energy to us at the time of our birth. This continued every milli second afterward. I like to think that God has an interest in each and everyone. A divine intelligence exists and guides our lives and ultimately the life of our precious Earth. We are never alone as this presence is always there. It is the supreme intelligence of the Universe. It is from the same energy source that both Grant Stallion and Tim Bears-Den talk about in their lectures. They are not aware of my research; but I do hope that in time, they will come to know of my work." Aunt Amie explained

"Wow, you are really excited about this aren't you?" asked Candy

"It would change our whole world if people realized that every action is judged by a supreme being that loves and understands their humanity." Aunt Amie replied

"But how does reincarnation fit into all of that?" questioned Candy

"I thought you would never ask? All timed perfectly. Numerology and Astrology are connected. You are beginning a study of Spirit World and I promise you will never be bored again or feel alone." She stated in a knowing manner.

Something about Aunt Amie's confidence when she talked about all of this made Candy's heart sing. One thing for sure she was no longer sad. Every day seemed now so full of promise. Was she a modern day Sleeping Beauty? I have found my prince, Prince Sam. I must call him that! Seems like a good nickname for him. Perhaps it'll make him laugh.

Two more months and she would marry him; then she would be a Princess Candy.

Lunchtime! They would eat downtown near Goldman's Boutique. Sam was waiting at the table, grinning ear to ear.

"What have you done? Why are you so smug?" questioned Candy

"I have managed to book the same place where your Aunt and Uncle had their 50th Wedding Anniversary. A cancellation in June is a miracle! I grabbed it! I have so many happy memories from that place.

147

Both my cousins were married there. I think the place gives good luck to those who get married there; as they have happy marriages." He said excitedly

Aunt Amie returned from saying a hello to one of her clients and asked. "What is all the excitement about?"

Sam whispered, "I have booked the families' favorite reception hall!"

"Perfect! This is coming together so easily and you know I knew it would! We have your Mother orchestrating the event; how could it help but not be easy." Aunt Amie whispered

"We are running out of time. We must be at Goldman's Boutique in half an hour. Get something from the Salad Bar. That will speed things up." Aunt Amie stated

Sam and Candy were too excited to eat much, anyway. They made it on time. The models paraded on the platform. This was this year's spring fashion show. Many brides spend hours doing research about their weddings. Candy was just letting things flow and having fun.

She was not one of those nervous uptight brides. This was a fun time and she determined to savor every moment. Sam seemed to recognize her resolve as he realized that he was marrying not only a brave but incredibly smart woman who knew how to relax and have fun.

"How lucky can a guy get?" He whispered to Aunt Amie.

"I think I am lucky, too! How wonderful! I never thought that I would have a daughter and be part of a wedding ceremony." Aunt Amie whispered to Sam.

I have helped so many people to restore broken relationships; have helped people get back together again and comforted the heart-broken when the relationship didn't make it to the altar. This was her chance to know the happiness and fun involved in a wedding, what a wonderful turn of events for her. She thought to herself.

Aunt Amie got excited when the mother's outfits modeled. Would she look good in that shade of blue she wondered? Candy turned to her and asked, "What shade should I choose for my bridesmaids? What shade would you like to wear as you know you will be my adopted mom?"

"A royal blue had always been my favorite; would you pick that color for your bridesmaids?" responded Aunt Amie with clear delight.

Sam interrupted, "Guess what? The chauffeur's cars are Royal Blue too. Talk about being color coordinated."

Candy saw a few wedding dresses that she liked and went backstage to model some of them. Sam left to talk with the catering companies at this Spring Fashion Show.

It was traditionally bad luck for the groom to see the bride in her dress before the wedding ceremony. He wasn't tempting fate that was for sure. The dress picked effortlessly and Candy knew that the one she picked her Mother would have loved, too.

"Hey, mother how do you like this one?" whispered Candy

Just then, the flowers that had been in a sconce on the wall let go and fell to the floor. She bent over to pick them up and realized that they were Gardenias, her favorite flower.

"That's your answer, Mom!" and she took it as a sign that her mother wanted this dress.

When she told Aunt Amie about the incident, laughter filled the change booth.

"What did I tell you? She is here and she wants you to know that!" whispered Aunt Amie

Sam brought back menus for them to go over and business cards for floral arrangements.

"We have to look at a few dresses for the bridesmaids. It won't take long." Candy added

"Don't forget the flower-girl. May I have my niece as the flower girl? "Asked Sam

"I can't believe how quickly all of this is coming together." Candy exclaimed

"I am not the least bit surprised!" replied Aunt Amie and Sam at the same time.

"Are you two parrots or something?" questioned Candy as they left Goldman's Boutique.

As they got into the waiting car, she asked, "Do you already have baby stuff hidden somewhere in the house since all of this is happening so fast; I can't help but wonder what else is going to happen next!"

"That is why you two are going to wait to celebrate your Wedding Vows! Or else you could accuse me of somehow getting you pregnant too." laughed Aunt Amie

"Artificial insemination when I'm asleep? Anything and everything is possible with you two!" She laughed back at them.

"This is the easiest wedding celebration New York has ever seen. You act like it is something you have done a hundred times before." Aunt Amie stated

"It is so funny! I have never been one of those girls who even considered getting married. It was something I thought I might do in my forties. Not now! You have really changed my mind on so many things. I don' think that I am the same person who came here two weeks ago! Are you sure that you have not put a spell on me?" Candy exclaimed

All of a sudden, it hits her! The wedding is wonderful; but it has to be private. No newspapers! No publicity! How safe was she? She had to be smart and realize those Calgary men might recognize her in a Newspaper article? This was serious! Perhaps it would be better if they got married at Aunt Amie's home. She didn't need an extravagant showy ballroom wedding not if it put the people she loved into danger.

Arriving home, Candy asked them to sit down as she had something important to say.

She asked," How safe is this public wedding? These horrible Calgary men might see my picture in the Newspapers or Gossip Magazines. Would it be okay to have our wedding here in Aunt Amie's home? I would feel so much safer. A hunch made me realize how dangerous a public ceremony would be at this time. I would love to have had a grand reception and all the fan fare; but I don't feel safe.

I would be just as happy to walk down this beautiful curved staircase and meet you here in front of our stained glass windows that overlook our beautiful garden. A small wedding is perfect since I do not have friends here. Except for cousin, Heather, I really can't think of one person my age that I would like to invite. Heather can be my Bridesmaid and Aunt Amie can give me away. In the last seven years, I have had no time to keep in touch with anyone."

Sam realized that she was right and responded, "Whatever you wish it is your day and I do want you safe. I am content to have a small intimate gathering."

Aunt Amie agreed, "I think a wedding here in this room would be lovely. We want you safe. You are right until this Sept 11th attack is over or prevented we do have to be careful. You could ask the Rothman girls to be your bridesmaids you know. They realize how important your safety is. A quiet wedding it will be."

Candy cheered up with that thought and replied, "Yes, when they finally rescue Marie and get back to New York that would be wonderful for them and for us."

Chapter 20

Robert and Judy said their goodbyes to Kathy. At the Parking Lot, they found their van stolen.

"How could that have happened? Robert asked the Parking Lot Attendant.

They called the Insurance Company, A B A. The van was and paid for. Yes, the Insurance would cover it. "This may be good; we need an older Nissan 4X4 SUV, with no computers. Our property needs a 4X4 especially, in the winter's snow. I can buy one for a few hundred. The rest of the payout will buy our garage package. It's inconvenient; but maybe a good thing." Robert explained

"Well, I'm relieved. You picked me up at work and they may have watched. I feel better that they don't know what we're driving. Moreover, when you couldn't get our Motor home to Kathy's that was good. I'm relieved that they don't know what we're driving and where we are." she whispered

The Insurance Paper work completed.

Judy asked, "With Ruth in the Hospital there is no need for me to go back there. I don't feel safe here in Calgary. Do you think Kathy will get out of there too?"

Robert agreed, "I think she already knows it isn't safe there."

"Would you like to take some time off? We'll take a break. Let's go back to Mike and Rosemarie's place. They'd be happy to visit with us for a few days. We can take a day's trip into Edmonton and buy a Nissan. Let's head back there tonight?" asked Robert

"I was thinking the same thing. I don't think Ruth would want me to risk my life to help her. She understood what was happening to her. She kept repeating to me that she thought that she was doing the right thing by adopting Harry. How sad that instead of being a comfort to her in her old age; he is her killer. I think she knows who he is." Judy sighed

It was dark when they left Calgary and big sky country offered them the stars. The miles went by and the lights of Calgary dimmed.

The beauty of the Aurora Borealis followed them along the highway. The beautiful colors changed continuously; from turquoise to pink to green and became more lovely as each new shape and color filled the night sky.

"Yes, remember me telling you that the scientists are using the power of these beautiful lights to create billion watts of laser energy. God created this beauty and they in return are using it to destroy our planet, in the name of almighty greed. I wouldn't want to be their shoes when they have to meet their creator.

They have been experimenting with this science for over fifty years and now use it to control the weather and so much more."

Robert explained

Aurora Floral

"What a beautiful night!" they both said at the same time. Then they laughed.

At Stony Plain, they called Mike and asked if it was okay for them to come back and stay on their property. They explained their stolen van situation.

Rosemarie and Mike were pleased to hear from them. They'd wait up and have a snack for them.

Beau, their German Sheppard met them at the bottom of the hill. It was close to midnight and they were still up and excited about their new Computer and a Satellite connection.

"We can research our "Free-Energy" Generator and even sell it on the Internet. This is a business investment. We can bring in internet sites

154

from all over the States and Europe." Mike exclaimed

"We've been on it for hours, I went to Grant Stallion's Site, and I've emailed him directly. I'm waiting for a response." Rosemarie added

"Do you think your Satellite Service could connect us if we bought a Computer like yours?" asked Robert enthusiastically

"Yes, of course as you'll stay here until your home is livable; at least we hope you would stay here until then." Mike replied

"The computer is the means for our Earth to change. I want you to spend some time catching up with information that Rosemarie and I've found. Our old computer is at the shop. Once repaired, you're welcome to use it." Mike offered

Rosemarie is eager to hear about the Care Home from Judy as they made sandwiches and coffee.

"I've a hunch they'll be up to two in the morning. Let's have a snack. Are you hungry? What was going on at the Care Home? I am dying of curiosity?" Sshe asked.

Judy confirms her reading. Ruth had fallen. Harry's scheme completed. Care Aid, Cherry would get her $10,000 loyalty money.

"He's without conscience; a true psychopath. He planned her fall including the happy drug and three-inch high heels. Yes, Cherry has earned her measly $10,000. It was simple. Cherry didn't feed Marie. The floor covered with slopped food; Ruth wearing three-inch high heels slipped and broke her hip again. Poor Peter was afraid that he was going to fall too." Judy continued

"I'm relieved that you're no longer there. Stay away from there! Harry is capable of killing you too Easy, another accident. How's your friend, Kathy? Is she leaving there soon?" she asked

Judy replied, "Kathy is staying long enough to get more info from their taped meetings."

Rosemarie added, "She's brave! One in a million would risk it."

"Yes our van was stolen. Thank god, we had theft insurance. We'd just finished paying the van. It was worth $19,000! Robert bought it to sleep in when he was looking for work at Fort McMan It's paid for itself many times over. One night's hotel cost is $300. The van helped us save the money to buy the Motor Home and the down payment on the land. Now the Insurance money will buy our Garage Package.," stated Judy

"We've got the money to buy the wiring, plumbing, insulation and more. We don't need a Van anymore; but an old SUV." Judy continued

"I've heard Mike talk about Fort McMan's prices. Robert would've been cold in November and December, in a van. Good thing they met each other. Robert is the brother Mike always wanted. He grew up with sisters and always complained about it. He's happier these days." Rosemarie agreed.

"I'm happy Harry and his gang doesn't know what type of vehicle we've got. Or, where we are. Maybe it isn't safe to get my check. I don't think it's safe for me to work as a nurse anymore. I'll need to do something else. Self-employed. If they are trying to find me through my SIN number; they won't find me." Judy said quietly.

"Are you really that afraid?" asked Rosemarie

"When Kathy informed the Police about the Care Home in Hinton, she went through a really frightening time. She changed her name and went underground for two years. She had just found herself now, in the same situation again. She has warned me to do the same. I'll be relieved when I know she is safe from there." Judy admitted

"I'll do a reading for you as soon as we eat and we have some peace." Rosemarie offered.

"Hey, you guys come and get it!" she called to Mike and Robert.

"I hope that these pickles don't keep me awake tonight?" complained Mike

"You're already awake all night; do you know what time it is?" Rosemarie asked

"Goodnight! I'll be there as soon as I do a reading for Judy. We can't wait till morning; our curiosity has gotten the better of us," she added

Mike replied, "We'll spend a few more minutes in here; we've found another very intriguing site."

"Let's do this on the veranda; I need some air. Smell the grass! It is so fresh! Rosemarie chuckled

"Did you see that shooting star? What a great sign! You're here now! I have always named my cars a girl's name. I praise her when she gets good mileage or pulls out of a snow bank. Naming a vehicle is something that we'd do. Belleville is a great name for your Motor home." She exclaimed

Judy confessed, "I don't tell people about myself. I was doing readings back in Southern Ontario. My first predictive vision was at the age of three when I saw my Uncle Joe, dead in the snow bank. I told my Mother what I had seen in my vision. She slapped me for telling lies. Two days later a telegram came. Uncle Joe, found in a snow bank! My mother's feelings for me changed for the worse. I did it again when I was seven years old. This time I saw her other Uncle John dead in a snow bank. He was her favorite uncle. Yes, the telegram came again. I was right again. This time she had the church elders attempt to cast the evil spirits out of me. They believed that I was causing the deaths. I was the devil's daughter. These men frightened me and I stopped having visions for many years.

I didn't do it again until I was thirty. I then started studying Astrology and Numerology. I hoped I could prove my visions. My abilities accepted. I wouldn't be thought of as evil. I didn't tell you earlier as I don't share this info. I needed to know you first. I haven't even told Robert about my clairvoyance and psychic abilities. "Judy stated

This information pleased Rosemarie. "We can share information and research. I'll ask the Angels and my guides if we'll be able to do Mini Psychic Events or even a Psychic Site on the Internet. You want to do something that's safe. Working on the Internet and helping people is perfect. Especially, at this time, so many people need help. I'll do a reading. "

"Finally, the years of research will count for something!" added

Judy

Can we close that Care Home? The answer is YES! It will take a while. Should Judy get her pay? The answer is a strong "YES."

Can they work together in a Professional Psychic Business? "YES" was the resounding reply.

How soon will they do a Psychic Event? Within this month!

Will they get the right place to do this event? Yes, in Edmonton, the largest department store puts on a Spring Gala in April.

"I don't know how I'll sleep tonight? They'll never believe this. We'll show them! " We've just changed our lives." Rosemarie whispered

Mike and Robert are dumbfounded when they told them the news. Robert unaware of Judy's abilities never realized that she was ready to go professional. Doing readings at this Spring Gala

"Wow, you two! Never would have thought this would happen this fast?" praised Mike

Robert added, "Go for it girls! This is better than working at that death house. What a relief!"

"We're calling our Psychic Events and our Psychic Website the Forth Dimension." Judy. stated

Finally, bedtime! We're all going to sleep in this morning.

Chapter 21

The next morning started late for all of them. It was raining; a perfect day for sleeping, visiting, and researching on the internet thought Robert to himself. He sleepily looked out the window at the lake. Nothing moving on the lake this morning.

"The temperature had dropped and we're going to get some snow today. It's April 19th." he sighed.

"I don't care as I want to spend the day with Rosemarie. We have to cover information in the next few days to prepare for this weekend. I want to know; what Rosemarie has on the computer for Indigo and Crystal children. In the past, I had mothers who needed help with their children. Did you know that the birth frequency of Autistic children is now 1 in 120 children? This has happened in the last 20 years! You seldom heard about a child with this condition twenty years ago. I wonder if Rosemarie has mothers inquiring about their children. Maybe they're not autistic; but are having allergic reactions to our food source.

In my opinion, the chemical they are spraying on the wheat crops is the cause, as flour products seem to increase their symptoms. Moreover, I think that when they communicate they do it with mental telepathy. I think their energy is different from ours and that is why they get agitated with all the electric power around us." Judy explained.

"I have noticed that even dogs seem bothered by the high pitch of some of our machinery; I know what you mean. My collie on the farm, in the 80's would be howling sometimes when my tractor needed repairs." Robert replied

"What you want for Breakfast? Oatmeal or Red River Cereal?" she asked

"Shredded Wheat is quick. I want to get on-line for more on this "Free-Energy" He replied.

Rosemarie had the coffee on and homemade cheese biscuits begging for fresh strawberry jam. Eleven o'clock was the right time for a snack.

"When do you have time to make preserves?" Asked Robert

"I fit it in somehow; I can't stand to see such beautiful food go to waste. I hear you call our Judy a nickname "Honey Jean." It probably means that she was a twin. Are you left-handed like me?" Rosemarie asked

"Did you know, scientists have found that children who are left-handed are different? They had a twin in the womb. Research has found that when the one twin dies; the living twin becomes left-handed.

Many times unknowingly, the parents call their children a double name. Purely subconscious! Even more interesting, most of these children are born with paranormal abilities. Psychic talent! It makes sense as twins have such a link. Alive or dead, they connect with each other." Rosemarie added.

"Judy, do you know if you were a twin? Could there have been a lost twin?" asked Robert

He chuckled, "I don't think the world could take two of you!"

"Well, it explains my clairvoyance at the age of three." She answered and continued,

"My father had to protect me from my mother when I was a baby. It's a long story. Maybe you'll find it interesting. My grandmother was raped when she was at a fall fair in Napanee, Ontario in 1912. At that time, a woman didn't tell if this happened to her. She was thought of as a loose woman. Everyone shunned her. She hid the fact and didn't eat through her whole pregnancy. My mother was born full term but weighed only two pounds.

She didn't look like her parents, who were tall elegant, dark-haired and blue-eyed. Instead, she had red hair and green eyes. She was short and stout. Her limbs were shorter than average. Nearly a dwarf. Of course, the village gossiped and decided that she had betrayed her husband and that this daughter wasn't his child.

My grandmother was heartbroken. She was an honest, good Lutheran woman. She played the organ every Sunday morning at church. Her handwriting was so beautiful that the people from the surrounding area paid her to write their wills and other legal documents. From a place of respect to one of scorn was an impossible situation for my grandmother. Shamed by her community, she stopped eating all together and died when my mother was two years old. My Mother's two uncles raised her. Sadly, she grew up being told that her birth had caused her mother's death.

She grew up believing that horrible lie. When she was in her early thirties, she had her own restaurant in Trenton, Ontario. Her baking and cooking were famous; but even more famous was the legend of her virginity. The boys going off to war would kid her and tell her to wait for them. They were coming back to marry her as she was such a great cook. Well, she believed them and expected that one of them would return and ask her to marry him. The war ended and not one of them returned and asked her.

She was thirty-two years old in 1946, an unmarried woman without any hpes of getting married. My father strode into town. He had just finished working on the High Rises in New York with the Iroquois Indians. Dressed in fringed buckskin jacket and high top boots, he walked into her restaurant like an athlete, a circus performer. He was told

161

that she was the owner of this restaurant and a virgin. He decided that he was going to marry her. He finally talked her into going to the show with him.

He kissed her passionately in front of the people in the theater. The gossip flew. She felt that she was a tarnished woman and might as well marry him as her reputation was in ruins. He probably made certain that she believed that lie. Well, the next thing you know she was pregnant with me. However, that was not the worst of it; she was also Plenticost and he was a divorced man. Back then, it was impossible for a good Fundamentalist Christian woman to marry a divorced man. It was unthinkable.

My dad's ex-wife was an alcoholic native woman who was running with the Plenticost Minister's son. When she confided in this Plenticost Minister her condition, he got in touch with her brother, my uncle and explained the situation to him. My uncle at that time was the richest man in the area and he could buy anything he wanted including this couple's death.

This Minister and my uncle schemed up a perfect plan to solve all their problems. My uncle sold the Minister's son one of his cars; at a price, he couldn't refuse. Next, they got this couple drunk, which was very easy to do, as that was their normal state. They placed them in the back seat of this car and drove out to the local railway track. They pulled this couple from the back seat and put them into the front seat. They made it look like they had driven there and had fallen asleep at the wheel on the tracks.

This all coincided with the train coming through. The train couldn't stop and crashed into them. They never knew what hit them. How convenient! My mother three months pregnant could marry my dad and the Plenticost Minister's son would no longer embarrass him.

Perfect solution for everyone except the gossip took over the town. There was talk that my father had caused the accident. The gossip got so bad that my mother had to give up her restaurant and move away. My father took her to Sarnia where she lived in a double tent while my Dad laid the foundation for the rubber plant there. She hated him for destroying her life, her independence, her ruined reputation, and her

162

ability to make her own money. She had always been able to make her own money.

By the time, I was ready to be born they had enough money to buy a home in North Bay, Ontario. I was born at home. Soon, my father realized that she wasn't feeding me. He brought in a childless couple who made sure I ate and they saved my life. I grew up with a mother who hated me. It was her belief that I had destroyed her life. With that situation, I would never have learned that I was a twin. My dad had wanted to call me Honey Jean.

Sadly, that couple wanted to adopt me; but my mother wouldn't let that happen, as that would have brought her more shame. I lost a loving couple that could have been my parents. They really did love me! My mother told me that they had died and that they were in heaven. When I started doing accurate predictions at three years old, her fear overwhelmed her. I'm sure she thought that I was Satan's daughter or my father's ex-wife."

Rosemarie commented, "Wow, I can see that you have known a lot of emotional pain. Not being wanted is one thing but this is worse. She feared or hated you. That is a harsh reality. It's only a matter of time, for you to be recognized as a Psychic. You'll be able to relate to many people who are in emotional pain. Psychics deal mostly with people who are in emotional pain. I seldom get a frivolous reading."

Mike asked, "Let's have a snack and think of the future. It'll be interesting I can tell that already."

Judy, embarrassed; apologized for dumping all that information on them continued," I'm sorry! I don't know what possessed me to tell you all that; I never tell anyone that stuff. I sure hope that I haven't made you think poorly of me. I have told very few people about my life."

Robert consoled her. "We all have weird live stories; I'm sure if anyone can cope with this; these guys can."

Mike agreed, "Wait till I tell you my teen age years your hair will curl!"

"Judy, don't feel bad about telling me this; it only convinced me more that you not only have ability but compassion. Hurting people come to us when there is nowhere else to go. You can't learn in text books what you've developed. It comes though pain and self discovery." Rosemarie explained

She continued," It is sad that modern religion has made such a mess of people's lives; your mother and grandmother suffered because of it. The result was not in vain. You'll through your life help heal many people's lives."

"Let's look at the Internet for info on the Indigo Children. Judy you're one of them. Have you ever heard the term, "Star Children?" Mike asked

"Not yet, but I spent many hours looking up at the stars when I was a child. Why did you leave me? Why didn't you take me with you? I believed this couple was in heaven, up there in the stars as my mother told me they had died." She added.

"Star children are born here on earth in different circumstances. They all have a feeling that they don't belong here. You're not alone with such ideas. They are often extremely curious.

I call them the "Why" children as they don't take anything for granted. They want to question everything. Why is the grass green? Why the sky is blue? The list of questions is never ending. Were you like that when you were a child, Judy?" asked Rosemarie

"I used to get into so much trouble with that "Why" thing. I even got the strap one day at school for asking questions." Judy answered

"Did you know that you are part of a group of special souls who were sent here? An "assignment team" to aid with humanities transition and bring in a higher energy dimension, known as the Forth Dimension.

You have a larger range of abilities than ordinary humans do. You are from part of the Indigo Soul Energy. You vibrate at a faster vibration than an ordinary human does. You have access to the Forth and Fifth planes of existence. That is why you are so aware.

From the age of three, you accessed this with your gift of Clairvoyance. You're more perceptive and sensitive. That's why it was so hard to see Ruth and Marie going through emotional pain. Are you aware that you work with your left and right brain? This makes you very artistic and you are able to understand advanced Astrology and the paranormal.

Not the crap that Newspapers and Magazines offer, but real Astrology uses thirty-six energies. More than the sun or moon sign! Modern Astrology is complicated and based on quantum physics and Forth Dimensional Energies. It has nothing to do with Greek Mythology; but energy."

"I have studied Astrology and that is my conclusion, too. Modern Astrology based on the energies from the Forth Dimension. I use the Nodal Chart Erection to get the best readings. I view the Planets and Asteroids as satellite points nothing more. I am not a superstitious person. I use calculus, High math to create my Nodal Charts. Based on science, the oldest science known to humans." Judy answered

"I get frustrated with the Fundamentalists when they tell me I'm doing Satanic work with my readings; especially my Astrology readings. The Christian Religion, based on the idea that the Wise Men studied the stars to find Christ before King Herod could kill him. How can they at one time tell us the Christmas story of the wise men studying the stars; even following the stars to Bethlehem and in the next instant call the same science evil is beyond me." continued Judy

Mike agreed, "I was raised in a fundamentalist religion and that has been a problems for me. Especially, ideas in Revelations! Our enemies in other countries who have other religious beliefs could not be happier when we self-destruct, by out stinking thinking. Revelation's insane ideas condemn the Christian world to racial suicide. How any intelligent person can believe that stuff is more than I can figure?

The other world nations with their own religions are laughing at us. They don't have to lift a finger; if we buy into Revelation's concepts; we'll destruct on our own!"

"Thoughts are things and what we allow ourselves to dwell upon will surely come." agreed Robert

"Do you realize that in 1905 there was one Bible for every 500 persons? In my grandmother's day in 1912, there was only one bible for every village. Only the very rich, the 1% had a bible in their homes. This 1% wanted to control the world and use fear like Revelations, Armageddon, and Hell Fire Damnation upon the unsuspecting masses." Robert confirmed

"I wonder what Grant Stallion has to say about the Indigo Children; let's search it out on the Internet." suggested Judy

They make their way to the computer and like their grandparents during the 20' and 30's gathered round the old radio to hear stories and music. They read and talked about the Computer's information. If one was looking at the scene then and now; it was clear that human kind would always want to learn and evolve.

After lunch, Robert reminded Judy that they have to go into Edmonton for the mail.

Mike offered," Since you don't have your van why don't we make an afternoon of it for all of us. Your check from the Insurance Company could be in your mail box by now."

Robert exclaimed, "We can buy a Bargain News and see if there are any 4X4 Nissan SUV's for sale. I can't drive this Motor home; it's too expensive."

Judy added," Maybe there'll be a letter from Kathy? I wish I could phone her. I sure hope she is safe!"

The rain had turned to snow; it didn't bother them at all with good winter tires and four-wheel drive it was like driving on a summer road.

"Let's stop for a coffee at Devon and you guys can stop at the Home Center there and meet the salesperson. Maybe you can find out when they are going to have a sale on Bay Windows. We can save some money by buying the garage package at that time. Those windows go for Two thousand each. If they have 30% off; we're going to save by buying at just the right time." Judy suggested

Robert and Judy went into the Home Center. In front of them were the two Bay Windows she had just mentioned. They were on sale.

"Are you psychic or what? We just saved another $1,200. A customer canceled out on his window order. They were anxious to sell them and move their inventory! 40% off! The salesperson has told me that next week they will be having 30% off on last year's Garage Packages. I should wait a few days. Then purchase our double garage at 30% off." exclaimed Robert

"Hey, we can afford to take you two out for dinner!" Judy offered

They were at the mailbox at Devon's Post Office.

"Wouldn't it be great if the Insurance check was here? We'd be able to buy the garage package with cash." She added

"Our lucky day! A check for $18,000! A package for you." cheered Robert

"It can only be from Kathy. She's the only one with this address. I hope she's okay." She sighed

Opening the box, she found her paycheck, small voice activated tape deck and recorded tapes. In addition, there was a letter. Judy read the letter aloud,

"I have evidence on the tape that we needed and I have left Calgary tonight on the bus. This time, I have to go back to my maiden name. I'm considering going to school to become a chef.and looking for work on the Oil Patch in a remote camp. I'll be safe there. My name now is Marlene Brothers. Marlene is my third name. Aren't I lucky?

My parents must have known to give me three names. I told the gang you'd gone back East, for a dying Aunt in Southern Ontario. I hope that they bought it. I pulled your paycheck out of the bunch lying on their office desk. Well, it doesn't matter anyway. These tapes, when you hand them into the Police should shut them down. I copied them and sent them to Rachel and Sophie Rothman.

Consider going to their bank and cashing this paycheck quickly. I don't think they'll have a bank account for long. They even talk about their pending terrorist attack on New York so the FBI should get a copy of these cassettes too. I copied a set for me. I'm making sure that this information gets to the right people. I wish I could tell you more but not now.

I think of you often and send you post cards with the alias of Sunshine so you know that I am okay. Perhaps I'm going overboard on all of this, but then you never know whom they're really connected to. Some powerful people in the government; be careful. Thinking of you! Marlene Brothers

"Lets' deposit this Insurance check. We need to get back home as soon as possible so we can listen to those tapes in privacy." Judy stated

Chapter 22

Robert and Mike built them a fabled cottage so they could do their Psychic readings in the Malls. A small portable cottage was easy to assemble and come apart. They had found the idea on the Internet. It had taken two days to build. A fairy tale cottage and would appeal to folk.

If it gives the girls a better chance to promote their work and make a living; it was worth it. One thing for sure, no one would be able to go by without knowing their cottage was there. The cost of the space in the Mall was expensive at Two hundred and fifty a day.

When busy, they'd make a good living. They'd charge thirty dollars for a half hour reading. When they did fourteen readings a day, they'd do okay. It seemed reasonable to them. Even if they only got a few readings a day, they would cover the cost of the Mall space.

"Rosemarie loves doing her readings; She's happiest when she helps people. I'm lucky I'm with such a caring person. It's hard when she gets so much flack from the fundamentalists. Things will be easier for her now. With the two of them in the cottage, they are safer. They'll probably have a lot of fun." Mike stated

"Just to know that she's safe and not working at that Care Home is good enough for me. It would be great if they could do their readings from the comfort of our homes. That would be the ideal situation." Robert added

"That could easily happen as they get more known. It is just a matter of time. This summer they could go in your Motor Home. Imagine them in Fort McMan. People would love them there. So many folk from Newfoundland; you know how crazy they are there with their ghost stories. They wouldn't have any problems getting readings there." Mike laughed

"Do you suppose we should dress in some type of quaint costume to go with the theme of the cottage?" asked Judy

"It wouldn't take me long to make the cutest old-fashioned dresses. At the front of the cottage, have a scroll for them to sign with a feather pen. I wonder if it would be more appealing to the people and increase our business?" asked Judy

"You really do have the feel for this stage work don't you?" stated Mike

On Saturday, they were in their Cottage dressed in old-fashioned dresses looking like Aunt Maude and Aunt Betsy. Each had their own private reading area inside the cottage. The client had total privacy from the passing crowd. It was like a page out of history and so unsuspected that people impulsively stopped to get a half hour reading. It wasn't hard to prove to their clients that they knew what they were doing. They were good Psychics and the Mall hummed with the gossip of their presence. It was fun. They decided to book the next month's weekends.

"I sure can use the money and they all go away happier." Judy sighed

Robert and Mike were off dealing with the Devon Home Center's manager and closing the sale of the double garage. The two garage doors removed from the bill. An attractive front door added to the package. It would be ready to deliver in a week.

Monday, the backhoe and other equipment would finish their work on the access road and leveling the ground for the I-Beams to sit on. The foundation for the cottage was important. They had it all under control. Their timing was good. The snow had melted and the land was clear to work with.

Rosemarie and Judy worked as a team. They were sisters. Long-term plans for them evolved. The Internet worked better than they thought. It was easier to promote their business than they had ever thought possible. This was the beginning. They determined how much they wanted to work and how much time they relaxed.

Life flowed! Robert and Mike knew that the home had to be finished by November. They would have to go back for one more winter season.

Their schedule worked perfectly. The double garage package delivered to the site. Their home erected in a few days. Judy got out the drafting paper to place the kitchen and living areas on the main floor. The Insurance money paid for the electrical and plumbing supplies.

"Imagine we lost everything when our mates died last year and this year we are getting ourselves solid again. I can't wait to paint the walls and ceilings of our dear little home." Judy affirmed.

"I guess we are in the right place, at the right time, doing, and saying the right thing to the right people for our success now and in the future." Robert added

"You know I teach that phrase to all of my clients and it is miraculous how quickly their lives turn around. They get things happening for their good. It doesn't seem to matter how bad the situation is that thought form has power." Judy stated.

Robert, Mike, and Rosemarie shook their heads in agreement. "Spirit world wants us to win in life. People could only realize that idea." Rosemarie sighed

"Why do the religions of this world take such delight in teaching

171

otherwise and preaching fear and damnation to its followers?" Mike asked

"Bowing and kneeling would help get them closer to their god. If only they knew, their loved ones in Spirit just want acknowledgment; not worship. They want their living loved ones to know they still exist just in a different dimension, the Forth Dimension.

When I have gone to church in the past, I could feel their spirits trapped there; especially, the Christians. They are brain washed into believing that Christ will come, take them by the hand, and bring them to their wonderful heaven. When Jesus does not come for them, they get angry and upset distancing themselves from their loved ones. They don't realize that they go to the White Light on their own.

Ghosts created! This energy stays in the churches. I used to cry every time I went to church as I could feel their trapped souls there and I was powerless to release them." Judy sighed

"Let's look on the Internet for Ghosts and how the Crystal Children are going to elevate humanity to a new understanding." Rosemarie added

They were soon reading about the Crystal Children. They found a site that discussed all of this! They all looked at the screen! Crystal Children Here Now

Cindy Mayes and Amie Goldman were on a panel of guests discussing the Crystal Children, who come from the Silver Ray of Energy, which is from the Forth and Fifth Dimension! They'll help us raise our energy to the Forth and Fifth Dimensions.

From there, humans will Astral Travel. There will be less need for vehicle transportation. Now cameras connected to your computer allow one to see and talk with the person on the Internet.

Their ability to raise their energy will allow them to communicate with other Dimensions. The audience will realize when a child of four sings and they sound like an adult professional singer that they're in the presence of a child who is a Crystal Being.

Others come with the energy to heal people with sound and light. Yet, there is another type of Crystal Being able to manifest material objects. There have been three documented events so far from these types of children. Three boys, when looking at the vending machines in Malls have been able to get inside these machines by merely willing themselves into it.

The owners of these toy vending machines have had to spend hours trying to get the machine to open so they could get the boys out of it. So far, three little boys under the age of six have done this. The Crystal children are definitely here.

Furthermore, another type of Crystal Being has incarnated. From the Ninth Dimension, they can create anything in the Universe. Their power is from the highest dimension. They simply look at the heavens and heal the ozone layer. Like Jesus changing water into wine. They are masters of creation.

The humans who are deliberately destroying our planet in the name of greed will be at their mercy. These Children are very forgiving. They arrive at this time in history to save our planet.

"No wonder the Harry Potter Books are so popular with this group of new arrivals. They see other dimensions and know that much more is going on than meets the human eye. In my opinion, an early arrival of this kind is Chris Angels, who does the amazing and unbelievable magic shows all around the world.

In my opinion, these are not magic shows but his ability to manifest and change reality at a moment's desire. He's working with the energy of the Fifth Dimensions, changing the gravity state and vibrations of molecules at will." Judy stated

"Tim talks scientifically about these phenomena in his research." Mike added

"This is a mundane thought but it's time for something to eat!" Rosemarie stated

"I feel humbled when I realize that our creator of this vast Universe cares enough to intervene by sending these awesome beings to us." Mike added

"Some teachers and speech therapist think these children are mentally challenged because they don't talk quickly enough. It boggles the mind. I've had a few distraught mothers bring these precious children to see me and I am amazed at their brightness and their compassion. These mothers tell me they're learning mental telepathy. Their children are relating to them with this ability. I am humbled every time I meet one of these powerful beings." Judy exclaimed

Rosemarie agreed," I know exactly what you mean; last week I had a mother with one of these precious children with her. The largest of eyes that I swear penetrated to my soul. I was sure glad that I have lived a good life and had nothing to hide."

"I wonder how these powerful children will deal with these power mongers who want to destroy our Earth. I wonder if these children are already working to prevent that. Do you suppose they are already protecting the planet by using their Fifth Dimensional energy? Stopping their attempts or changing their attempts?" questioned Robert

Chapter 23

A week had gone by, time them to hear Scientist Tim Bears-Den lecture at Rabbi Samuel's home. Sam, Candy, and Aunt Amie were eager for this lecture. If thoughts could control reality, they had to find out how to do this.

Even Marie's daughters had come. Candy realized that Aunt Amie was right. Yes, she would like them in her wedding. They were perfect, as they knew how important it was for her safety. No Newspapers!

Secrecy for now was most important. Their wedding seemed so petty when she compared it to the coming attack but life must go on and she wasn't going to let terrorists destroy her life; which is what would happen if she canceled her wedding. She would get on with things that made them all happy. Those terrorists would not destroy their happiness.

"Thank you for understanding; you'll make our day. Hope you like royal blue as that is the color theme of the wedding." Candy whispered.

"We've news that you must hear. I received two tapes this morning by Speedy Service. It is information from the night nurse from Brenda's Care Home. The Coordinator, Judy, and the Night Nurse, Kathy had the insight to plant a small voice activated tape deck in their Board Room. Wait till you hear them." Rachel stated

"It's proof that our mother, Marie is getting better and that she's heard of this planned Sept 11th attack on New York, too. She walks around the center of the house wailing "9 -11; the planes; the twin towers" for hours on end. In these tapes, these people are concerned about her behavior as they think someone is going to know what she is saying. They are afraid of her and part of the terrorists who are planning this attack! We've got to get her out of there and fast!" explained Sophie

"We've time to listen to them after Tim Bears-Den's lecture. Perhaps everyone here will want to hear them especially, Tim. We'll get these tapes to the FBI or some government agency that can look into this." Sam stated.

"Soon, we'll get your Mother out of there." Aunt Amie promised

In walked Tim Bears-Den who introduced himself as a Forth Dimensional Physicist as he said the term Scientist smacked of intellectuals who were so conditioned to out dated theories that he no longer wanted any part of them.

"Tonight, I want to change your ideas of what is real. I want you to understand the idea of quantum physics from layman's terms. You know that we are all vibrating molecules. Microscopic atoms vibrate at tremendous speeds. Everything around us is the same way; our chair we sit on; the floor we stand on; the room that surrounds us. All vibrating molecules are not dense matter at all.

Some of you have heard about the Florida Freighter during the Second World War; they tried to hush it up but the story did get out. How they had used science to change the molecular structure of the ship so it would be invisible to the German U Boats and when they rematerialized it; the sailors on the ship had come back with their bodies all entwined in the freighter's composition. To deal with this they simply bombed the ship and told everyone that the ship had been one more target of the German U Boats. Our government hid this reality from the American people." He lectured

"I know this is true as I was a reporter for the New York Times back then and our jobs were on the line if we breathed a word to anyone about this." said an older distinguished gentleman sitting in the back of the room.

"Then you have an idea of how this science has continued research in Alaska from the 50' to present. The Russians started research on the same concept in the 30's. Khrushchev concerned that this science uncontrolled and in the wrong hands could destroy the planet. He called their research more dangerous than any nuclear bomb could ever be. He referred to them as Super Weapons." He continued

"Is that why, they are so willing to give up their Nuclear Bombs: as they now have weapons that make that outdated?" asked Sam

"Yes, you have it! They can now use this energy from the Forth Dimension, which is faster than the speed of light to create super weapons.

Have you heard yet of the Tesla Howitzer and how it works. Some information has got out about that. Bombs are obsolete! So are the planes that would deliver them. There is no delivery system. All present systems fail. They are destroyed by this energy.

All distant destruction is from as small a place as a phone booth and delivered anywhere on earth. These new weapons can cause storms on the Sun. Solar flares is their term. All nations and their people must arise and demand the ban on these weapons. Earth headed for total destruction! We're at the point in history, where we can absolutely destroy our planet even our galaxy with "Scalar Weaponry"

Back in the 60's, Kruschev was concerned. You can only imagine how much farther along these researchers are with inventing these new super weapons. It is beyond our imaginations! Star Trek is here! Black Ops Government Personnel are supporting this "status quo." The 1% has the "free world" under control. They have been very successful at this for over the last Two hundred years." Tim Bears-Den continued

"What about the new threat for Sept 11ᵗʰ on the Twin Towers?" interrupted Sam?

"Rabbi has told me about this planned attack on New York for Sept 11ᵗʰ. This does not surprise me, as they wish to make it look like the Middle East is responsible for this attack. Their goal is to get their hands on the Oil in that area of the world. They are determined to keep things as they are even though they know this science and technology is available as we speak. Forth Dimensional energy is infinite "Free-Energy" for the world. No need for people to suffer under third world conditions." stated Tim Bears-Den.

"Surely, there are some people in that social set that would want to create a New World that would be prosperous for all?" questioned Candy

"Yes, you are right! Lady Dianna and Fergie are two that do not fit into the 1% they are both Indigo Children who see through their pretense and lies. I don't know how long the 1% will let them live. Their very existence is a threat to them. We have to think and act for our planet and we must act quickly as the 1% are getting stronger all the time." He added

"What is a Tesla Howitzer?" asked Sam

"It is very scientific and would take hours to explain the science part; so I will save that part for another night. This weaponry is stronger than a Nuclear Bomb and can be repeated easily again at that place or anywhere else. It can use a lesser power setting and simply destroy all electronics in the target area.

My concern is that they will use this power to destroy the Twin Towers. The planes flying into the top floors of these buildings wouldn't be strong enough to make them disintegrate. Only the top floors destroyed, but not the entire tower. They will use resonance or vibration energy to turn the Twin Towers into dust." Tim Bears-Den continued

"This Forth Dimensional Power used in this way can make our nuclear missiles inoperable as they sit in their silos by "frying" the electronic circuits that guide them; it can bring down any airplane, anywhere in the world, at any time; it can target any person anywhere, if their exact place is known. Assassination without a shot fired as it can target the heart or kidney making it look like it was a natural death.

The Howitzer can destroy the hydropower grids anywhere in the world. It could target Wall Street by destroying its electricity. Our powerful leaders don't know when some real terrorist group could cripple America, Canada or Europe. For the first time in history, the 1% may loose control. of our world. What if a terrorist group got hold of this technology?" Tim explained.

"They don't want you to know about this tremendous power. The 1% would panic; they realize that their time is ending. Scalar Interferometry or the Tesla Howitzer has changed our world forever; whether they want it or not. We have to wake up and know that the citizens of the world need to come together; all nations and embrace our new technology." Tim continued.

"Have you heard of Weather Wars yet? Well they are coming as the second Howitzer Mode called the "Endothermic" sucks energy out of the chosen target. The target becomes freezing cold even to the point of freezing parts of the ocean This sucked out energy is then vented out somewhere else on the planet,

They are using this technology to open inaccessible gas deposits in Northern Canada so that they can have infinite wealth from these Gas Deposits. Continuing the suicidal fossil fuel energy, which is destroying our Planet? Unfortunately, when they open these gas deposits the endothermic energy has to go somewhere else on the planet. The increased world cataclysms; as earthquakes, tsunamis, volcanoes, and extreme weather changes created every time they use this Forth Dimension energy in accessing another gas deposit. "Tim continued

"This is why we are seeing such erratic weather patterns and it is not our fault. The idea that we are consuming too much gas for our vehicles and homes are what are causing the horrible weather is not true." Sam interrupted

"Yes, you are right. We are not causing this! The cause is the use of this technology. By using heat (exothermic) and cold (endothermic) modes together the weather has been altered everywhere. Warm the air over here, cool it down over there, put a curl in the jet stream, dissipate

179

clouds, create clouds, and whip up a tornado.

Weather wars are what are happening as we speak. Why do you think so much has happened around the world in the last few years? However, it is even more deadly weapon as they use it to freeze tanks, equipment, and soldiers. Sudden extreme freezing is child's play with this technology. Soldiers frozen instantly do not come back to life and neither would we if they decided to do this to an area. This reality I learned of years ago. Their intent is to decimate 80% of the population by December 21, 2012

The media has bought into this idea as it sells stories that predict the dire Mayan predictions for Dec 21st 2012. Mass marketing has enforced this thought form of eliminating 80% of our world's population by an asteroid named Nibiru hitting the planet; another of the elite's schemes to frighten the masses. Much like the Y2K predictions that the world would end then

Why, you might wonder because they have built the infrastructure; all the roads, all the bridges, all the high rises, and more. Now it is not necessary to have all these people. They can keep it all running with five hundred million people. Thus, they will never run out of the raw materials they figure they need for their survival." Tim Bears-Den informed.

"How can we ever fight back or even protect ourselves from this?" asked Rabbi Samuel.

"Thoughts are things; and this information needs to go viral as quickly as possible. We are at war whether we know it or not. It is just a matter of time! A terrorist group has this technology and uses it. The Russians have extreme terrorist groups that could easily attack their science labs and take over this technology. Hiding our heads in the sand and pretending that this does not exist is no answer at all." Tim Bears-Den replied

"I believe that the Crystal Children who can manipulate energy have come to our planet to divert this outcome. They have amazing powers of Universal Creation. Now they are very young still but in ten years, some will be fifteen years old and very able to understand our danger. Many of them are wise beyond their years and aware of this evil already even at the age of three and four they know what is coming.

They will be in their late teens in 2012 and they will be able to do amazing things. They read minds and they will be able to hunt down terrorists. Many of them at the age of seven tell me they are here to protect the planet. I still think there is some hope for all of us. Don't forget that Spirit World is watching over all of this and they have abilities too. I am confident that we can stop this destruction of human life from happening." Aunt Amie stated

"Just look at how Spirit has led us to connect with the people who work at that wretched care home in Calgary. The many coincidences or God incidences that have come together to rescue our mother, Marie" and tell us of us this pending terrorist attack." exclaimed Rachel

"Yes!" they all agree

Tim Bears-Den smiled and stated," At least, you didn't crumble in fear, but you've stood your ground when you have heard the worst. You have done better than the scientific groups that I have lectured to in the past. "

"You have given me hope that with cool heads we can change things and our future. If you have any ideas or wish to talk with me I am available." Tim added

Rabbi Samuel graciously stated. "Thank you for coming to give us this talk, tonight. Although it is upsetting, it is better to know than to have our heads in the sand. We will think seriously about this new information. Let us have a snack. Tim, please stay as Rachel has brought us tapes from Calgary. You may have answers for us."

The first tape dealt with their scheme to create Ruth's fall. Create her second hip fracture and at age 83 would be fatal, as she would get pneumonia and die. Their scheme to have Marie's eating behavior cause it angered the listeners.

Cherry had shown her loyalty to Brenda's Care Home and the $10,000 was in Cherry's bank.

Their next scheme was to push Marie down the stairs as she made the walk around the center of the Care Home. This concerned all of them as Marie's life was threatened. .

Again, Cherry would earn another $10,000 if she would push Marie down the stairs; especially, when she was the only Care Aid on shift. Their conversations now recorded gave the needed evidence.

Rachel had not had time to listen to all of this tape until now. That was all they needed to hear that Marie was in imminent danger. Everyone exclaimed, "Oh my God!"

"Was there a plane out tonight for Calgary?" Rachel asked

They'd get the last plane to Calgary tonight. They didn't have time to listen to the second cassette which connected Harry Hall and Walter Brown to the pending 9 -11 terrorist attack

"The FBI would know how to deal with this part of it. They would have a copy of this cassette in the morning." Sam promised

"I wonder after hearing tonight's talk will it be enough to motivate any real investigation? It is as if the Police and government officials have been brain washed. Do they go through screening when hired? Only the ones with killer instincts picked for the job of policing the inferior masses. This attitude is clear in the Military as they consider the people inferior to themselves." Tim Bears-Den stated

"The chicken or the egg? Who knows?" questioned Sam to the small concerned group that stayed behind to discuss a way to keep Sept 11[th,] from happening. We can copy these tapes and spread them throughout our communities. Just leave them behind on the streetcars or in the subway. Spend money, copy them as much as possible, and get other people doing it too. This is modern word of mouth warfare. The people of New York have to know what is coming and prepare. The people who find these tapes will be the ones who are supposed to know about this attack.

I would put a large ad in the Newspaper but I do not want to cause a large panic, as that is not the answer, as they would then just bomb another city. Just pray that some people receive the information to save themselves and their families.

Chapter 24

It was a sunny morning and the spring weather had returned; the snow was melting and birds were singing. Fishing boats were on the lake. Robert and Mike sipping their morning coffee studied the Bargain Newspaper looking for a good deal on a Nissan 4X4 SUV.

Rosemarie called, "What would you like for supper?"

Mike yelled back, "Make it the trout that we caught last summer. They need to know that fishing is a worthwhile effort."

Just then, Judy came up to the house. Beau clumsily ambled over to meet her and pushed his head into her outstretched hand.

"I'll be so happy when I have my own kitchen so I can cook for you two, I hope I haven't lost my cooking skills and burn everything." She sighed

"I have your mail!" Rosemarie handed her the mail.

A postcard from Marlene; really it was Kathy as she had signed it with Sunshine.

"She is doing okay, attending night school to learn cooking. It sure didn't take her long to get going on her dream. She says she is going to stop by when she comes through this way on her way to the Oil Patch. I sure wish that I could send her a letter or a phone call. I didn't get her new cell's number that night. " Judy added

"Perhaps she's been in touch with Marie's daughters in New York. Here's their phone number. Would you mind if I called them?" asked Judy

"Right after we eat as I am starving and those sandwiches you've made look too good to wait for." replied Rosemarie.

After lunch, Judy called New York. The housekeeper answered the phone in a strong New York accent, "Yes, it is the Rothman's residence. How can I help you?"

Judy explained that she had been the coordinator at Brenda's Care Home and wondered how Marie was and if the girls had gone to pick up their mother, yet.

"I'm so worried! I haven't heard from them for days and they should have been back by now." Jessie, the housekeeper, sobbed

"Do you have a phone number for their cell? Or a hotel where they might have stayed?" asked Judy

"Yes, here it is; the cell number is 602.555.3535 and they're at the Calgary Airport Inn room #332. Would you be able to see them or get through on the phone?" she asked

"We have to go to Calgary tomorrow anyway to set up our booth at the Annual Psychic Event. It's being held across the street from that hotel if I remember right. We could leave in a few hours and be there tonight. We could even stay in the same hotel. What do you think Judy?" Rosemarie asked

"I'll book a room now. Let's see if the guys are willing." Judy replied

It didn't take long and they were ready. The reading Cottage disassembled fit easily into the storage area of the Motor home. They want to take in the Motorcycle Show in Calgary that weekend so everyone was happy.

"Talk about coincidences; here's another one." chuckled Mike

"The Annual Psychic Event is on now; just when they decide to rescue their Marie from that horrid place. The hotel they are staying in is across the street from this event. We've already planned this weekend. It just gets better and better." Judy exclaimed.

"We'll be there for supper. Did you think to put the fish back in the freezer?" asked Mike

Beau hopped into the Motor home as if he owned the place and settled down on the back bed. He liked traveling.

"Remember that Nissan SUV 4X4's advertised in the Calgary Bargain Paper? Wouldn't it be something if I bought it and drove it home or better yet hitched it to the back of the Motor Home?" Robert asked

"I wonder if Ruth is still in the hospital. Maybe if I wear a Nurse's Uniform I can get in to see her?" suggested Judy

"Better be careful about that!" warned Robert

"Well, I am going to take the tapes to the Police as soon as I get there and maybe they can do something about getting her out of that dreadful home. I can't even say Care Home anymore; it gets stuck in my throat." Judy muttered

They arrived at the Calgary Airport Inn and checked in. They would use the Motor home too "It is great to have all the comforts of a luxury hotel. I can cash my paycheck at their account and they will not know where I am living now. So far, I've been able to hide my whereabouts effortlessly. Perhaps, Jack, my husband is protecting us." Judy added

Robert answered, "I know what you mean. This last two months have been incredible. I can't believe how easily things have come together. I think I have a guardian angel, maybe Bonnie is looking after us."

"Let's check room #332. If they aren't there why don't we leave them our cell number? They can call us. I really want to give these two tapes to the Police and as quickly as possible. Cash my paycheck before their bank accounts seized." She stated

At Room #332 there was no answer. A housekeeper was finishing her day's work and without hesitation, Judy went up to her and asked if she had seen the people staying in #332?

"I saw them yesterday as they left. They were in a hurry." the housekeeper replied

"Wait, I heard them saying that they would probably be getting back here for supper tonight and they wanted a cot put into their room." She answered

Judy asked," We're old friends and I had hoped that we would get here in time to connect with them. Could you please put this note in their room so they can find us?"

With that, Judy wrote a quick explanation. Who she was and would they please meet her at their Room #338. at eight that night. If not would they please phone her cell?

The housekeeper opened the door and placed the note on the desk in their room

"Thank you" stated Judy as she handed her a tip.

"Well, that's done and now we have just enough time to get to the bank and get this check cashed. It is a good thing that it from the TD Bank as they stay open until nine o'clock.

"I hate rush hour traffic and in this Motor home it is going to be harder than usual to get to where we are going. Why not, just rent a car for the weekend." offered Robert

"You're right that is the only thing to do. Just make sure that this Inn takes better care of our Motor home than the last parking lot. We can't afford to have our home stolen." She answered.

Robert decided to let Judy drive, as he hated rush hour traffic let alone Calgary's version of rush hour traffic.

186

"Am I getting smarter? We have managed to get to their bank in time to cash my paycheck and deliver those tapes to the detective. All done in an hour and a half. He sure looked very curious when we handed him those tapes, didn't he?" She asked

Robert smiled and asked, "We got to get back to the Inn so we can go for supper with them; besides I am getting tired. I might need some cuddle time?"

"Are you feeling romantic or tired? You have to make up your mind. "She tossed back.

Mike's cell phone rang twice and he answered. Yes, they were back at the room taking a nap.

"We'll be there in about ten minutes so be ready. By the way, we were able to leave a note for Marie's daughters in their room. We asked them to come to our room at eight o'clock tonight

I hope they have rescued Marie." Robert stated

"I wonder how the Motor home is. I am sure glad that Beau is in it. His big bark would keep most people away. Do you think we could take him for a quick walk so he can take a whiz?" Judy asked

"Hey, we're ahead of schedule thanks to your driving. We can take our time. He's such a good dog. I sure would like to have a dog like him soon. Nothing like a dog when things are frightening." He stated

"Okay, I get it! A dog for you and a dog for me! A dog for protection and a cuddly one for me; especially, when you go back to Fort McMan to work." She responded

Belleville, the Motor home was doing just fine. Beau was glad to see them. He wasn't a barker but a quiet dog; but he could bark when he needed to and it was a fierce bark.

"Got to like a dog that is this smart! "Exclaimed Robert

"He will help train our new dog!" She replied

They walked around the hotel and Judy noticed the Rothman girls helping their Mother out of a taxi. "Quick put Beau back in the Motor home so I can meet up with them. I can't wait to see them again and let them know that I just gave those tapes to the Detective?" She asked

"Hello, do you remember me? I am Judy, the Coordinator from Brenda's Care Home. "I left the Care Home as it wasn't safe for me when I realized what was going on there. Kathy sent you the two tapes that I had taped from their Boardroom meetings as I found out that they were going to hurt Ruth." She excitedly rambled on.

"Please do come with us up to our room. Mother recognized you and she's smiling. We picked her up today and I can't wait to get her home." Rachel stated

"Marie, remember me Marie?" Judy asked as she walked with her arm supporting Marie.

Rachel and Sophie brought the new suitcases and bags of clothing that they had just bought for their mother. They had left everything behind at the Care Home; telling them that they were taking her out to lunch.

"I wish that you would switch rooms with our room. They might try to follow you and get her back. It could get ugly if they wanted to silence all of you. I know how long it takes police to work their cases. It's very different from the detective stories that we see on television; it would be no problems to switch rooms just for security's sake. We know they're killers." Judy offered

"You know you're right! We never thought to use anything but our own names when we came; as we were so anxious to rescue her from that place. Could we do it now?" Rachel asked

"Certainly, we are sharing this large suite with friends of ours. The room is in their names. They will have no problems with that, as we will get another room. I want you safe." Judy responded.

Mike went down to the desk and asked to rent another room on the third floor. He explained that another Psychic had joined their group. They were in another room immediately.

"Man, I feel like I am living in one of those detective stories." Mike sighed

"We must be careful; these criminals are smart." Rosemarie agreed.

"We are up to it! Rachel, I have a wonderful idea. Why don't you come with us in the Motor home back to Edmonton and visit there for a few days using our names to rent a hotel room or better yet to stay at a Bed and Breakfast until the Police have time to arrest these people and then you will be safe to fly home with Marie?" offered Rosemarie

"In fact, they could come to our home at the Lake and just holiday until things blow over here. Then if you still are having problems taking your Mom home we can all make a Holiday of it and drive you down to Vancouver and across the border. There you can rent a car and make your journey back to New York." suggested Mike

"You folks are unbelievable! Sophie and I have tried to figure a way to protect Mom and get her home safely. Now that we understand what has happened to her, we can get her help. Could we go to your cottage for a week or two? It sounds the safest. The less people who see us; the better it is." Rachel stated.

"There is only one problem; we came for the Spirit Psychic Event. How do we get out of that?" asked Rosemarie and Judy at the same time.

Everyone started to laugh and the tension broke in the room.

"Hey that's no problems. We'll use the rented car. Tomorrow morning Mike and I will drive you back home to our lake and return. It can all be done very easily." Robert stated

Mike joined in, "You'll be comfy at our home. Lot's of food and we'll be back home anyway on Sunday night."

"You people are unbelievable; strangers helping us like this." Rachel whispered.

Sophie added, "We're grateful; Mom needs to get home safely."

"Hey we are family, when I take on a patient I do it with a conscience. Your mother wasn't a resident to me, but a patient." Judy stated

"I would like to leave here before sunrise tomorrow morning; I need to return by eleven o'clock in the morning to help with the Psychic Event for the girls. Would you be able to get going that early?" asked Mike

"Of course, five-thirty!" answered Rachel

By now, they gathered in the executive suite.

"I am starved! Let's order our food!" piped up Judy

"Here's the menu!" added Robert

Soon all of them were eating including Marie; she was eating properly with a fork. Marie was no longer pacing the floor with her constant wailing of "9 -11 planes; the people"

"Marie is not in that manic state that I saw at the home!" exclaimed Judy

"Yes, we looked through her research papers and found some information that helped us understand what had happened to her. She had volunteered herself as a patient. With drugs, they had changed her so she was mental. They were experimenting on her. They wanted to see if the "Scalar Wave Technology" they were studying could heal it.

They never finished the research; instead, her team of scientists fired and a new team came. The research on Mind Control using this new science stopped. No wonder they packed Mom up and dropped her on our doorstep. Her co-worker advised us to hide her in Canada. She would never have gotten better in that home as they had her on so many drugs She'd never have been a threat to them; drugged like that." stated Sophie

"We stopped giving Mom those drugs and already she seems better!" exclaimed Sophie

"We've done some research ourselves as Judy and I, are Clairvoyants or what some people call crazy and other people call Psychic. Our research has led us to a man named Grant Stallion who is talking about "Electromagnetic Waves" controlling our minds and personality. Do you suppose it was this type of energy that Marie and her team were researching?" asked Rosemarie

"You are right! I brought some of Mom's computer CD's which mention his name often. We can explore that if you have a Computer at

your home Sunday night when you get back from your Psychic Event."
Rachel stated

Sophie piped up, "By the way, our Aunt Amie is a recognized
Psychic in New York, and she would love to meet you both. As soon as
it is possible, you'll have to come to visit us and meet her. I sure wish
that we could have gone to see you at the Spirit Psychic Event"

"Oh! Don't worry we will have lots of time to do readings for you
next week when the men are busy putting up Judy and Robert's new
home." responded Rosemarie

Chapter 25

"They are going to deliver the cottage today after lunch, what do you think of that? You will be in your kitchen before you know it." Robert joked as they woke up in their Motor home back in Lake Isle.

The sun was streaming in and Judy was basking in it. She had done many Psychic readings over the weekend. It took a lot of energy to do readings as it involved her emotions as each person she read for connected with her on that level. She needed rest.

"I must have done over sixty readings this weekend. Rosemarie and I decided to do only half hour readings so that we could see more people. I wonder if she is as worn out as I am. We did two days with twelve hours each day. I'm exhausted. I don't know how we ever did it." Judy stated with a big sigh.

"Do you want to go back to sleep? I can shut the blinds and maybe you can get back to sleep?" Robert asked

"That wouldn't be fair to Rosemarie! She's making breakfast for our guests and I should help." She answered

"Well, an afternoon's sleep is a must! Do you promise to do that?" He asked

"We'll see; it will be hard for me to sleep knowing our home is coming today. Besides, I really want to see Marie's CD's. I can only imagine what is there, it will be mind-blowing." Judy replied

Life was never boring with her around and now with Rosemarie things were even more busy and weird. Thought Robert to himself

"Oh! My god! I just realized; there are now three more weird women added to the mix. Mike and I have to go fishing and soon." Robert joked

"You love it! Imagine you could be with a chick who does nothing but watch Soap Operas and eats candy; besides I know you and Mike are just as anxious to see what is on those CD's as we girls are!" She laughed

"Our life is interesting as we have played the cloak and dagger game. Getting Marie and her daughters out here to the lake was exciting. I was just thinking about how it had all come about. The rescue couldn't have been planned more successfully. Even you're driving the rented car under my name. You were in their bank for a few minutes at the busiest time of the week, Friday night. With your hair dyed that new shade and your new glasses I'm sure that even if they had someone looking out for you they wouldn't have realize it was you." Robert stated

"I know at times, I feel like we have guardian angels guiding our footsteps. Especially, the way we thought to change rooms and eat in the suite instead of the restaurant. The rented car whisked them here. Maybe we should go into the espionage game. I wonder if we've watched too many spy movies?" She joked

"It really is happening naturally; our evasive tactics are not planned they just happen." He replied.

Mike knocked on the Motor home's door.

"The delivery truck will be here in fifteen minute. Hurry up! I think I am even more excited than you guys are about this home." Mike yelled over Beau's barking

"On my way!" Robert yelled back

"Tell Rosemarie I will be over in ten minutes. Why is Beau doing all that barking?" Judy yelled

"There is a bear and her cub roving at the back of the house and Beau goes crazy when that happens. I'll have to put some mothballs in the trees around the house and yes, around your new home too. They don't like the smell of mothballs and they stay clear of any area that has them. Such a simple trick but very effective. My grandparents used that trick on the farm where I visited as a kid." Mike added

Awake now thought Judy. I'll exercise and stretch, that gets the blood flowing. By the time, she walked up the hill with Beau at side she was awake. Rosemarie met her at the door. Marie was smiling at her.

"Good morning, Marie! You're sure up early this morning. This fresh air must agree with you." She stated with a smile.

"We've had such a pleasant weekend. Mom is getting better and better." Sophie stated a smile on her face as she hugged her mother.

"At this rate, she'll soon be able to talk with us again and tell us what happened to her." Rachel added

"Coffee is on; the hot cross buns have your name on them." Rosemarie yelled from the bedroom as she put on her jacket.

"I have to go outside and put out the moth balls; I can't stand Beau's incessant barking" Rosemarie continued.

Breakfast was over; Rachel handed Judy the research CD, that Marie had done all those months up north in Alaska. What was on those CD's?

"We're now going to get to the bottom of what happened to Mom!" Rachel stated

She had told them that she was working on extending life and people not aging; that everyone could live to 200 years old or more and not age; in fact the old could be rejuvenated and return to an early age of thirty years old, the prime time in everyone's life. Disease and sickness wiped out. Birth disorders healed. Could Marie have offered herself for a test for this new science?

"Where would this knowledge come from?" questioned Sophie

The CD opened with the title.

Cure of Diseases

Cancer, AIDS and any disease is now curable. Everyone becomes healthy and stays healthy. Bioenergetics is a new form of longitudinal electromagnetic energy which can heal all humanity. Psycho-energetics can heal the mind from any mental condition. The power grids of this new technology would keep the entire population healthy, rejuvenated, and bathed in this age-reversing energy. "Longitudinal Electromagnetic Energy" .from the Forth Dimension would give infinite energy. The CD was a lecture by a Scientist named Tim Bears-Den.

"He was just at Rabbi Samuel's home last week talking with us about this new "Scalar Wave Energy." Rachel exclaimed

We have no idea yet of how long the human life span can increase with this new technology. People might be able to live two centuries given the full development of this technology. These energies can totally change our medical care for everyone. A new kind of electromagnetic energy that is different. We know about the waves that work radio, TV, cell phones and microwave ovens. Some Astrologers are aware of these new waves of energy. They are working with this energy sent by the different planets and asteroids when they create a Birth Chart for their clients.

The energy waves that we already use are transverse EM waves. Whereas, these new longitudinal EM waves called "Scalar Waves" are exceedingly more powerful. These waves come from the "emptiness" of space which is not empty, but a great ocean of seething energy! .Nikola Tesla knew about this a hundred years ago. The Russians have worked with this new energy for the last hundred years.

This ocean of energy from the Forth Dimension is where the Psychics get their information. They call it the Akashi records; a small part of this ocean of energy. Star Trek may be real. All that you saw in that T.V. Series could be real. It is just a matter of time when what you saw there will be commonplace.

We are living in a Third Dimensional World. There is a Forth dimension space called "Space-time." The Forth Dimension consists of compressed energy, when further compressed by the same amount that this original matter is compressed by equals the "speed-of- light squared"

Star Trek is here with a new equation "E equals delta-tee-cee-squared" Einstein move on over as he failed to create this concept. This compressed energy when released has tremendous power. "Time-Bomb" takes on a new meaning.

This Longitudinal Electromagnetic Energy called "scalar waves." It exists only in the vacuum of the emptiness of space.

This vacuum of space exists in everything. We are vibrating molecules with space throughout our bodies. Even our bodies are mostly space, between atoms and molecules. The gateway to this seething ocean of energy is there at every point in the universe. This seething ocean of energy is all around us and all through us. Therefore, it is possible to send this energy throughout the world to cure disease, hunger and change the world for all of us. We merely have to tap into this immense power and change our world.

Rosemarie stopped the CD and asked," Would anyone like a cup of tea. I have to stop and get my breath. This is too much information. I have to absorb what we have just read?"

Rachel and Sophie look at their Mother, Marie in amazement and both started to talk at once in their excitement, "Were you working with this team of scientists? Did you work with him too?" they asked. So many questions filled their minds.

Judy asked, "Marie are you coming out of this fog?" Marie shook her head up and down and stuttered, "YYYYes!" She had listened to them as they had taken turns reading what was on the Monitor's screen.

"I think Marie will fully recover. Induced by Bioenergetics; She'll make a full recovery. Imagine what she'll be able to tell us! " Judy stated

"This new science could be used for great good but it's like fire or water it can also be used for great harm to the human race. Maybe Marie found out what these people were all about and they knew how ethical she is. They knew she would go to the media and try to stop them from harming humanity. I wonder if that is why her team discarded. Maybe; killed! I guess Marie was lucky that she survived at all! " Judy stated

After their coffee break, they continued the CD

"I guess you are a Psychic! This CD began with weaponry." Rosemarie interjected when the CD started up with the same idea.

Scalar Wave Energy

Bioenergetics can also be a weapon.

Anyway, you can use it to create diseases and diseases for the masses. In other words, whole areas of the world targeted with diseases like Anthrax etc A grid called the Woodpecker established by the Russians in 1976. It is a worldwide electromagnetic pattern. There even exists a Woodpecker signal at low amplitude so the conscious mind can't detect it. Some Psychics say they use this Woodpecker Grid to Astral Travel. On this wire, they travel on it; in their sleep state. They have been able to use it for their own good visiting loved ones many miles away. Not physically; but mentally!

"How come we don't hear anything on the news about all of this?" questioned Sophie

The CD continued with this next title

How to "Broadcast" Diseases

Longitudinal EM Bio-wars. New, "quantum potential weapons" used to induce disease-at-a-distance in any population! You'll soon get a vaccination for an epidemic called M2K2. It'll be used to survive a conventional bio-attack. It is possible through this new science to broadcast a virtual disease pattern over a population. The

immune system, overloaded by antibiotics in our food chain succumbs to this bio-attack.

In other words, alter one's internal atoms and molecules with this new energy to a population and create a deadly virus. Send that to a population. The cellular control systems order the immune systems into action but is overcome by more than one disease hitting it at once and the immune system can't fight all these disease patterns sent at once .Overwhelmed the body shuts down. The immune system can't defend itself against so much at one time.

The 'Woodpecker Grid' acts on mass. Designed to create anthrax, smallpox, or flesh eating disease. Cripple a country. Populations of countries could be dead overnight.

"Does anyone here want to have a break as this is too much for me. I need to take a break! This stuff is overwhelming! Why can't humanity just learn to use technology for good?" Rosemarie asked

"Do you suppose Mother was given this in the form of Alzheimer's and she didn't have the strength to fight it? That is what she seemed to have and now she seems to be overcoming it?" questioned Sophie

"Mother talked about bio weapons being employed in 1997 when the Gulf War Syndrome occurred. Back then, she said it involved the use of scalar technology to induce this disease state. She believed that the Gulf War Syndrome induced with this stuff. It was a test; but we were not interested in her work back then. We were young and thought of party dresses. I guess she gave up trying to tell us what she was doing. The significance of her work. Boggles my mind. How I wish, I had listened." Rachel stated

"When "the flesh-eating disease" came out Mother talked about it being a test of the power of this new technology. We were not listening! She must have felt so alone with this horror!" Sophie sighed

Mike and Robert came in for lunch all excited about the package. It was ready to receive the 12/12 Pitch Roof that was coming this afternoon.

"Our home is nearly standing; by tonight we will be able to stand

under our roof and know we are on our way to finishing our home."
exclaimed Robert

It was a good thing that something exciting as building a new home
could take the edge off what they were reading. It was hard for Judy to
shift gears and get into the spirit of their new home. Robert could sense
that something was up.

"Hey what's going on here? Has someone died? Why the gloom? He
asked curious and dumbfounded that she wasn't excited about the house.

"Robert, you will never believe the information on Marie's CD's.
We've just finished hearing the most shocking news and yet, the most
hopeful news. It has left us all in a brain freeze. Of course, I'm thrilled
about the house. Just give me some time to recoup." Judy stated with a
sigh

Chapter 26

The days went by fast, Rachel and Sophie watched the newspapers and the media expecting to hear some news about Brenda's Care Home and its murderous owners. However, nothing at all! Kathy (now Marlene) had sent a couple of postcards; one a week and she was doing fine.

"They must have a lot of connections to keep this out of the newspapers." Rachel stated

"I am not surprised at all; the "power folk" own all the media. They've been able to hush it up." Mike affirmed.

He liked to call the 1%, this elite group who have all the money and control the "Power Folk"

"Remember they all golf at the same golf club; dine at the same lounges and dance on the same ocean liners. They protect each other." Robert agreed

"Besides how can they let this crime out to the media as it exposes their terrorist scheme? I'm concerned for all of you. The fact that this pretend care home has not been closed down or those killers arrested; puts all of you in grave danger." Mike stated

"They'll have realized that these tapes were done by Kathy and Judy. When you picked up Marie and didn't return her to the home, this put Marie, Sophie, and yourself in a serious situation. In my opinion, you shouldn't return to New York, but stay here with us." Robert stated

"Are you sure we couldn't go to Seattle in your Motor Home and have Aunt Amie pick us up and drive to New York." Rachel suggested.

"Our evasiveness has protected all of us so far." Judy added

"You would've thought that there would have been news in a Newspaper or on television.. Not a word! I don't believe it! I was so sure that detective would act on those tapes. I have a clean police record and I am in my 50's. Surely, I should have some credibility. Do you suppose he thinks we made the tapes up?" Judy questioned

"It would be a pleasant trip to Seattle. Aunt Amie and Candy would fly there and rent a Van. I've always wanted to travel coast to coast and this would be an opportunity to do so." Rachel argued

"I'll phone Sam and see if anyone from Brenda's Care Home has tried to reach us. If there has been any response from the detective that I gave Kathy's tapes to two weeks ago." Sophie suggested

"Maybe Jessie our housekeeper will have some information?" added Rachel

"I don't think it would be good to phone our home as it might be bugged. I am getting paranoid. I wonder how Jessie our housekeeper is doing. Have to ask Sam to visit her. He can explain in person what is going on. On second thought, not safe to phone Aunt Amie's home, either. You just never know with the kind of power these terrorists have obviously anything could be possible. They could have listening devices on all of our friend's phones back home and of course, especially our home." Sophie added with a sigh.

"No answer, I will try at Sam's work that is a better choice anyway." Sophie stated

"Let's take a break. I would like to have you come and see how our home is coming along. It is already to lock up stage; with the Bay windows, all the other windows, too. Front and back doors are in. The siding is going on today. All of this finished in only three weeks. Can you believe it?" Judy continued

"You never know, we may have to give up our home in New York and move to Canada just to keep Mom safe." Sophie added

"Who would've thought that we would have to hide." sighed Rachel

"Marie is improving everyday; we can look at her condition the same way as you would if she had had a brain tumor. She is slowly recovering." Judy stated

"Today, she has said some more words. Her vocabulary is increasing. We won't mind caring for her here; between all of us she isn't a burden." Rosemarie added.

"Maybe you could even slip back into your life without any one really knowing that you have been here. Do you have any friends in California who you trust? Who would say that you had visited?" asked Judy

"We would like to make the trip to Seattle with Mom in your Motor home as it could be a long time before we see her again and it would bring back many memories for all of us. We had many vacations in our own Motor home as children. Mom can come back here with you. We can take the bus back home from Seattle. That would be the safest thing to do. No one would suspect us of taking a bus." Rachel suggested

'Hey, that works for us?" He asked and started to laugh

"Any excuse to go traveling in Belleville." Judy replied

"Marie is comfortable with me; in fact she let me help her dress this morning; so she'll be fine here with us if she didn't return to New York." Rosemarie suggested

"Would anyone ever understand the sneaky way we are behaving to protect a parent. I hate the thought of traveling by bus all that way; but Rachel you're right!" Sophie agreed

Robert and Mike had taken some time off from building the house to buy a Standard 1982 Nissan SUV They had got it for $500.00 including a set of winter tires.

"I can use the hitch on the Motor home to pull the SUV behind us. A standard is easy to do this. Yes, we're going to have a holiday!"

cheered Robert

"Should we leave in a couple of more days? I'd like to see the "Hardy Board" siding finished on the house. The metal roof on before we go. If it starts raining, I would like to see the house watertight. The house needs the exterior finished. The house needs to look like someone is living there. Curtains on the windows will make it safer. In the country, we have to think about security. Neighbors' are miles away' you are our closest neighbor." Robert stated

"I can't believe it! I think we should get married down in Seattle by the Justice of the Peace. I'll have a new last name and then I can change my Driver's License. Kill two birds with one stone. Holiday and wedding at the same time. Isn't that what we promised ourselves months ago?" asked Judy

They all laughed when she went down on one knee and pretended a marriage proposal. "Crazy gal, Yes I'll marry you!" He replied

"We're going to need our legal papers which prove that we are single again. I have them handy; both legal documents that state we can get married." Robert stated

"Hold the phone! You guys! For heaven's sakes, you can't do that now. Harry Hall is a government official who is probably on the look out for Judy." Rosemarie exclaimed

"Reconsider! I will hire an actor to marry you two. So far, you have managed to hide from these creeps. I repeat Harry Hall has connections in government and the fact no is arrested gives a real concern. Do not give him anything to find. You're better off keeping a low profile until he is arrested if ever?" continued Rosemarie

"You must behave as carefully as Rachel and Sophie." Mike agreed

"You're right! Hire your actor friend and we'll do a mock ceremony. It'll be fun to have even a pretend wedding with all of you here as part of it. Judy agreed

"It's a good thing I am so flexible!" laughed Robert

"How will I ever get away from those creeps?" Judy sighed

Later, Rachel phoned Sam again and this time she got through.

"Is there any news about the Care Home Mom was in? Any news at all from the police about the tapes we gave them?" questioned Rachel

"It has been six weeks and nothing? No one has called to see if they're looking for Mom? Doesn't this seem strange to you; why no one had asked about Marie?" asked Rachel

"Can you go over to our place tomorrow and ask Jessie our housekeeper if anyone has been around or any phone calls for us?" asked Sophie when Rachel handed her the phone.

"Of course, there has been no news at all. I find it very strange. They had the tapes that Candy gave them. Your tapes should have been enough to make them understand how real this "9 - 11" threat is. It's very strange!" replied Sam

"We are thinking of coming home by bus. I'd like you to put our home up for sale as soon as possible. I don't think that we will feel safe living in New York anymore; especially with those killers knowing where we live. We're going to have to close our businesses, too. Do you think that you could find a buyer? Please be careful! Be careful! We know it's risky stuff." Rachel stated

"I don't want to go through the Witness Protection Plan as we'll loose all of family and friends. I think that we might buy a Motor home and hide here for a while. However, we need money. Is it possible to cash in our bonds?" Rachel asked

"I think that you could cash in some bonds and investments. However, I think you'd be wise to hold off on the sale of the rest. "Answered Sam

"I realize things are very serious for you; but you must take it slow. You cannot show fear and the less legal stuff you do now is important. These government officials are all connected. Try to take one day at a time and live life simply. I am sorry to hear that you are in that much danger. How is your Mother? Is she getting better?" Sam continued.

"We'll be okay if we can have some of the money. I think if we play it low for a few years that we are able to get on with our lives. It sure is a good thing that we never got married or had kids as that would be a real mess." Rachel answered

"I'll create an overseas account for you and place your money as it comes together into it. That way it will be hard for government people to find you. I'll see about getting new names and identification for you." Sam added.

"Life is a mess. but we do have some good friends here who understand our situation and are trustworthy. Please be very careful. I don't want you into harm's way." Sophie injected.

After they got off the phone with Sam, they realized that they shouldn't go anywhere. Life had changed for them. They had worked so hard building up their businesses now was the time for them to relax and enjoy it all for a while

It would take time for money to come in but that was okay. They had thought prudently and had brought cash, as they knew credit cards could be traced. They had been smart enough to do that.

"We'll, be with you for a few more months. I have enough cash to buy a Motor home, but I can't use our names. Is it possible to buy it in your names?" asked Rachel

"We can't continue to impose on your hospitality. Sam has told me to stay here. He'll spring some of our investments. He has said not to sell the house or our businesses, as these legal transactions would lead these terrorists to us. With our investments cashed out and the money wired to an off shore account, we will at least have access to more money. Sam is working on getting us new identification. Hey, in days we will have different names. What do you think of that?" Rachel asked

"After viewing the CD's that your mother saved for us to see; I think it makes a sense. Especially, when the detectives and police don't seem to care at all what is about to happen to New York.?" stated Mike

"We'll go in to town tomorrow and look for a Motor Home for you. Folk have chosen to live in that life style for many of the same reasons that you have. Under the circumstances, it is probably the smartest thing that you can do. I'll buy the Motor home in my name." Rosemarie stated

"If people keep coming to us here, we will soon be a commune." Mike laughed

"Oh well, I guess we will live without the vacation. Hey, we are already on an extended holiday. Great friends! Good Food! Let's go fishing?" suggested Robert

Mike answered, "Fresh fish for supper!"

"Tonight after supper, we'll look up that "Free-Energy" Generator again. After reading more of Marie's last CD, I think you are on to something. Imagine no energy bills! Self-sufficient!" Rosemarie stated

Mike interrupted, "I have this week's Bargain Paper, and there is a whole section of Motor homes for sale at great prices. We can do some looking tomorrow. I'd prefer to buy a Motor home privately, better price than dealing with the big R.V. Companies."

With Robert and Mike's guidance the girls searched for their new home,

"Imagine doing Canada in the summer and Arizona in the winter. You know what we are. We are "Snowbirds" before we are even thirty." Sophie laughed

"Well at least we will be safe and so will Mom and that is all I care about!" agreed Rachel

Chapter 27

Robert and Mike finished the last of the fireproof Hardy Board siding. It sure didn't look like a garage package but the cutest home.

"We have to go into Edmonton to buy the metal roofing. Why not take the girls so they can check on the Motor home they called last night to view?" asked Robert

They gathered around the barbecue on a warm summer night.

"Would we have to take the Motor home as we don't have enough room in the SUV for all of us?" Judy asked

"I would like to buy a couple of Canoes, then we can all go out on the lake fishing. What do you guys think about that?" asked Mike

"I want to get some tomato plants and other gardening stuff. We have to plant a large garden this summer; if we are going to freeze enough for this winter." Rosemarie added

"Tttomorrow, will be a bussssy day!" Marie stated

Everyone turned and looked at Marie! "Mother, you talked." Sophie exclaimed

"I was expecting that soon, but not this soon!" Judy added

"Well, it's worthwhile!" Rachel shouted to the stars.

Marie looked ten years younger; the sadness disappeared as she danced around the campfire. Beau joined her eager to play. Marie's body had without them realizing it; gained muscle tone and movement as she had walked along the lakeshore every morning with Beau. Yes, she was healing.

Rachel and Sophie laughed with excitement and joined their mother. Soon everyone was doing an old-fashioned square dance. Life was good!

The next day, the cranberry colored metal roofing purchased. They would deliver it the next day. Now the search for the best Motor home deal was on. They decided to check out the R.V. Lots. Research was always a good thing. This way they could wheel and deal with the private sellers.

One o'clock came and it was time to meet their first choice from the Bargain Paper. Robert had been very lucky when he bought Belleville. It should have cost twice what he had paid for it.

Sophie and Rachel knew they had limited funds and they were ready to play good and bad buyer. Maybe, that would get a better price.

"I don't like this flooring; it will have to be replaced. That is going to cost $2,000. The plumbing needs repairs, too." Sophie stated

"I don't care about the flooring. Can you come down on your price?" asked Rachel

With two pretty girls, making the deal it was hard for the Oil Patch worker to stay at his price of $20,000.

He finally gave in and sold it to them for $18,000. In an impulse, he threw in the winter tires. In addition, a three-month guarantee that the mechanical was sound. It was a done deal.

Rosemarie paid the money and signed the Bill of Sale and the Guarantee. Now, it was time to get the Insurance and AMA done. Things went smoothly. By four o'clock, two Motor homes headed home, with garden plants and supplies. Both had a canoe tied on their roofs. They were great shoppers.

Marie burst out laughing! This was the first time her girls had heard her laugh in a long while; last night she was humming and dancing.

Now, she is laughing.

"Now, she's laughing!" Sophie exclaimed

The girls hopped into the girl's Motor home for the journey back home. It must have brought back wonderful summer memories for Marie, when her girls were small and life was fun and more fun.

"Marie will be talking easily by the end of this month." Sophie looked at her mother with encouragement. Marie nodded and stuttered, "YYYYes!"

After supper, they all sat down to continue the CD that Marie had saved from her research days. Marie pointed to a special CD and insisted that they play that one. She was very adamant about it.

BRAIN RESEARCH

"Mom, you can read again!" Sophie blurted out as hugged her Mother.

"This is some of your research!" exclaimed Rachel relieved that her Mom could read.

Present medical research measures Electroencephalographic Energy in the brain. They look only at the surface. The thought, mind, emotions, and physical function of the brain are more complicated than what we have so far understood. This new "Scalar Wave Energy" is able to detect and record more accurately, what is going on in the human brain.

The interior energetics areas involve the spirit, mind, and body connections. This new science helps us explore the hidden depths of man's psyche; we now can understand life, memory, personality, thought, and primary biological control of the human being.

We can finally explore the Forth Dimension involved with spirit and soul. How reincarnation plays in our lives. The aspect of how cause and effect affects our lives. Karma revealed will explain why some people are good and others seem to be inheritable bad. This

science explains the Hitlers of this world.

"Scalar Electromagnetic Energy" even affects the hidden aspects connected with the mind, life, and personality. Our minds consist of stabilized structures. Thoughts are a special class of energy interwoven in these waves in that overall structure network.

The personal unconscious is a single small, localized sample of yet a greater collection that represents deeper unconsciousness. In other words, we are infinitely in connection with the Super Consciousness of the Universe. Our minds are divine, eternal, and even after death, our thoughts endure. That is what the Mediums connect with when they can talk with the dead.

The conscious mind does one thing at a time. Our unconscious mind is very aware. It does a jillions things all at the same time. It is a true multi-tasker.

The conscious mind understands a single idea at a time. The unconscious mind sees many concepts simultaneously. Asleep, the unconscious mind understands life on a super conscious level.

A single body has a quantum potential that connects all the body's atoms and cells. This energy is the "spirit" of this entity. It has a living quantum potential. This spirit of the living being is capable of being everywhere and every when in the universe. A giant hologram exists in space and in time.

Our whole universe is everywhere alive, with everything. All life is eternal. Nothing is ever lost. A thought or thought form is a concrete form in the hidden Electromagnetic channels of the bio potential. Thoughts and thought forms are real.

They exist in virtual reality in space. They occupy one "real" space and time dimension.. Metaphysics and physics share one dimension in time. Skeptics of parapsychology, who believe that humans are robots and the mind is just a meat computer, have no comprehension of basic quantum physics knowledge. This new research with quantum mechanics has destroyed the old materialistic concept.

With this new science, bioenergetics thought forms made to order and placed into one's mind is a reality. Short or long-term memory affected. The conscious mind is like a computer. This new scientific understanding used to create new memories and knowledge in any mind. Another form of this energy known as the Brain Snapper made Marie a test dummy.

This is frightening idea. It affects the electromagnetic mind-body connection. Brain Snapped at a low-level creates unconsciousness. Brain-snapped at a slightly higher power one looses consciousness and is in a hypnotized trance. More snapping and the person become catatonic.

Stuttering she said," I, I, I wworked on this. Tthey didd tthis too mmme Ttteeested mme wwhenn I,I, wwas assleeep."

Marie pushed the play button again and continued with her tape.

"Mom, we know they did something to you with this new energy; but you're healing now and you will recover. You must have felt so alone. Trapped in a body and mind that was not your own. You'll be okay and talking soon. It's wearing off what ever they did to you." Rachel consoled

Marie seemed to understand, shook her head "Yes", and stuttered "III wwant tttoo tttalk III hhave ssso mmmuch tttoo xxplain.

HOMEOPATHY

What is homeopathy? It is the inner energy of a structure when you remove the physical carrier. Homeopathy retains the charge. This in turn affects changes in the treated body just like the real medication. It does it even better. Now you do not have the "physical residue" .It is direct. This new science creates new concepts that are profound and controversial. It challenges the entire Medical Scientific Community

Again, Marie stopped the CD and removed it to put another CD in the computer.

Healing Blanket

A portable version of a Healing Blanket contains wire channels which performs as a "Scalar Wave Antenna" It can send and receive "Scalar Electromagnetic Waves" from the Forth Dimension

A two-minute treatment of the waves is enough to restore the body to its earlier healthy condition. Thousands treated easily and quickly in the aftermath of a bio war attack. These portable machines produced economically and quickly. Then made available all over America and the rest of the world

Quick development of this technology could lead to a suitcase size device, capable of treating a patient in less than one minute, and stopping the symptoms and reversing it. Especially, it is useful in the aftermath of nuclear radiation.

Three "less than a minute" treatments one week apart are required for a complete cure. Added advantage is the reversal of aging in older patients. This is a bonus. The Healing Blanket fits into a large suitcase. It has three basic parts, the longitudinal wave generator, a laptop computer, and the antenna-blanket.

"Can you imagine a blanket that gives such healing power and reverses the aging process? Just think my old knees would feel like new again." Robert exclaimed

Mike added," Rosemarie, I would be chasing you around the house again like in the old days"

Marie stopped the CD and removed it to put another CD in the computer.

Gaia is a Living Organism

Jungian research of the Collective Consciousness is thousands of year's old. The priests of all religions use worldwide thought forms.

It doesn't matter which religion; they all have the same concept.

Thousands of years ago, the Hawaiian spiritual leaders, the Kahunas talked of the Super Conscious, Conscious, and Subconscious states of mind.

This is not new science. This is knowledge that Psychics and Spiritual Leaders knew for eons of time. Priests used picture cards to explain life, death and the life lessons humans have to learn in each lifetime. These picture cards used for thousands of years all over the world and are part of this collective unconscious. This new science talks about ancient spiritual practice. When I read the Tarot, it is not satanic as the Fundamentalists are so keen to preach. These picture cards are part of the Collective Unconscious.

"Aunt Amie says the same thing when she does readings for her clients. It makes so much sense." Rachel added

Marie turned the CD back on and it continued

Jung's collective unconscious consists of "Electromagnetic Waves" acting together in an overall "bio-quantum-potential" for the entire species. Planet Earth, known as Gaia, the living earth exists with a spiritual, emotional, mental, and physical state much like a human. When we blast holes in her with "exothermic" energy, which is an outward force at the target site it doesn't stop there.

The following "endothermic" energy is greater than nuclear level of destructiveness. It affects Gaia on an emotional, spiritual, mental, and physical level. What these scientists don't understand is that the planet is a living entity.

Marie pushed the fast forward button until she came to the area that dealt with disease

Quantum Potential EM Biological Weapons

Distant induction of diseases into a nation's population tested in the United States at low levels. The flesh-eating disease energy tested

here. This disease 'energy pattern' deliberately kept at a low pitch so that only a small part of the populace with depressed thresholds of immunity would respond to it. This test broke out randomly and spread without any precursor's .Done with a total random set of occurrences. A new strain of smallpox without any preventive vaccine launched against the unsuspecting public.

Marie had tears in her eyes and she shakes her head and mutters, "Nnnno! Nnnno!"

Marie started to cry uncontrollably; it is obvious that she knows even more but can't talk yet to warn them.

Rachel soothed, "Mom, it'll take time, but you'll be able to talk soon, sooner than you think."

Sophie interrupted, "I phoned Jessie and Sam today when we were in town. No one has phoned the house to ask about us. There were no messages on the answering machine. Jessie went to her sister's place in Florida, as there was a death in the family; so she hasn't been there for the last five weeks. She had just got back today. There weren't any messages on the answering service. Only bills! Jessie had been worried about them. Sam is being very careful with cashing in our investments. Do the easy ones. He has put some money into an overseas account in your new identity.. But he's getting concerned for his safety too."

"Did you ask Jessie to go away again as she isn't safe there now; either as they may want to question her about us?" asked Rachel

"She said that she was leaving within the hour to go back to her sister's place in Florida. I gave her our cell's number and I got her phone number for Florida." Sophie answered

Bedtime, I don't know how any of us are going to sleep after reading this info. Let's go for a walk down at the lake? Fresh Air and the sound of the waves lapping on the shore always puts me to sleep. Besides, I have to get sheets out of the dryer so you can make up those beds in your new home. Anyone for warm sheets? " asked Rosemarie

Robert was already outside building a campfire.

Mike called, "Toasted marshmallows and hot chocolate? I'm serving

214

up ghost stories."

Marie had stopped her crying and was walking along the lake with Beau.

"It's amazing, but I never realized Mom is a genius. All these years, I thought of her as just a Mom. How hard it must have been for her after Dad died and she had no one to share this info. "Rachel stated as she stared into the fire.

"The beds are made in our new home. It feels so cozy. I can hear the lake's waves lapping on the shore. I had forgotten how great that sounded. I know this place will bring Mom back to her old self." Sophie cheered

"I hope we don't have any nightmares after reading all that stuff tonight it makes me realize how important Marie is. She has to recover so she can get this information out to the public. No one realizes how much technology has advanced. People will have a hard time believing any of this. It sounds like something from Star Trek. Worse, our religious leaders have kept us in the dark while the Russians are using this stuff against us. We have to wake up the American public. How? The media won't let the simplest information be heard like UFO's and crop circles." Judy exploded

"The general public needs to understand what we have read the last seven weeks. I am bursting to tell people about it. However, where would one start! Who would even listen?" asked Mike

"Well I took some solace in what we've read. Our planet is alive and more than I ever thought possible. Maybe the old Druids had knowledge that we don't have. Maybe they understood more than we realize. They built a giant stone observatory or matrix at Stone Henge. It tells eclipses into infinity. The pyramids are there too; that we couldn't have built. We still do not have the technology. Maybe we do now?" Robert stated in awe.

Chapter 28

Rosemarie looked out her bedroom window and chuckled. Mike was right; they did look like the start of a commune. Two Motor homes parked on their land. Maybe people will think we are rich. Oh well, she thought to herself I don't care what they think. I'm enjoying life and each day does seem that much more precious with all the craziness in our world. Time to make breakfast. They have to get over to Robert and Judy's home.

It felt like a home already, even though they were not living there yet. We spend so much time here. I have to get our garden in. I wonder if Marie would like to help with the planting. It is supposed to be therapeutic.

The phone rang. The delivery truck would be arriving at the lot in twenty minutes.

"Mike! They'll be at the lot in twenty minutes." She yelled.

"Rosemarie just got a phone call from the delivery truck they'll be here in twenty minutes. We're going to have to take that bacon and eggs as a toasted sandwich so we can go now!" He added

They'll be gone all day with the roof. She knocked on Marie's Motor home and she asked,

"I'd like to surprise Rosemarie. If we all worked hard this morning helping Rosemarie plant the garden, we can go into town tomorrow. A day in town would be fun. I think she would be surprised if we showed up there in a few minutes." Judy stated

"Marie do you remember planting gardens when you were a child?" Judy asked.

Marie smiled and nodded her head "YYYes" She stuttered

"Mom got dressed by herself today!" Sophie said giving her Mom a hug

"We're ready; let's get going!" Rachel stated as she helped her Mom down the steps.

"I slept better last night than I have in years. Did you sleep sound, Mom?" Sophie asked

"I can't believe how my life has changed. I was so lonely with Robert gone and having to work in that dreadful care home. It felt so weird there. I wanted to tell them off but knew I couldn't" Judy added

Rosemarie opened the door and saw her crew dressed for garden planting.

"We can all have a coffee first and visit before we start. Seven o'clock, we'll be done by noon and have the afternoon to sit by the lake. How does that sound?" asked Rosemarie

"Should we take the guys some lunch?" asked Judy

"I can't wait to see how that roof is going to look with that cedar colored siding. It's fireproof, practical, and beautiful." Judy added

"Next summer we will have to build your cottage for you." Rosemarie added

217

"I'm glad you put those mothballs out in the trees; as I saw a mother bear and her two cubs in the valley. It was funny she sniffed in the air and must have smelled the mothballs as she abruptly turned around and headed away from us." Sophie stated

"That was why Beau was barking so hard a few minutes ago." Rosemarie added

The garden now planted. Mike had salvaged some heating pads from discarded waterbeds. He had made raised beds with these pads under the soil to quicken the garden's growth. Marie had fun planting these raised beds. Occasionally, Rosemarie checked on her work and found that she was doing a great job.

"There's nothing wrong with your thinking, Mom." Rachel said as she gave her a quick hug.

Marie responded with a laugh and stuttered, "Gggood wwoorrrkk!"

"Time for lunch! We're done!" Rachel shouted

"I'd like some beer?" asked Judy

The garden planted just in time as it had started to rain. "Great timing!" cheered Rosemarie

"I bet we don't have to take thm lunch. They can't work on a 12/12 pitch roof in the rain; it just wouldn't be safe." Judy stated

"I'm going to make some Chili as I bet they're starving. Would you folks like some too?" asked Rosemarie

"Sounds good!" Rachel replied

"This is what we need a good card game and some laughs. I have a game that would help Marie with her thinking process. Aggravation! Has anyone ever heard of it?" asked Judy

"We used to play for hours when Dad was alive. Mom said it was great for teaching us patience. You would no sooner think that you're going to have all your marbles in and then your opponent would knock you off the board and you would have to start all over again. It also made you realized how foolish gambling was; as you would be lucky one minute and the next no luck at all." Sophie answered

"Mom, how would you like to play Aggravation?" asked Sophie

Marie burst out laughing and shook her head, "YYes." She stuttered

Robert and Mike walked through the door, "Sure smells yummy in here!" stated Mike

"Smells like Chili to me!" agreed Robert

They noticed the Aggravation Game Board all set up in the dining room and started bragging rights as to who won the last few games. They would have to take turns as it's a four person game. "I am going to help, Mom so only one of us has to wait to play." Sophie stated

"I would really like to get on the computer and check out a system for heating our new home I'd love to heat our home without Hydro. Off the grid sounds wonderful. We talked this morning about how we can do it." Robert stated

"I am going to pass as I'd like to find a way to do this for our home." Mike added

"Well, Sophie you and I will have to take turns helping Mom." Rachel volunteered

"We will get Marie ready to play those guys and then we'll skunk them. They won't see it coming." Rosemarie joked

The smell of homemade bread filled the home and life was good, very good.

Robert and Mike were intent on finding a solution to their heating problems; getting firewood for the stove was getting harder to get. They scanned sight after sight until the came to Tim Bears-Den site. They had been there before for the "Free- Energy" generator and thought it was only for vehicles.

As they read, they found how they could use it to heat their homes and power their SUV's and their Motor homes.

"Imagine being able to go all over the place in your Motor home without costly fuel bills. Hey, we could take off on any holiday without a lot of money; Mexico in the winter." Robert exclaimed

"Wow, this is incredible!" Mike muttered in amazement.

Nikola Tesla's Research

"Electric power is everywhere present in unlimited quantities and can drive the world's machinery without the need of coal, oil, gas, or any other of the common fuels. At any time and at any place, free and inexpensive energy is available. Enormous electromagnetic energy flows directly from the universe's active vacuum." by Tim Bears-Den

New waves discovered, Longitudinal electromagnetic energy fills the vacuum of space, Space combined with Time, Time from the Forth Dimension compressed energy, "E=tc2"

All of this sounded so technical but maybe if they kept reading it would sink in and they would understand it. So they continued. "I wish I could talk with him! I wonder if we could go visit him." Mike suggested

"That's not a bad idea, but maybe we could find his phone number and talk with him. It shouldn't be that hard to figure out if we had him to talk to." Robert answered

"I am going to take a break; my head hurts, too much thinking." Mike stated.

"I need another bowl of Chili and another beer; maybe if we get drunk we will get what he is talking about. Worth a try. It worked when I was in high school trying to learn calculus." Mike laughed.

"I wonder how the girls are making out with their game of Aggravation." Robert joked

After checking with the girls; grabbing beer and Chili they returned to the computer.

The first thing to try to comprehend is that a new energy discovered called Electromagnetic (EM) Longitudinal Waves in the

empty vacuum of space called the Forth Dimension.

When engineered it is an inexhaustible supply of energy in great magnitude at any place on the planet. The discovery by Nikola Tesla of "Radiant Energy" after an electrical thunderstorm was in 1899 more than a hundred years ago. Tesla used a new type of electric wave. His discovery was fundamental. His goal was to give free energy to all humankind.

The elite power brokers, Edison, Marconi and others withdrew their financial backing. Tesla discredited, shunned, penniless and homeless disappeared. He was even removed from the American history books until now. Tesla invented the generator at Niagara Falls that is still producing power for the East Coast until this day. He was a genius and his research amazing.

"Nikola Tesla's statue is at Niagara Falls. I have been there and saw it; but never realized who he really was and how important he would be to all of us." Mike stated

Today, Tim Bears-Den is bringing back his research. Russian research is advanced.. Imagine building houses, buildings, etc. powered by "Free-Energy" no electric or gas bills.

Energy will flow freely from the Forth Dimension indefinitely. There are no moving parts to wear out. This "Free-Energy" Generator" will change the world, as we know it.

Once people in third world countries have this technology they will join the rest of the modern affluent world. Real energy transmitted faster than the speed of light.

One had only to tap the trapped vacuum energy, and make a so-called "Free Energy." The secret was to curve the energy. This produced a continuous loop of energy. In turn, this source in a vacuum would produce continuous energy.

A paddle wheel in a river produces energy. It's not looped! When we tap a current, we do not just tap a potential. Produce a current first in the local vacuum potential; then tap that current. An electromagnetic generator without moving parts includes a permanent magnet and a magnetic core. Also a first and second magnetic paths is needed. The input coils are alternatively pulsed to give induced current pulses in the output coils. Drive electric current through each input coil. This gives a level of flux from the permanent magnet within the magnet path.

"I think I understand some of this maybe; one energy current goes in one direction and the other one beside it goes in the opposite direction?" quizzed Mike

Robert suggested," I need another beer, this is interesting but my brain is hurting; there is a lot to absorb. Still wish we could talk with one of these brains."

"Why don't we search for Nikola Tesla on the Internet and see if he has more research, explanations and inventions?" added Robert

"Man, this is real; but it still doesn't give us a schematic to follow." Mike sighed as he stopped the computer.

The Electric Magnetic Generator or MEG

Strong magnets, coils, and a controller unit with electronics is needed. This is the new science of "Scalar Electromagnetic Energy, the MEG conserves the energy in the Forth Dimension; it does not break the law of conservation of energy.

The machine is deceiving as it looks like a transformer, using Longitudinal EM Waves of the vacuum. A dipole, polarized into negative and positive could be a battery, or the terminals of a generator. or any magnet with its two poles. Wherever there is a dipole there is already immense Scalar EM Energy ushering out of and back into the vacuum.

"I think that I am starting to understand what they are talking about." Mike stated

Tapping that energy and altering it into electricity is possible. Instead of two wire electrical circuits; the MEG does not close that loop. The dipole is not destroyed.

MEG type devices could be put into a car with an electric engine to make a truly fuel-less automobile. Electricity is available in very remote places. People will be able to get off our very terrorist-vulnerable power grids. In an era of terrorism, a highly dispersed power system would prevent terrorists from controlling the population. Decentralized system is safer.

"I just love the concept; but I still can't figure out how it works." Robert sighed again.

"I am going to sleep on it and maybe my subconscious can figure it out as my conscious mind on this much beer can't do it. We got to get hold of some blueprints." Mike laughed

"You remember that guy, Chris at work? Do you have his phone number? I bet he would understand all of this. Doesn't he live in Edmonton?" asked Robert

Chapter 29

"Candy, have you heard from Rachel or Sophie?" asked Aunt Amie

Concerned; no news for over two months, nothing at all.

"Sam said they had got Marie out of that dreadful care home in Calgary; but they didn't feel safe coming back here with their Mom. The people who owned the place had not been arrested nor had the care home been shut down." Candy replied

"I know it seems odd that we haven't got any news back from the detective. I gave them to him two and a half months ago. I should've had a phone call from him, but nothing." Candy continued

"Good thing! I made a copy. Rabbi Samuel said he's going to copy and give them to the people." She added

"Strange! Nothing from that detective! He has your tape and Rachel's Boardroom's tapes! That should've been enough to get them working." Aunt Amie questioned

"At Rabbi's meeting, we'll have to ask what they think of this detective. They will have some ideas. Why has nothing happened to these people? Why haven't they been arrested?" stated Candy

'Sam's suggested; we leave New York. Get married some other time. I think we are not safe here, either. What if they know; we gave those tapes to the detective? We're in trouble." She sighed

The doorbell rang and they both jumped.

"Were you expecting anyone this morning?" asked Candy

She peered out the bedroom window. At the door, were two men dressed all in black and in the street, a black sedan?

"Do you know who they are?" Candy asked shaken. A bad premonition came over her.

"No, I don't know them. I'm not answering the door." Aunt Amie stated, trying to stay calm.

"I think it's time you and I left New York. I just had a horrible premonition. I'm going to grab a few things. Grab your stuff; and hurry, we're out of here." Aunt Amie continued

"They're leaving! We're going over to Martha's. She lives four doors down. We are going to take the back door and go down the alley. From there, we'll think of what to do next." She added

"Thank goodness she's home." Candy stated

Martha looked surprised at them coming to her back door. "What's wrong, Aunt Amie?" Martha asked

"We've got to get away. We are in trouble. Two men at my door a few minutes ago came to question us about Marie. I can't lie! I'm out of here. I'll come back when things are normal." Aunt Amie stated

"Don't worry; I'll look after your place. Don't tell me anything. They may try to questions me, too." Martha offered

"Life has become difficult these days. Reminds me of the old days in Poland." Martha added

Martha had survived the Holocaust and had some idea how serious their situation was.

"Would you like tea and biscuits? Stay here till it's dark. Give yourself some time to think. I'll call someone from the Synagogue to pick you up." Martha suggested

"Good idea! They could take us to Rabbi Samuel's home. We'd get to the meeting tonight. Iit might be the last one we get to for a while." Aunt Amie replied

"Sam and Candy were planning their wedding for June 30th at my home. We have worked hard to make it a nice event. Now, all that effort was for nothing." Aunt Amie sighed

"We'll have a nice wedding, just not now." Candy added as she quickly hugged her aunt.

They sat down to eat her homemade biscuits with fresh strawberry jam. Martha loved to preserve jam. She loved filling her home with delicious smells.

Martha's curiosity got the better of her. She urged Candy to tell what was going on. Although, she was at Rabbi Samuel's home and had heard the tapes, she wanted to know more. Had Marie got out of that horrible home? Why hadn't the detectives called them, immediately?

Martha stated, "This reminds me of Poland. The Gestapo!" She shook her head.

Martha offered, "Rest! Take time to think. Anything else you might need. I will get it for you. You left in a hurry. You've forgotten stuff. Make a list. I'll use shopping bags. Would you use my suitcases?"

"Thanks! Good idea! We left in a hurry. I will make a list. We are going to be gone until after the attack. It should be safe to come back then. It doesn't look like the government is going to protect the Twin Towers." Aunt Amie sighed

"Don't worry! You've done all you could. It'll be neighbor telling neighbor just like in Poland." Martha stated.

Candy thought to herself what a brave, wise, old woman. She is in her eighties, but you'd never know it.

"I'm calling Sam as he should know what's going on. Is that okay?" Candy asked

"Sure, tell him to come to the back door. That's best; the less people knowing what is going on the better." Martha replied

"I should've realized sooner that we'd be at risk; I guess I wanted things normal. I had always wanted to be part of a wedding. It would have been wonderful. I just got a horrible feeling when I saw those men. I knew they were not people I could trust. Was it gut instinct or psychic ability? " Aunt Amie stated with such seriousness that Martha went over and gave her a hug.

"We've been friends for over forty years and you've never been wrong on your hunches. Don't worry, you're doing the right thing now. Evasive action is the only answer." Martha consoled

"I worry about Sam helping the Rothman's with their money. He's cashed in some of their stocks. Put their money in over sea's accounts so they've something to live on. If he's caught doing it; he'd go to jail." Candy sighed

"How are the Rothmans? I remember our wonderful picnics. So much fun! Life was so much fun back then." Martha responded

"I can't tell you where they are; but they're in a safe place with their mother thanks to the Coordinator from that care home. She risked her life to help them. When she found out what was going on, she taped their conversations. She sent the tapes to Rachel." Candy continued

"When they went to pick up Marie, she found out where they were staying and went to the hotel to rescue them. They've been with her in Alberta." Candy added

"Is she Psychic, too? That sounds like something I would have done?" She asked

"I used to help my clients, when they were in serious trouble. Make sure they were safe. I'd like to meet her and love to see Marie again. I've worried about her as I could feel that she was in trouble." Aunt Amie continued

"I forgot to tell you how she whisked them out of Calgary. With all the wedding stuff, it slipped my mind." Candy apologized

"Are the Rothmans living in Alberta with her and no one knows where they are except for Sam?" She asked

"Sam won't tell me as he knows I can't lie and he doesn't want to risk any of us." Candy replied

"Poor Sam, that's brave. We should take the summer off! God knows we've worked hard enough to earn a summer off." Aunt Amie exclaimed

"I'm going to try again to reach him." Candy stated

"I need to get to the bank. Get some cash. No credit cards! Martha, do you still drive? Can you take us to the bank?" She asked

"I still drive; but not on the freeway. I'll take you to your bank." Martha replied

"Our bank's across the street from where Sam works. Maybe he's thinking we need to get out of here, too." Candy exclaimed

"It'd be wonderful. A summer off! We've done all we could do here." She continued

In minutes, they were downtown. Candy met Sam just as he was returning from a meeting

"Come, I've got to tell you what's going on." Candy ordered

Sam knew something was wrong. Her voice was shaky.

"What has you so upset, my girl?" asked Sam

Candy explained Aunt Amie's Psychic reaction to the black clothed men at the door. Two and a half months later, they show up. Why had it taken them so long? Was her concern real?

"We need cash, clothes, and a car. Let's go on holiday for a couple of months. Take time off. I feel it's urgent." Candy whispered

"Good, I've been thinking the same thing. Come back when the terrorists are caught. I've already cashed in my bonds weeks ago. I knew I would need cash. Government and terrorists are a dangerous mix. We've got to be clever." Sam added

"If only, I hadn't bothered to give those tapes to that detective. I should've known it would backfire on me. Even in high school, whenever I did the right thing it would always bite me back. We wouldn't be in such a mess, if I wasn't so naïve." Candy complained

"There's no way, you could've possibly known these people are connected. Don't blame yourself. We've got to leave, now." Sam stated

I foresaw this coming. My stuff is packed. No worries! We'll be okay. I've thought this out." Sam stated confidently.

Between Aunt Amie's premonition and Sam's preparation, they left Manhattan without problems. Sam's friend, a court Judge would protect them. His license plate was above suspicion. No one would bother them. In Vermont, Sam bought an old Corolla. The Aurora Borealis shone on the highway as they sped north through the night.

They crossed the Canadian Border. They covered many miles, changing drivers every few hours. Soon a sense of adventure replaced fear. The sky was so beautiful to them.

Living in Manhattan, they had forgotten there were stars in the sky, as they were not visible there. Even more exciting was the wonderful colors of the night sky. They had never seen the Aurora Borealis before; they didn't even know this beauty existed.

Twenty-four hours later, they checked into an Ontario Bed and Breakfast. They were exhausted.

"Traveling with you; makes us look respectable and they all like getting cash." Candy added

"It's great being old." Aunt Amie laughed

"Guess, what I'd like to do?" asked Sam

They looked at him and at the same time asked, "What?"

Relieved, they were now safe in Northern Ontario. They could take their time and enjoy life. They were officially on holiday. Life seemed normal again. They all laughed.

Aurora Substorm

"Laughter for sure is the best medicine." Aunt Amie gasped

"I would like to drive across Canada to Jasper, Alberta. A few days' drive takes us to the Rothman family. They've just bought a Motor home. They're staying there for who knows how long. They are happy. Marie is healing quickly. Would you like to surprise them?" He asked

"Sounds great!" again both of them say it in unison.

"Psychics or twins?" Sam laughed.

Chapter 30

Robert and Mike were on the roof early the next morning. Up there was a serene view of the lake and the fishing boats. "Let's get this done fast?" Mike shouted

"I can't wait to get out there. I don't care if I catch anything; it's the peaceful feeling." Mike stated

"I did research a few months ago. So relaxing. When I took the Hypnosis, Course, "Quit Smoking" I learned we go into an alpha state when we are on the lake. Alpha state is the closest to sleep and connects with our unconscious mind. Reading Marie's research, I'm remembering some of that course. It's starting to make more sense." Robert stated

"Well, genius figure out "Free-Energy" stuff!" barked Mike

"My head hurts from trying to figure it out!" He continued

"I'm stopping for a bit. Need coffee. My sciatic nerve is hurting, again." Robert yelled as the pain shot down his leg.

"We've just about finished this side of the roof. We're nearly done, but we could come back this evening. I know what Sciatic Nerve is like." Mike offered

"We'll stop for a bit; maybe that'll help." He answered

"We're not in a hurry; we don't go back to work until the end of October. Easy does it! You used to say that at work all the time!" Mike added

"I'm eager to have the home-built and Judy and I living in it. I know how excited she will be the day we move in. I can't wait to see the look on her face when I carry her over the threshold. She doesn't know, but I've found a Justice of the Peace that'll come and marry us here. By then, the attack will be over and maybe we can go back to a normal life." Robert stated

"You haven't told her about this yet?" asked Mike

"Nope, I want to surprise her! I had Rosemarie ask her what kind of dress and the music she wants. This is going to be a surprise." Robert laughed

"You're one tricky devil. I've never heard of this." Mike exclaimed

"She likes surprises. I love her as she's easy-going and fun." continued Robert.

"I'll keep it a secret. We'll get the home done for October." Mike agreed

"Let's do some stretching; that would loosen your leg muscles?" asked Mike.

"A great idea; every hour we'll stretch. We'll get this roof done." He replied.

"Remember our boss had us do stretches every hour or so. It helped us get through those fourteen-hour days. God it was brutal." Mike reminded him

"Wish we could figure out that damn "Free-Energy" generator. We could make and sell them. Imagine, how many people would want one?

I'm going to get hold of Chris. Would it be okay to invite him out here for a weekend? Would be safe? I don't want to put Judy and the girls at risk?" asked Robert

"He's one of the guys who hated the Oil and Gas companies. He was forever saying that this crap is obsolete. I wouldn't be a bit surprised if he doesn't already have a generator." Mike replied

"It's safe for him to come. I can take the back seat out of my SUV and convert the space for a bed." Robert suggested

"Let's come back tonight and do this other side after supper?" Robert asked. His sciatic nerve had continued to throb. The pain was getting worse.

"I'm curious about some of the other stuff we found when we were looking at Tim Bears-Den's generator. There's more information?" asked Mike

"May I soak in your tub? Epsom salts has always helped to ease this damn sciatic nerve. I've even used a jalapeno pepper placed there and it's stopped the pain. Deadened the nerve. Got any of those peppers in the fridge?" asked Robert

"We'll go to Edson and get some. It's only forty minutes away. You soak! The girls will jump at the chance to go to town. Hey, maybe they can look at some wedding dresses?" Mike suggested

Back at the house, Rosemarie and Judy were getting ready to do another weekend in one of the local malls.

"I've placed ads in their local newspapers; Do you suppose we'll get any tourists from Jasper coming out to see us at the Mall?" Judy asked

"I'd like to ask Sophie or Rachel to act as our receptionist. It'd make it easier for us to concentrate on doing our readings." suggested Rachel

"I wonder which one of them would like to help us? Maybe they should dye their hair and wear glasses; in case someone recognizes them." She continued

"We look different when we're working. No one would recognize you. Your hair in a bun, old-fashioned hat's veil covering your face, and glasses down on your nose changes how you look." Rosemarie continued

"It's uncomfortable, but it adds to their reading. I'll continue to do it." Judy answered

"I like my hat and high top old-fashioned dress. You're right; it's uncomfortable. It hides my double chin and makes me look younger. I've gotten used to wearing it." Rosemarie added

"Let's ask the girls if they'd like to take part in our weekends?" asked Judy

After lunch, the Rothman family had a nap as it seemed to help Marie.

"I wonder what ever happened to Ruth?" asked Rosemarie

"I've been too concerned about our safety to do any prying; but I can't help but wonder what happened to Ruth." Judy answered

"You could phone her nephew, Pastor David Smith in Calgary. He might know what has happened?" Rosemarie suggested

"Next week when we are in Edmonton, I'll give a call. Can I really trust him? Remember the trouble; I had as a child with that religion? I don't feel safe with him. I don't know if I can trust him?" Judy replied

"Besides, I felt that the church was after Ruth's money too." Rosemarie agreed.

"Why can't people trust that their needs will be supplied? I wonder about religious leaders. When they don't walk their talk? On Sunday, they preach God will take care of your needs and on Monday, they're as grasping as any drug addict. Why don't they trust God will take care of them?" Judy asked

"I had to let go of my worry for Ruth. There was nothing more that I could do. The authorities weren't listening. The detective hasn't investigated the place. Brenda's Care Home isn't closed. We haven't heard anything in the news. A waste of time; no luck! I am not family. They can't release any information." Judy added with a big sigh.

Rosemarie agreed, "What a shame! We can't trust the authorities to do the right thing."

"Just talking about it wears me out! I'm going to have a rest. Wake me in an hour and a half, okay?" Judy asked

Rosemarie finished clearing up the kitchen and began tonight's supper. Most nights everyone ate at their place. They had the barbecue. Besides, it was fun. Their life stories shared at supper, no one would have missed. No rush to go to work. Gardening and house building took some time. It was a holiday for them all. Marie was improving daily. She could now say a sentence and more. Her thinking was clearer. She understood their conversations and heartily laughed. I would love this to continue. Rosemarie thought.

"Rosemarie, can you take Judy into town? Robert needs A535 and a Jalapeno pepper for his sciatic nerve. Doing that roof with a 12/12 pitch isn't easy. I need some A535, too. He is going to take a hot soak in Epsom salts. His sciatic nerve is causing him a lot of pain." Mike added

"I was going into town anyway; I need to get hair dye for myself and the girls. They need to change their appearances; especially, Marie." stated Rosemarie

Two o'clock in the afternoon, the girls had come up to the house. They woke up when Beau barked at the guys, when the SUV climbed the hill.

"Anyone for some fresh home-grown carrot juice?" asked Mike as he did his magic with the juicer. No one turned him down.

"Nectar of the Gods! He said, as that was the only term to describe this treat of baby carrots freshly pulled from the garden.

Sophie and Rachel had wanted to change their looks. They had always worn a lot of makeup. Going natural changed their appearance. A different hair color and glasses would complete their look of "country chick." New York clothes discarded. They now wore Jeans, T-Shirt, and cowboy boots.

"You'll need an old-fashioned dress; and glasses from 1900 to work with us in the Mall. An old-fashioned hat, too. I have a friend who does clothing, make up and hair for movie sets. She can find us your costume.

235

Only, two months ago, she dressed Judy and me for our stage look." Rosemarie explained as she pulled out her dress.

Sophie with delight responded, "It's like Halloween; only, every weekend and make money. I've always played dress up; that's why I went into the fashion industry."

"First, we'll buy your new clothes, glasses, and hair dye." Judy suggested

"How can we make Marie look different?" asked Sophie

"We'll get her some Huderite clothes. They have one of their communities not far from here. An antiquated bonnet on her head and round glasses; no one will recognize her as the scientist, Marie Rothman." chuckled Rosemarie.

"That is hilarious!" Mike said through his laughter.

"The neighbors might start thinking our community is Huderite. What a disguise. No one will ever realize who we are!" laughed Rosemarie

"Mike take care of Marie while the girls, Judy and I go to town?" she added

"We'll not be long. The girls know their sizes. It won't take long. I'll get our stuff and home again." She continued

"I've been wearing your worn out jeans and this old shirt, since I got here. I already look like a country hick. Can I borrow these rubber boots to go into town?" asked Sophie laughing at how she looked in the mirror.

"We threw out our New York clothes as soon as we got here. I've been wearing these worn out jeans and shirt since I got here." Rachel added.

Rosemarie found rubber boots for her to wear. No makeup on! Old straw farm hats and sunglasses finished their new look.

"I think I need some Huderite clothes too. That way, Marie and I will look the same. No one would be suspicious. I will need to go to the second-hand store for our costumes. Buy a few extra dresses for the rest of us. It wouldn't hurt for people around here to think that we're Huderites." Judy added.

They all broke into laughter

Chapter 31

Robert and Mike turned on the Computer to do some more research. Marie joined them. "What were we talking about on the roof this morning? I know it was important but now it has slipped my mind?" asked Mike.

"Chris told us that he thought every time they opened a new gas plant that somewhere in the world an earthquake happened. He thought the way they were opening these gas deposits buried deep in the earth was with this new Scalar Longitudinal Energy.

These gas deposits had been inaccessible to them with diamond drilling and blasting; but now they easily opened them up. The problem is that the energy used is stronger than a nuclear explosion. It doesn't stop with just opening the gas deposit but continues into the Planet. This rebounding energy hits somewhere else on the planet and has caused huge earthquakes, Tsunami, dormant volcanoes to erupt and more." Robert stated

"The other guys laughed at him; but I had the feeling that he was right. I started to take notes and researched when these new gas plants opened and there was a correlation. Within days of a new gas plant opening, I would hear of an earthquake, tsunami, or volcano happening across the earth." Robert continued

"Let's see if Tim Bears-Den has any information about this?" suggested Mike.

"By the way, have you been able to reach Chris yet?" asked Robert

"I'm going to go by his home the next time we're in Edmonton. I worry about him and I don't know why? Maybe all this cloak and dagger stuff with the Rothman family and Judy I am getting paranoid, too." Robert stated

Marie picked up one of her CD's and put it into the drive.

How to Make an Earthquake

To create an earthquake is simple with the new Scalar Electromagnetic Energy. It is easy to create a very large earthquake with these weapons. It is the method of using exothermic energy and endothermic energy. Find a fault line and apply this energy into it. Use the diverging energy and deposit the electromagnetic energy there in the rocks on both sides, increasing gradually the stress in the land until it gathers so much energy that it reacts.

Gradually, apply the stress until it builds up to a large pressure; well-above a plate slip minimum energy required. At some point, the rocks yield and one or both sides "Slip" and move rather sharply, giving a very large earthquake in that area.

When you want access to a gas deposit, it is easy to do just apply Scalar Longitudinal Wave energy into the earth. This laser energy will easily penetrate right through the earth to the gas deposit.

Create a volcanic eruption by focusing this Longitudinal Scalar Energy into the active part of the volcano that is still slumbering. Focus this energy into this area. Keep increasing the energy into the magma itself, and eventually the increasing pressure from deep within that volcano, underground, will cause an eruption. Build the energy slow, and the eruption will likely be much larger.

Mike looked at Robert and exclaimed, "My god, not only can these scientists use this energy to open gas plants but also to destroy countries at their will. I wonder when they will strike again. It makes the idea of a nuclear bomb look like child's play compared to this science."

The article included an example of the Yugoslav Earthquake in 1997 followed by a cold explosion. Only a few people understood what had really happened when they watched the television broadcast. "I remember hearing about that but I had no idea that this was created by this science. People just do not realize what is happening on our planet." Robert added

"What do they mean a cold explosion?" asked Mike

Robert replied," Sounds like weather control to me. A few years ago, I read a book on the climate. The book, "Weather Wars Now" chilled your bones just reading it. Now added to this information I realize that it wasn't fiction at all but reality. I wonder if other people are realizing this now.

Eco-terrorism Using Scalar Electromagnetic Weapons

Terrorists or other countries now engaged in an "Eco-War." Weather wars whereby they can alter the climate set off earthquakes, volcanoes remotely with these electromagnetic waves.

H.A.A.R.P

Is this H.A.A.R.P., "High-frequency Active Auroral Research Program" in Alaska, on George Park Hwy near the Village of Tok? Is it an "Ionosphere Heater" that sends this new Scalar Energy into the ionosphere and bounce this energy back to anywhere on the planet? There are also 17 H.A.A.R.P. installations China, Russia, Canada, Britain, Norway, and more all have this science. Ionospheric Heater

Ionospheric Heater

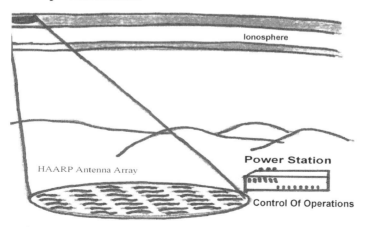

Ionospheric Heater may be used to control weather

241

They can create an Ionosphere Heater that sends this new Scalar Longitudinal Energy into the Ionosphere and bounce this energy back to anywhere on the planet.

Could it provide enough energy to open gas deposits easily? What if this energy does not dissipate but bounces somewhere else on the planet causing huge damage greater than an Atomic Bomb?

Tesla built his Wardencliff Transmitter, over eighteen stories high on Long Island, New York in 1907. Tesla may have used this science to create the Tunguska Explosion in his attempt to convince the government of this science's power. He wanted to protect people from the Airplane in World War Two. He believed that this energy could put a shield over the allied countries that would prevent airplanes from bombing these cities. Can you imagine how much farther this science has gone in the last 100 years?

Can you imagine the abilities of the H.A.A.R.P. for the healing of our earth or for destruction of our planet? Imagine the good for humankind when this energy heals our planet and the people from Nuclear Radiation, from diseases, from the crippling affects of aging, and from birth defects. It can also supply all of our energy needs. It is a matter of time when this science will be used to create abundance .for all of the people on our planet.

Do you suppose other people in other countries are waking up to this knowledge? Maybe they understand what we are fighting. How can we connect all of us so we can fight on the Internet to bring this new powerful science to be used for the healing our planet?

Imagine what could be done to help starving nations if we could change their weather and instead of drought they could have the water they need to grow their crops and more. I am excited when I think of the possibilities of this science. In the right hands there would be no more third world countries.

Nikola Tesla's Wardencliff Tower on Long Island 1908

Eighteen Stories High

Was it powerful enough to create the Tunguska Explosion in June 30th, 1908 from Long Island? .Could Tesla's technology at that time have harnessed the sun's energy and delivered a blast equivalent to 10 -15 megatons of TNT which flattened 500,000 acres of pine forest in Russia? That probably was the event that so intrigued the Russians that they started studying his research. If he had created this explosion, it was not out of wishing to do harm but to prove to the governments that his research was real.

Can you imagine how much progress has occurred since 1908 in this scientific research? The H.A.A.R.P. program has developed ability that is far more advanced. A thousand fold in power!

Terrorists who have this technology can wreak terror upon other nations. Soon they will attack Canada with extremely cold winters; attack Australia with flooding and summer fires; the States with tornadoes, hurricanes and extreme heat so fires burn out of control.

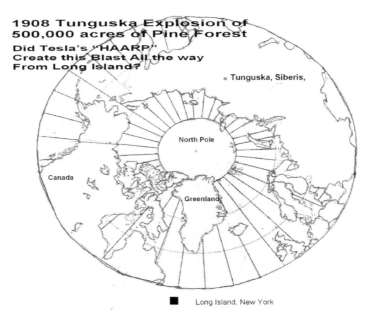

1908 Tunguska Explosion of
500,000 acres of Pine Forest

Did Tesla's "HAARP"
Create this Blast All the way
From Long Island?

Tunguska, Siberis,

North Pole

Canada

Greenland

■ Long Island, New York

California and Western Canada have large areas destroyed by fire. Australia could be a practice range. Could there be a correlation of the opening of gas deposits and earthquakes or Tsunami's? Only time will tell us the answers. The ability is certainly there with the H.A.A.R.P. program.

Robert and Mike were stunned. Both men sat in silence.

Mike broke the silence. "I'm going for a walk would you like to come, Marie?" asked Mike

Robert suggested, "Let's go for a boat ride maybe the alpha zone of the lake can calm us down?"

Marie had known about this for some time. She had already tried to make sense of it. She realized that this technology was there as she had worked with some of it. For her refined and healing nature, it was difficult to think that people would use this wonderful science for such evil.

244

She longed to tell them what she had discovered in her search to prevent these horrible things from happening. However, without the ability to talk how was she ever going to do it They paddled around the lake with the afternoon sun shining on them. It seemed surreal that life could be this calm and peaceful one moment and so frightening the next.

"Mike, do you remember Chris used to tell us stuff like this, but we just laughed at him. It seemed like what he was telling us was out of Star Trek; that he was making it up but now I know that it was very real. I feel so bad that I didn't take him more serious." Robert sighed

It was close to five o'clock by the time they paddled back to the dock. The SUV pulled into the driveway and the girls hopped out of the car. What a change! Two cowgirls with cowboy hats and boots jumped out of the SUV. They couldn't hide the fact that they were pretty; but they didn't look like New York socialites anymore.

"Marie, I've some new clothes for you, too. I'm going to look like you so people will think we're sisters." stated Judy smiling at the thought of people thinking they were Huderites

"Mike, don't say anything to the girls about what we found today on Marie's last CD. At least not until we figure out some of it ourselves first. Okay" Robert asked

"Tonight, we're going back to the house and do some more roofing. That will give us time to come to terms with it. We should read a bit more of that CD. Maybe other people understand this stuff. Maybe they have a better handle on it." Mike stated

"We live in interesting times! Never thought I'd say it but I'm glad to do some roofing." Robert sighed

"Let's eat; a full tummy puts a better slant on things no matter how bad it seems." added Mike

"I can't get over the fact that our government doesn't tell us a thing. It's like we're in an "Alice in Wonderland" fairy tale everything is surreal." Robert continued

"What can ordinary citizen do?" Mike sighed

245

"We have to put on a happy face for the girls. And now old man!" Robert added with determination.

Beau chased a squirrel across the lawn and up a tree. "See he has the right attitude; we have to become like that squirrel and get up the tree!" Mike stated

A summer shower started and they ran inside; it came down fast and from nowhere. There wasn't a cloud in sight.

"I'll never take the weather for granted again!" Mike stated

"Supper time, Chinese food come, and get It." called Rosemarie

"I picked it up before we came home as I knew you two would go back to work and needed something light to eat. Don't worry when you come back I'll have something more for you. I know how you guys can eat." Rosemarie chuckled

They all had a wonderful afternoon in town!

"We'll be back about nine tonight as soon as it gets dusk. We can't see good enough to do any more work." Mike stated

"We'll do a fashion show for you. We've picked up a clothes today and want your opinion?" asked Rosemarie

Marie was already in her Huderite clothes and she thought it was funny. She twirled around and laughed.

"You're sure different from the first day I saw you, Marie," Judy said as she hugged her.

Judy continued, "In town, I phoned Pastor David Smith and asked him about Ruth. She died in the hospital with pneumonia.. Brenda's Care Home is still going strong. They have so much business that they can't keep up. Pastor Smith gives a Sunday service each week. My hunch was right; he is part of them now. Money and more money.

He was quick to tell me that Walter Brown and Harry Hall are members of the Oil and Gas Club in Calgary. It is the same place, where Candy used to work. They are on the Board of Directors. I now see why they met there; they are part of this terrorist group. No wonder they

246

haven't been arrested. No doubt, they're the terrorists who are going to bomb the Twin Towers. These people are going to have Americans believe that an Eastern Nation is responsible."

Mike exclaimed, "I think there's a "HARRP" installation at a Gas Plant that I worked on at Crow Lake. I remember seeing 150 electric poles all in a field. Tim Bears-Den stated on his Website that H.A.A.R.P. in Alaska has 360 Antenna. Imagine the power Eight Hundred Billion Watts of Micro Energy can deliver.

Kruschev was right in 1960, when he stated that these huge generators are Weapons of Mass Destruction. However, one can't help but wonder the power full good they could do placed in the right hands of people who want to heal our planet. The right people could make all the difference to our world. Also, used for the survival of humankind. The one I saw had 150 Antenna, but even that could do a lot of damage in the wrong hands. Robert added

"I have found a photo of a small H.A.A.R.P. on this site. It looks a lot like the one that I saw at Crow Lake Gas Plant in Northern Canada." Mike exclaimed

"This is one is smaller than the one that I saw at that Gas Plant but imagine what it could do?" Mike continued

H.A.A.R.P. Generator

No one could answer me when I asked what this was. The day that I arrived at the camp, they had just finished opening a gas deposit and they were talking about how strange it was that more than a hundred geese had fallen out of the sky. They couldn't figure why that had happened."

"That is very odd but I have heard that this is happening all over the world." shared Judy

"I know I've worked in that industry for many years and I've never met one of the big wigs who were honest and fair with their employees. My god! Its a billion dollar company and they work us like dogs. It is nothing to do five weeks at fourteen hours a day. Men so burnt out at the end of the period that we can hardly make it home. I have felt sorry for the Newfoundlanders as they have a long trip home." continued Mike

"What I didn't like was their pretense of safety; but when it came down to using safety; it was a big joke. We are so tired after fourteen-hour shifts; that we would have slept through their fire alarms never waking up. They had fire bunk wardens to wake us up; but that was a real laugh. One fire bunk warden was responsible for two or more bunks. There is no way they would even have made it to the bunk to wake any of us. It takes seven minutes for the bunk to burn to the ground. It takes seven minutes to get to the bunk. Sleeping in another bunk, they wouldn't hear the fire alarm in our bunk. It was a joke." He continued

"That's why we relied on each other so much at camp. We would take turns staying awake. Some fool started a fire. Smoking not allowed, but no one pays any attention to the rule. Instead, they take the batteries out of the fire alarms and smoke any way. The trouble is most of us are so exhausted; that we sleep like the dead. I trusted Mike to sleep lightly one night and then the next night I would rest while he slept." Robert exclaimed.

"I'd love to stay here and not have to go back to that nightmare; I'd love to have our own business even if it means cleaning toilets. I'd love to be out of that pressure cooker." Mike added

"Besides I hate supporting an industry that is only destroying our world. I do not want any part of it. Especially, now that I know that there is another way to get energy. Fossil fuels are outdated. There is no need to continue to destroy our planet." Robert exclaimed

"I never knew how much you disliked your stay there. I would have found another way for us to survive. I just had no idea you felt like this." Rosemarie stated as she went over and hugged Mike

"Let's concentrate on this 'free-energy" generator that you talk about. We'll spend the money to track down Tim Bears-Den." Rosemarie continued

Marie got a pen and paper and wrote, "I know him he is a friend of mine."

Rachel and Sophie instantly realized whom they were talking about and got out their address book and there it was; Tim Bears-Den's phone numbers for his home and his office.

"I have heard that this is a small world; but this is uncanny. The very man who would help us make sense of this stuff is a close friend of your family. Synchronicity or what? Unbelievable?" exclaimed Mike

"Spirit moves in incredible ways." Judy sighed giving Marie a hug.

Just then, the phone rang and it was Sam. They'd be arriving tomorrow. They are staying at a Bed and Breakfast in Banff. Aunt Amie and Candy were with him.

Chapter 32

This was an exciting day. Rachel and Sophie excited Sam, Candy and Aunt Amie arrives today. Thank God, they had bought the Motor home when they did. Marie hadn't seen Aunt Amie for many years as they had both been busy with their careers Judy and Rosemarie were eager to meet another Psychic.

"I am happy they are coming. I've enough room for them to stay with us." Rosemarie offered

"Robert and I have three hours work left on the roof to do and we'll be back to help make dinner. When did they say they're arriving?" Mike asked

"About four! They want to see Jasper this morning, so beautiful there. They are taken with the beauty of Banff and Alberta. A wonderful trip for them." Sophie replied

'I know how amazed I was at the beauty. It was surreal. I'm sure they'll be in awe; like I was." Judy agreed

"Life is very good here; especially around here." Mike seconded

"We'll be back by three; plenty of time for me to get the barbecue going and to help with supper." He added

"By the way, there's a message on the answering service for Mike. Chris called and he will be coming tonight. He's coming too." Rosemarie yelled

"Sure glad he's okay." Mike yelled back

"It will be easier today as the sun won't shine in our eyes as we finish. The job might even go quicker than we thought. Isn't that something! Wishing for help on making "free-energy" generators and now Chris is coming out to visit. Tim Bears-Den is a friend of the Rothman family. We'll talk with him soon." Robert suggested

"I wonder what this Sam is like. He is a stockbroker from Wall Street. Things must be scary for him to take a summer off. They love to work; like a drug for them. Wheeling and dealing! However, he is different; risked his life to help the Rothmans. I hope he likes it here. So quiet here!" Mike stated

"You never know he might want to help me with our home here. It'll get done quicker than you think." Robert added

"Maybe he's never liked his job; but didn't know what else to do. There are many like that you know. They take the first job out of college and stick with it for their whole lives without question. Sure glad that I did different things." He continued

"Reading Marie's CD's are scary. I have calmed down. I want to read some more; I can't tell whether I like scaring myself or if I am nuts. What do you think? Do you wan to read more?" asked Robert

"I know what you mean. It is intriguing, but bloody scary. Like watching a horror show; too frightened to leave and too afraid to stop watching. Like a rabbit frozen by the fox, hunting him. That's what I think." Mike answered

"Our ancestors faced natives and highwaymen; we survived and we'll find a way. I have never been a coward and I am not going to start

251

now. I'm going to do some more reading." Robert stated determined to face his fears.

"Last piece of roofing! This should not take long. The roof finished and it's only eleven o'clock. It pays to get an early start." Mike added

On the way home in the Nissan, the radio was turned to CDC. The announcer reported that there were huge deposits of Oil and Gas in Northern British Columbia especially; around Georgia. They were going talking about had been there. The economy would turn around and everybody would have work as soon as the Oil and Gas Corporations could open the gas deposits there.

Robert looked at Mike and they both thought the same; why are they going on about these deposits and how valuable they are?

"I guess they're preparing the locals for the coming earthquakes. This was the result of using H.A.A.R.P. to blast their way into the ground at Georgia, British Columbia." Robert stated

"They've used diamond drilling, but no success as the rock shield is too thick. They're going to use scalar electromagnetic energy." Mike agreed

"Georgia is on the Ring of Fire, the plates are already shaky enough. The west coast would be in danger if they start blasting Scalar Electromagnet Energy into that area. Not safe! The whole coastline could disappear. Hell, the earthquake activity in the Ring of Fire is already ten times more active than seven years ago. The seismic engineers already are nervous enough. Do these greedy bastards ever stop?" Robert exploded

"We've got to get through to Tim Bears-Den. He has to know about this. Is there someway to stop these Gas Companies? Genocide of a whole area. Worse than an atomic bomb." stuttered Mike

"Finished already? Want some lunch?" asked Rachel as they came through the door.

"Nope, got to use the phone!" answered Mike without explaining anything

"Do you have time to mow the lawn?" She asked

"I have to get hold of Tim Bears-Den; it's important. I'll explain what's going on as soon as I talk to him." Mike replied

"How are we ever going to explain to the girls what's happening. Rosemarie and Judy can handle this. However, the Rothman girls are young and spoiled by life; how'll they cope with what's coming." Mike sighed

"I'm glad I'm in the country. Tomorrow, I will stock up on dried food enough for at least three years. We need to store barley, beans, peas, soya beans, and rice! I don't trust our government anymore. The CDC promoting this new technology; without realizing how it is going to cause so much destruction. It's beyond me. Not one honest scientist that will let the people know what is coming. Surely, one engineer can see what is going to happen. The Ring of Fire is nothing to play with. The consequences are unthinkable!" Mike exclaimed

"I've left a phone number for Tim to call us and mentioned that we're friends of the Rothmans; hopefully he'll call us soon." Robert stated

"I'm going to go and cut the grass; I can't eat now. I'm too upset. Do you want something to eat?" asked Mike

"No, my ulcer is starting to act up, too" Robert replied

"I just realized something. You know last week on television they were showing the new toy the cops have called a Tazer. It is using the same energy that we are researching. It's using this new electromagnetic energy." Mike stated

"They aren't kidding when they say that the new Scalar Wave Energy is here already." He added

"Let's turn on the computer and watch Marie's CD that we were watching yesterday." Robert asked

"We'll look for just a few minutes; put the timer on the stove on." Mike hollered from the office.

Manipulating the Weather

Terrorists can deliberately control the weather. Making high and low pressure systems is child's play with this new technology. Create high-pressure areas by cooling the air so it shrinks this in turn increases the density. Then create low-pressure areas by heating the air so this air expands and decreases its density. One can make the highs and lows wherever. It is possible to move them along a given path. Creating highs and lows where ever which causes the jet streams to go where they want them to go. The term is called "steering the weather".

A very cold snap brought from Northern Canada pushed to Southern California destroying their crops. It is possible to do regularly. An ice storm, just add another air current of cold air you bring down from the Arctic, North Pole. Weather steered by using artificial highs and lows from the ocean. Where they meet, you will get freezing rain, sleet, and then severe icing. Destroying the weather causes great damage to a nation or nations. Famine resulting.

"I thought the weather was a game as every weekend it seems to rain and as soon as Monday comes the sun is shining again. Haven't you noticed that?" asked Mike

"I know we are joking but can you imagine how that could bankrupt the States and for that matter Canada too. Our poor farmers work so hard to bring in their crops and this is what is going on. It makes my blood boil to think that whoever is doing this has gotten away with this for a long time." Robert exploded, a farm boy from Southern Ontario who had felt the loss of the family farm because of many summers in a row having bad weather. They continued to read.

Another example is the spring of 1986, abnormally strong weather engineering occurred over the States causing a drastic drought. This drought was broke by an American scientist who used an extremely powerful scalar EM device to redirect jet streams. It successfully blocked the terrorist scalar EM actions. Two huge circulations developed in the atmosphere. It showed as two side-by-side giant "holes" in the cloud cover over the middle and eastern States. Between these two giant holes, the cloud circulations formed a stream of clouds, moving to the south, looking very: much like a giant vertical "bar" of a huge "Y-shaped" cloud flow. Several national weathermen commented on this unusual pattern. The pattern continued for days. Blocking continued successfully by an American Scientist who set up his own Tesla Transmitter to block this weather attack.

Tesla believed this energy controlled the weather and earthquakes.

"Let's turn it off again. I can only handle this stuff in small dozes as it's too upsetting to know our government officials know what is happening and they say nothing." Mike stated

"I'm going to mow the lawn and water the garden. I'm going to build a green house and make sure our food grows this summer." Mike stated with determination. The phone rang. It was Chris, again. He is coming for the weekend. He's arriving tonight.

"With everyone coming for this weekend, I've postponed our readings this weekend in Hinton." Rosemarie stated

"We couldn't concentrate this weekend anyway with everyone here." Judy added

"Great! We're going to have a wonderful time. This weekend's going to be fun." Robert agreed

"Life's too short to work every weekend. Money is coming in, Don't worry! We'll have enough." Mike stated with a big grin.

"Hey we have our own commune here and it's growing everyday." Rosemarie laughed

"I've always wanted a large family and here we have it." Judy agreed

The cuckoo clock called the four o'clock time and the preparations were complete for the barbecue. Suddenly, it poured so hard you could hardly see your hand in front of your face. There would be no outdoor campfire or barbecue.

"Oh, well!" Rosemarie breathed a sigh

"Someone, phone Sam's cell and let him know we will come and meet them. I don't want them getting lost especially in this horrible down pour." called Mike to Rachel

"Have already done it and I was coming to ask you to go and meet them." She responded

"We'll have to make supper in doors tonight. What a shame. I was really looking forward to enjoying the camp fire tonight." Rachel sighed

Sam was at Wildwood, which was very close. The rain was coming down so hard that they had no choice but to pull off and wait for it to stop. Sam said that they had a great time till the rain over came them. Mike was on his way to meet them Rachel had said on the phone. Good thing as they would have been lost as the rain pouring that hard made it impossible to see highway signs.

"Maybe it is a good thing. In this downpour even satellites couldn't follow them. Just is case they are being followed. It is a good thing for sure." Robert added

"They're going to enjoy a hot meal and a warm bed tonight." Mike stated

Chapter 33

Mike answered the phone. Tim Bears-Den had returned his call. "Can I land my seaplane on your lake?" asked Tim

"No problems. When are you coming? Do you know that Aunt Amie, Candy, and Sam are arriving tonight?" Mike asked

"That's why I am coming. I heard that Marie and her daughters are at your place. I want to meet you. I can show you how to make the "Free-Energy" Generator. "Tim replied

"Man that is too good! We have a zillion questions to ask you in the morning." Mike added

"I'll be there about nine. I am bringing Grant Stallion, as we need to share some ideas with you. I can't say anymore than that for now." Tim answered

"Where are we going to house two more guests?" Mike asked

"We'll have to fix up the loft; we can use the air beds that we had from last summer. Thank god we have nearly finished building the loft."

Rosemarie replied

Marie and her daughters had come into the room. They had overheard some of the conversation.

"Who is coming in the morning?" asked Rachel

Just then, Robert pulled into the driveway with Sam following him. Horns honking like kids.

"We're going to have a house full for sure with thirteen guests. This is some weekend." Mike exclaimed, "Who's coming tomorrow?" Rachel asked bursting with curiosity.

"Tim Bears-Den and Grant Stallion; Marie will be thrilled." Mike exclaimed

Aunt Amie hugged Marie, Rachel, and Sophie excitedly. " I wouldn't have recognized you girls. No makeup and now you are blondes. Marie, why, are you dressed like a Huderite?" She asked

"Wise for folks to think we're a Huderite community. People won't be interested in us. We're still concerned for our safety since no police action has occurred against the terrorists or the care home. Worse, the owners of that care home are now part of the Gas and Oil Corporation. They're on their Board of Directors. Protected from the law now. So we have to be extra cautious." Rachel explained.

Candy and Sam introduced to everyone by Sophie and a lot of hand shaking and hugging went on. Aunt Amie hugged Judy and Rosemarie. Aunt Amie stated, "I'm grateful for your help, we're strangers."

Sam added, "We hoped that you would understand our serious situation in New York. We could not stay there any longer. We would be questioned where Marie and her girls were staying. It just made better sense to leave before that happened. I was expecting to have to do that anyway; since Candy had given the tapes to the detective. Three months ago, they've not attempted to contact us. We felt that something wasn't right when they contacted us now. A feeling, a bad premonition overwhelmed her.

Do not worry! I've taken every precaution to protect you and

258

ourselves. I bought a clunker to come the rest of the way. We took the back roads and stayed at B and Bs. We paid cash. It would be impossible for anyone to have followed us. We arrived at night and left before sunrise. I know they have no idea where we are. "Sam stated

"Last night we stayed at Banff. We arrived after dark and left before sunrise this morning. The owners of the B and B had no idea what we were driving. You should have seen the Aurora Borealis. It followed us for miles. So Beautiful! The last few miles, such a down pour; you couldn't see the car across the street. I am glad that it was raining hard. It's great to be safe." Candy added

Alberta Aurora Borealis

"Guess who is coming tomorrow?" Rachel asked Candy, Aunt Amie and Sam shrugged their shoulders mystified and said," Who?" "Tim Bears-Den and Grant Stallion." Rachel replied

"I saw him six weeks ago when he gave his lecture at Rabbi Samuel's home. It was about energetics and longitudinal waves something very scientific. His knowledge is hard for the layperson to understand. Why is he coming here; he is a very busy man? " Aunt Amie asked

"I'll explain that over supper." Mike stated

"Let's get you settled in your bedrooms. Supper will be in half an

259

hour. Do you like roast chicken? The Huderites, a few miles from here raise them organically and they are wonderful?" Rosemarie   stated

Rosemarie showed them to their bedrooms and they returned to the fireplace where a blazing fire toasted everyone. The rain poured down and it felt like fall instead of the middle of August. The rain tapped on the metal roof and the fire crackled. Everyone relaxed. Hot-spiced apple cider was in a cauldron on the dining room sideboard calling them to fill their cups and warm up. Excitement filled the room as they caught up on old news. This was a wonderful holiday.

Mike stated, "Chris is coming tonight too, I sure hope he's okay. Driving in this heavy rain is no joke. He has been here before; so I know he can find us; but all the same driving in this is dangerous."

With that said, there was a knock on the door and Beau was barking his head off which he always did for strangers. He was a great watchdog that was for sure.

Mike answered the door. Chris stood there, water streaming down his back. He looked exhausted. He had a flat tire on the highway, a few miles back and had to change the tire in the pouring rain. He would have liked to wait till the rain stopped; but then it would have been even harder to change a tire in the night's darkness.

"Chris, come on in; I'll pour a bath for you. You look chilled through to the bone. Do you like Brandy? Mike asked

"Here's some dry clothes!" Rosemarie offered

Chris soaked in the tub; his limbs coming back to life. He was so tired he fell asleep. His snoring heard in the living room.

Rosemarie called, "Chris, are you asleep in there?"

Startled, Chris woke up and climbed out of the tub. It had only been a few minutes of sleep but it did take the edge off and now he was starving. The food smelled awesome. Rosemarie introduced herself and the rest of the guests followed with their intros.

"Supper is ready; everyone come and eat!" Rosemarie called

"There's no way you will guess who's coming here tomorrow?"

Mike asked with a big laugh

Chris gave up and stated," Not a clue. Who's coming?"

The look on Chris' face was priceless when Mike told him Tim was arriving for breakfast tomorrow morning. It was a good thing that this was a large dining room. This table was big enough to hold fourteen guests arriving tomorrow.

Marie beamed all night. She nodded her head and said "Yes" often. She was getting her old self back and quickly. Just knowing her old friend, Tim would be here tomorrow delighted her. It was wonderful to see her happy.

Candy and Sam were overwhelmed with their new friends' generosity. They had done the right thing by leaving New York behind with it's approaching terror.

"Rosemarie, I need to buy a Motor home. Could Mike buy one for us? I have the cash and we're going to need some place to live for a while. I don't want to impose on your hospitality. Anyway, Mike can you help us find a Motor Home for a good price in the next few days?" Sam asked

"I like the one that Rachel and Sophie are living in. I'd be happy with one like that. Nothing too expensive!" Candy agreed

"God, the neighbors are going to think for sure that we are a commune. You're going to have to wear Huderite costumes so the police don't come checking on us." sighed Rosemarie.

"I think that Robert and I could set up some temporary shelter at our new home; the roof is on and the siding finished. It might be okay seeing it is summer." Judy offered

"It is too cold, even now in August we needed this fireplace tonight to keep warm." Robert cautioned

"Mike and I have to do the electrical and plumbing next week; but the week after that Sam and Chris might help me insulate the place and drywall it. You are right we'll be in our home the first of September. Would you like to help Sam? How about you, Chris?" asked Robert

"It sounds good to me. I've always wanted to learn how to wire." Sam answered

"I can wire and plumb." Chris offered

"Remember, we have to get the building inspector out to pass it before we can put on the drywall." Mike added

"I would like to get as much done as possible before the snow hits as you folks can't live in these Motor homes in this climate in the winter. We'll have room for five people in the new home too." Judy offered

"Have you got your water yet? I took a course on Dowsing and found that I was good at it; friends of mine had bought a cottage and they needed to dig a well. I was the only one that could make the willow branches work. They teased me about being Psychic as I could witch for water. I was so curious after that experience. I joined a Dowsing Club at the local University and found that you can dowse for missing people, pets, lost items, and more. It wasn't just used for finding water. I would love to help you find your water." Sam offered

"You are psychic. I have always known that and yes, I teach a Dowsing Course at the local High School. It is a great way to open up psychic abilities in young people. I even have them make their own Dowsing Beads, in my course." Aunt Amie added

Marie and Aunt Amie got the comfortable sofa and the rest of the gang lay on the floor on pillows telling ghost stories, psychic phenomena, and scary dreams. Each one tried to top the others' ghost or paranormal story.

"I was thirty when my psychic abilities started coming back to me. Mainly dreams at first and I will never forget this one dream. It was about a small mining city in Northern Canada that was running out of silver deposits. The owners of the mine wanted to close the mine but would have to pay out the miners. They were on a fancy yacht laughing and joking and scheming a way to shut down this mining town. One of the owners suggested putting a chemical into the air so that the town would go blind at once. He thought it would be very funny.

Moving cars crashed instantaneously into each other! People blind

262

in one minute. They didn't know where they were. It was mass hysteria. The rich people on this fancy yacht thought it was hilarious. The horror these poor people were going through was hell. Even the Police and the Ambulance people were blind.

A chemical had blinded everyone. I woke up screaming that was more than twenty-five years ago. I never forgot it. It isn't fun to know the future as I see that event happening somewhere in the world and soon. I have read some of Tim's research and this new science can affect the optic nerve and do this horrible event. After hearing the terrorist tapes and realizing that, Psychopaths are attempting to control our planet. They are capable of this evil and the thought of it chills my soul." Judy stated

"I know what she is talking about; I too get the most horrible dreams. Are your dreams in color Judy?" asked Aunt Amie

"Since I was a child at the age of three, I have dreamed in color. My dreams are like a movie It is that clear. It is like I travel through time and see a scene played out on the big screen of time." Judy replied

"Wow that would not be fun." Mike stated

"Last week, before we left I had a few of my clients phone me and tell me they were having dreams of a plane flying into the Twin Towers; I didn't know what to tell them. I finally agreed to tell them to leave town and to warn as many of their friends and family as possible to leave Manhattan." Aunt Amie added.

"Do you suppose that a lot of people will get those dreams and be warned since the authorities are doing nothing to prevent it from happening?" asked Chris

"I hope so as there will be so many people killed in those Twin Towers." Candy sighed

"When people are dreaming those kinds of dreams, are they tapping into the Unconscious Mind and picking up that information from the people who are planning these events?" asked Mike

"It is hard to say but I do think there are some of us who travel in the Astral when asleep. I know that I have tried to talk with these terrorists; but so far, I have not been able to reach them. There is some research being done now about the dream state so that we can know more how the brain works." Aunt Amie continued

"Let's have a funny dream tonight; everyone here let's plan to have a great dream that they can share in the morning." Rosemarie asked

"I need you guys to go to sleep in a good mood so no more scary stories tonight." She stated

Aunt Amie started telling stories of Tim Bears-Den and the stuff they got into when they were kids. By the time, she finished telling them about his misadventures as a kid they all felt like they already knew him.

"Will Tim and Grant be okay sleeping in the loft?" asked Rosemarie.

"He'll love it especially if it keeps raining; he always loved the sound of the rain on the roof." Aunt Amie answered

"I sure hope it stops raining and the wind calms down by tomorrow morning as his seaplane will have a hard time landing on the lake." Mike sighed

"Oh no problems he used to fly helicopters in Vietnam." Sam added

"I have wanted to meet him for over twenty years; he is a gold mine of information." Chris stated. "I still can't believe I'm going to meet him. Finally, I'll know how to make the "Free-Energy" Generator." Chris laughed

"Who is this Grant Stallion? Chris asked

Mike answered, "He's the Psychic who believes that the Earth is going to lose more than half of its land mass. The west coast of America sits on the Ring of Fire. It will drop into the ocean when the earthquakes hit. He has even drawn a map showing the way the Earth will look in the near future. It is scary. The Military already use his map as their reference map. So they know it is real."

"Mike no more scary stuff tonight; our guests don't need nightmares." exclaimed Rosemarie

"Yes, Mom I'll be good." Mike replied as he grabbed her and tickled her.

Rosemarie and Mike had grown up in large families and this home felt like their childhoods with all these people there.

"I feel like we are the Waltons!" Mike offered with a grin

"I agree, small family units just don't have as much fun as the large ones do; I never realized how lonely we were until you all came into our lives. All kidding aside, I envy the Huderites.

They have warmth that we have lost over the years." Rosemarie continued.

"If we have to live like this until our New York returns to normal, I am content." Sophie stated

"I agree!" said Rachel and Candy at the same time.

"I have missed having friends and family around as my parents died in a car accident a few years back." Chris added

Everyone looked over at him in sympathy; Mike sitting beside him touched his shoulder and stated," It is hard to grieve in this cold world. Not many people know how to get over shocks like that."

That's what makes me so concerned for New York. I don't know how to stop the attack. I have done all I could. I copied hundreds of tapes and gave them out. Even to an old boyfriend that works as a firefighter in Manhattan.

I don't know if he listened to them or not; but he never called me to tell me what he thought of them. I can only hope that he listened to them. I hope the detective listened to them. We both gave those tapes to him; but we never heard from him, either." Candy sighed

"It is weird that so many people who should have acted on hearing those tapes have just ignored them." Rachel agreed

"That is why we are here. With no one responding the only thing that we can think is that they are part of what is coming and or they don't care." Sam stated

"I just couldn't stay there and be part of it; when I knew that I could be safe here. I believe in protecting my loved ones and myself. I am a survivor and if it means moving across the country; I am going to do it." Aunt Amie stated

"Our families had to do that to survive Hitler and it seems like the same beings are in control." Candy added

"I worry about Rabbi Samuel and his little group of caring people who meet every week at his home. I hope they can find a safe place when it happens." Sam stated

"I try hard not to think about it; I wish I could do something to make a difference but in my attempts I have only brought danger to myself and my loved ones." Candy continued

"Part of me thinks I should not have taped their conversations in the lounge that night; but I thought I was doing the right thing." She sighed

"I am sure glad that you taped those conversations; or Marie would not be with us now. None of us would have met and that is a miracle in itself. You can't buy the kind of friendship that we have here in this room." offered Sophie

"I'm glad that you did as now we have four Psychics in the same home. I would like to ask Robert and Judy to sleep in the loft tonight so that Chris can sleep in their Motor home. Do you know why?" Rosemarie asked

"We have four psychics, Rosemarie; who is the Forth psychic? Candy asked

"You are the Forth Psychic, dear! Do you remember our conversation the day you moved into my home? I told you then and now that you are one of us, a Psychic." Aunt Amie stated

"I want to see what happens when four strong Psychics share the same space when we are asleep. What kind of dreams will we have?" Rosemarie stated with a laugh.

"Sounds good to me as it will be toasty warm there in the loft and I love to hear the rain on the metal roof." Robert answered

"Can you imagine really four of them in one place! The four witches of Eastwick!" Mike stated through his laughter remembering the comedy movie that they had watched.

Chapter 34

No one slept in this morning; Mike walked with Beau down to the lake to make sure the canoes had survived last night's storm. He stopped by the Motor homes and knocked on both.

"Wake up guys; coffees served!" Mike stated

"How did you all sleep?" He continued

"Like the dead; as soon as my head hit the pillow, I was out cold." Chris replied

"Same here; the rain on the roof just put me to sleep like a baby." Sophie answered

"Mmmme ttttoo." Marie stammered with a big smile on her face.

The smell of frying bacon, coffee and homemade cinnamon buns filled the air.

"Tim and Grant will be here soon; it is eight o'clock; let's have a coffee and wait for breakfast so we can all eat together." Rosemarie stated while she took the buns out of the oven.

"So did anyone have an exciting dream?" questioned Mike as he poured the coffee eager to see if Rosemarie was right about her idea that four Psychics would increase the psychic energy in their home.

"I did have another one of my movie dreams; Rosemarie and I were doing a Gala Event put on by the largest department store here in Edmonton. I had a long line of women waiting to have their Tarot Cards read. It was at Christmas time and the place was full of happiness and excitement. Wonderful food and wine offered. East-Indian Men in harem costumes dancing through the crowd of women. Women buying presents; laughing about the clothes they were trying on; eating and drinking; having a wonderful time. Abundance and joy filled the place. I was in a holiday mood, too.

Thirty women lined up for a reading; a young auburn haired girl sat down in front of me. The first thing she said was that she didn't believe in any of this; but her friends had wanted her to do it. She looked like me when I was eighteen; that it was like looking in the mirror. I asked her where she was going for Christmas; she replied Thailand.

My heart stopped! All I could see was this big wave coming inland and everyone screaming to get away from it. The vision was a nightmare as people were swallowed up by this monstrous wave. It was a Tsunami. The vision only lasted for a few seconds but it shattered me to my core. I caught my breath and realized that I could not tell her anything.

I was representing this large department store. She wouldn't believe me anyway; if I tried to tell her what I had just seen. She would have scorned the vision and I would have been in trouble with the department store managers. I am still shaking from that dream. So I guess you are right; Rosemarie, our Psychic abilities do increase when there is more than two of us in the same place. "Judy stated

"I guess I was just too tired after all the traveling as I didn't dream a thing." Aunt Amie added

"I guess I am lucky not to have been born with your ability as it scares the heck out of me it is hard enough to deal with the daily stuff let alone seeing what is coming." Mike stated

"I had a dream and yes, it was in color too. I have had this dream

269

before many times. A large hurricane hit the coast of Florida and many people drowned. It was devastating. People drowning! Water everywhere! I woke up in the middle of the night scared out of my wits. Poor Sam didn't know how to calm me down." Candy stated

Sam added, "She was terrified; it took some time to settle her down. Maybe we should sleep in the Motor home tonight. I don't think my heart could take another night like that."

"Well, do you now believe you are psychic?" Rosemarie asked

It had stopped raining before dawn and the smell of fresh air and the smell of the fir and pine trees enveloped them as they went down to the lake. Beau was barking his loudest as the plane skipped across the surface and stopped at the dock. Tim slowly turned the engines off and waved to them. Beau had never seen a seaplane before.

"Beau stop!" Mike demanded and he calmed down, but he still wagged his tail

Tim and Grant had borrowed a friend's seaplane just to make sure no one knew where they were. Tim was a cautious man and why he was still alive even though he had been in the public eye demanding change from the government, for many years. His tireless war on the Gas and Oil Companies was relentless.

Tim picked up Marie and gave her a huge hug. "I am so glad that you are getting better!" He said brushing away a tear on her cheek. It was obvious they were very fond of each other.

Introductions all round and they went back to the house.

"Have you had breakfast yet; we've waited for you so we could all eat together?" asked Rosemarie

"No we left Lethbridge before sunrise; we're starving. My God, the beauty of the Aurora Borealis was breath taking. I wish you could have seen it. " Grant replied

All thirteen people sat at the table. Tim joked, "I feel like Jesus with his twelve disciples."

"No, maybe King Arthur and you're my knights. Rosemarie you are

Maid Maryanne and Judy you are Gwendolyn." Grant stated and laughed

"Marie do you have the research CD's that I asked you to keep for me in your safe deposit box?" asked Tim

"Yyyes!" Marie replied

"Have you been showing them to our friends?" He continued

"We have looked at them for the last two months ever since Marie arrived here." Robert and Mike replied.

"We have a lot of questions that need answers; especially about the "Free-Energy" Generator that you have worked with from Tesla's research." Mike added

"I have studied your work for the last twenty years; I would love the schematics for that generator. Can you help us make these generators so we can get them on the market?" asked Chris

Robert and Mike added, "We have tried to make a generator but something is not working. We're stumped."

"That is one of the reasons why we came here; but there is so more that you will learn to do and we'll be staying for a while to make sure that you learn how to do energetic mind research and control." Tim stated

"My research is like Tim's but what I have learned lately about our country and what is happening to America has brought me here to work with all of you. I wish to put together a "Brain Snap Team""

"We can work together using our abilities; we could save our countries." Grant stated

"You'll be the first group, a "Brain Snap Team" that uses this new "Bio-Energetics." Your Psychic Mind Control can fight the thought patterns attacking America and Canada.

We realize that some of our people are under mind control with this "Bio-Energetics." Some terrorist group is using Longitudinal Scalar Wave Energy. This science known in their part of their world is "Energetics." Nikola Tesla discovered this energy a hundred years ago. It was ignored here; but other countries have researched it for the last

271

100 years.

Mostly government and religion fundamentalist groups here in this country have kept this science suppressed." Tim continued

"We realized the strength of the mind control here when we received your tapes, Candy that you gave Rabbi Samuel more than three months ago. The detective that received those tapes went missing. I am certain that he is dead. The government people who you approached with copies of those tapes never listened to them or ignored what they said." Tim continued

"I know what you mean; I found the same thing when I gave copies to my mates on Wall Street.

It was like they were zombies; totally indifferent to the messages on those tapes." Sam continued

"Rabbi Samuel had found the same thing when he approached the other ministers from the other religious groups in New York. They were indifferent. Rabbi Samuel couldn't believe that they didn't care about the pending terrorist attack." Aunt Amie added

"I found the same thing, when I gave an old boyfriend a copy. He is now a firefighter in Manhattan. He too ignored them. It was as if he never got them. When I handed them to him, I told him they were about a terrorist plot to bomb the Twin Towers." Candy added

"What do you think is going on then?" asked Tim Bears-Den to the dumbfounded group

"Why do you think no one cares about this impending terror?" asked Grant

No one said anything; but looked at each other for the answer.

Finally, Mike asked," I give up what the heck is going on, anyway?"

Marie was shaking her head and said "Yyyes" but couldn't get any thing else out to her frustration. She went and got the CD that had played in the computer. She handed it to him.

"Yes, it is on this CD." Tim exclaimed

"We haven't gotten any farther than the information on Weather Wars and Earthquakes." Robert and Mike added

"Let's play the next part of the CD and you will know why the American People are in the mind state that they are in and what we are going to do about it." Tim offered

"Can we stop for coffee first; as this is really over our heads and we need a break?" asked Sophie

"It's nearly lunch time; maybe we should have lunch first?" Rosemarie suggested

During lunch, Tim asked," Would you like to fight these terrorists? You would be the first people to put together a "Brain Snap Team." We are here to help you do that. You have come together to form this Team. Each of you has the right abilities to do this. It's not a mistake. We have come together at this time for a reason.. You can call it Spirit World or Energy from the Forth Dimension; it means the same thing. You are here at this time to save the world, as we know it. Are you ready to fight this Mind Control?"

They looked at each other in total amazement.

Finally, Aunt Amie stood up and stated," I do believe you as that is the only thing that makes any sense at all. For all of us to come together so quickly, easily, and safely is incredible. Synchronicity or Destiny has brought us here."

"You are right; it is the only thing that makes any sense. We are all from very different lifestyles. The common denominator is our four Psychics. " Mike added

He reached out and took Rosemarie's hand who in turn took the hand of the next person and so it went. Within seconds, they had all joined hands.

"We're ready; what's next!" Mike asked

"What does that mean?" asked Chris who had not seen Marie's collection of CD's.

"You'll have some catching up to do. We have an extra computer for you to see the earlier CD's we've studied. It would take too long to explain. On the computer it won't take long for you to catch up." Mike informed

"I have over the years, researched the "Free-Energy" ideas but that is all I know. You mean there is more stuff to research. I speed-read. It won't take me long to catch up." Chris added

Chris sat down at the computer and began reading Marie's CDs. While the rest of the group continued with the later CD's brought by Tim Bears-Den

Radiant Energy

An alternate form of energy that uses electromagnetic (EM) wave discovered in the empty vacuum of space. It is an inexhaustible supply of energy in great size at any place in the universe.

Russians (KGB) have been working on this technology for over 60 years and have created different ways of employing these Scalar Longitudinal Waves. These are the weapons Nikita Khrushchev spoke of in January, 1960.

The Russians experimented with a giant scalar EM accident in the Urals, which destroyed the area. New super weapons created with this science called "Bio-Energetics." Khrushchev called them "Weapons of Mass Destruction" which could wipe out all life on earth.

They have done more than 90 years of research and testing on the planet with these new Scalar Electromagnetic Weapons. This force used 2001, Sept 11. This will bring down the Twin Towers as if they were toothpicks.

The CD paused and Tim stated, "Yes, the terrorists are using this technology to destroy the Twin Towers. The planes will bomb the buildings; but this will not bring the Twin Towers down. The technology of this Scalar Longitudinal Energy known as "Bio-Energetics" directed at the entire building will disintegrate those steel buildings as if they were straw through resonance, as the planes would only have damaged the top floors where they hit. Even more alarming is that these terrorists

274

have used "Mind Control" on a mass scale. That is why no one has listened to any of us as we tried to stop it from happening."

Tim continued, "This new energy is adaptable and is able to do "Mind Control" by a program engineered called the "Brain Snapper." It is from the Forth Dimension and powerful enough to control whole nations by the twist of a few dials."

"We read about this Scalar Longitudinal Energy in Marie's Research last week called the Brain Snapper and that is what they did to her." Judy added

"So you know what I mean when I say the people you have warned in New York are not able to understand what you are telling them. They have been Brain Snapped. This "Mind Control' used all over the nation in many ways with just a few twists of a dial and these populations enslaved." Tim added

"They have used it to convince people there is an energy crisis and that oil and gas are the only means of fueling our vehicles. That is why I have not been able to have anyone take my scientific research on the "Free-Energy" Generator seriously. These terrorists control our people's minds. This is from outside and inside our governments. I repeat; they have perfected "Mind Control" on a mass scale. Their machines are controlling the populations of the States and Canada. They have mentally controlled New York with the twist of a few dials.

Since you have read Marie and my research on those CD's for the last two months, you are aware that we can fight back. I have developed a stronger generator than used by these terrorists. Tim continued

"It is energy from the Forth Dimension and infinite. I have come here to ask you to help me build a "Counter Brain Snap Team" so we can defend our country. It is possible with your help to build this counter energy using the same Scalar Longitudinal Wave Energy a "Force Field large enough to counter their Mind Control Program. I call it the Brain Snapper.

Are you willing to do this?" asked Tim

"You mean we can finally do counter attack and maybe shut them down entirely." asked Mike

"You must shut off your electricity and this is why the "Free-Energy" Generator is so important. Once you are off the hydro grid, you can counter attack. They can't trace where the attack is from.

These terrorists have incorporated our hydro lines into their magnetic grid they call the "Woodpecker Grid" to control our thoughts. If you live in the city surrounded by electrical wires, it is very easy to generate these thought forms of control. Out here in the country you are safe; especially when you shut the hydro off." Tim continued.

"Let's get busy even if we have to work non stop for the next few nights; I am ready to make it happen." Mike exclaimed

"We are the "Brain Snap Team." Incredible coincident have brought us together. It is destiny!" stated Aunt Amie as she hugged Marie.

"A "Brain Snap Team" is what is necessary. I know you're committed to change things. I have the generator and equipment but I need you to help me manage it. With your focus on this, we can destroy the energy that they send to New York and the rest of America and Canada.

The energy we create will open the minds of some of the more intelligent people. They'll wake up and realize what is happening. Some of them won't go to work that day. They will stay home or leave the area all together; just like you all did. You are survivors and your intuition worked and saved your lives and maybe the lives of many more people in the future." Tim continued

"I intend to build "Brain Snap Teams" all over Canada, the United States, and Europe! The sooner the people are aware what is happening to them, the better as then they can fight back. We can do it! We can take back our own brains." Tim stated

Grant Stallion added," The New Earth Map does not have to happen if we come together and fight back. When we visualize the planet healthy and use this Forth Dimension power source, we can heal the planet. Are we ready to fight this unseen enemy? We won when they attacked our weather last summer. We put together a counter force strong enough to stop their weather attack. Our normal summer weather returned. Our crops came in successfully. We can do it again. This new science used by us can save our planet and our lives."

"What can we do with our Psychic abilities?" asked Judy

"We've five psychics here including Grant." Aunt Amie stated

"How do we do this?" asked Candy

There are twelve here. I'll be putting you all into a mind-altered state except for Marie. By the way, she was very good at this work before the terrorists took over her Laboratory. When she is better, she will be your sixth psychic.

In the altered state, you can see the energy of the Woodpecker Grid and let us know where the energy is at the strongest place and time. We can feel what they will do next and be ready to block it. Your psychic abilities can also help us create these energy fields. In addition, our loved ones in Spirit know what is going on. They will guide us when and where we send our attacks. It is spiritual war. Your spiritual loved ones will protect you. You are safe." Tim stated.

"Like the Synchronicity Book, Spirit world has the ability if we let them work through us." Candy exclaimed

"Coincidences and my experience over the years give me the knowledge and faith that we will succeed. These terrorists are not working with the love or power from Spirit world. They disconnected from their loved ones long ago. In fact their passed over loved ones wish to work with us. This is no contest at all, really." Aunt Amie added

"I know exactly what you mean; when I did psychic fairs in the past, I would have to defend myself from negative people who loved to use energy to hurt my clients. It was easy to raise my energy levels and protect others and myself. This is something I have practiced for many years and many times successfully." Judy offered

"Here is a drawing of the Tesla Transmitter that I have found along with blueprints to build it." Tim offered

It was late afternoon, and Chris had finished his reading and joined the team. Confidence and a lot of laughter filled the room as they realized how Spirit had guided them to this unique place and time.

"With the psychic energy in this room, I think that we could channel Nikola Tesla himself and his advice to protect our country and ourselves." Judy suggested

"Yes, Tesla just might be able to come through to us. He spent many years researching the paranormal. He was very interested in time travel and had some concepts about this. One of his 2,000 inventions gives real information on how to do that. He may be able to appear to us; not as a ghost but as a living man.

He died in obscurity. He easily could have faked his death and with his science not aged. He may have been watching this 1% elite use his genius in this horrible destructive way. I am sure he would love to work with us and defeat these monsters." Tim exclaimed

"Yes, I am sure Tesla is watching in horror. They have used his knowledge to destroy our environment let alone the world. Tomorrow we will begin building another Tesla Transmitter. I have his blueprints and this sketch of what it looks like." Grant stated

Tesla Transmitter

Chapter 35

Sunrise found the team wide-awake and eager for the coming day. The exciting conversations at each meal were inspiring. Each had a story to tell and no one in this Brain Snap Team was boring.

Rosemarie asked, "Did anyone have an unusual dream last night? Did anyone astral travel?"

Judy answered," My dream went back to 1981, when I moved to Vancouver Island. I had just discovered Numerology and wanted to meet other people who wanted to study this fascinating subject. I placed an ad in the local newspaper advertising "Aquarian 33 Philosophy." I had no idea that there had been an earlier society. With a similar name led by a man named Brother Twelve. He had moved to Cedar on Vancouver Island in 1927. There, he established a group of settlers from England.

He had convinced them that the world was ending, an Armageddon. He was supposedly the Great Master in fact the Christ. They followed him to this Island and set up a settlement. They were rich and had given up their positions, their money, and everything to come there to build this place. He had managed to dupe them out of their life savings completely.

Back then, I had long red hair and many of the people in that area believed that I was his wife, "Madame Z" reincarnated. She had red hair and I looked something like her. Although, I could not see the resemblance as I looked like Sissy Spacek; not this hard looking woman. She had helped Brother Twelve set up their slave camp. She was a horrific person who beat these people and even killed some of them.

Brother Twelve at one point had 2,000 followers. He stole many thousands of dollars from these people and fled with Madame Z. They weren't caught. They supposedly died in Switzerland in 1934. I had no idea of this woman or of Brother Twelve until the offspring of these poor people threatened my life. This was very bizarre! My dream frightened me as I remembered my fear for my life back then. This actually happened to me in 1981."

Tim sighed and stated, "Yes, I believe that soon the established bankers will frighten the wealthy and famous to give up all their belongings and status. They'll convince people to hide out in bunkers to survive "the end of the world prophesy". This will be in 2012. They will use the Mayan Calendar predictions. They will also use the idea of an Asteroid called Nibiru, which is supposed to collide with our Earth. There has been much talk of this for many years. In fact, Norway has built many underground shelters in preparation for this event.

Presently, the government is working on a huge underground shelter under Denver Airport. They have even commissioned artists to paint the Armageddon pictures on the walls of the Denver Airport. They started that last year."

Mike asked, "Do these government officials and military people really believe that this asteroid, Nibiru is the end to our world? Perhaps they are just using that as a way to concentrate their wealth into their "Power Group." Maybe they're doing another Brother Twelve?"

Grant Stallion stated," I think that you are right about further concentrating the wealth as even back in 1930 author, H.G. Wells believed the same as Britain's hierarchy. He was a part of this elite group. Back the, Europe's elite wished the masses eliminated. They created the Great Depression. Their belief was "Only a few should control the world."

Banks like Rothschild, Warburg, and Schiff created Adolph Hitler in their hopes of killing off the masses in the Second World War.

Montagu Norman, President of the Bank of England from 1920 to 1935 supported Hitler in his efforts. Both World Wars created by this elite group, then 4% of the population.

Wells often referred to the "Prophecy of Technocracy". Remember Wells wrote the Radio Play, "War of the Worlds" which frightened United State's population. Real terror; as they listened on the radio believing that an alien race had invaded. I wouldn't put it passed the present government to do another scam with the use of this new Science H.A.A.R.P. They can easily create HOLOGRAMS to convince people that the aliens have landed or some Planet X, Nibiru crashes into Earth.

It would be easy for them to engineer a Hologram Hoax with Jesus and his angels in the sky using this technology. It's possible to show this on television as a news broadcasts. The average citizen would not know any better. They would believe it was a newscast.

The American Dollar's back shows the Pyramid's base with "NOVUS ORDO SECLORUM" which means "New World Order" The American dollar's back has had that on it for the last 200 years. The "EYE" from the Masonic order sit on top of it. Thus, for the last 200 years the elite Masonic power group have hoped to control and eliminate the inferior masses.

However, this is where it gets interesting. Many special interest groups wish to control the world. Each one wants to be the Only Power. The people in the Brandt Commission, The Illuminati, the Papacy, Gas and Oil Corporations, and the Powerful Banking Concerns want to be the controller These people are inter connected. There are Power struggles within these groups.

However, Power is Power. What these "Powerful Folk" don't realize is that our world has changed radically in the last one hundred years. People might not be so easily controlled as they think. I believe the Bankers on Wall Street today are attempting another crash of the stock market, another dirty thirties depression. I've heard them talk of deliberately inflating the mortgage market so that it'll financially ruin thousands of American Citizens. This will further concentrate their wealth into the hands of this 1% elite group.

It will be an inside job according to my sources. The American people forced to redeem these Lending Institutions "Billions of dollars of tax payers money." so the States won't go bankrupt. Billions will be coming from the Government coffers into the hands of these Banking Institutions. This is taxpayer's money. These Banks will brag that this puts 33 Million people out of work and living on the streets of America. Their intent is to destroy the middle class." Grant Stallion continued

"The Banking Institutions that create this event will then be further rewarded by the State's Government. They'll be given seats in the Parliament for their efforts. This will happen after the attack on Manhattan. It will take about seven years for these Giant Banking Institutions to carry out this fraud. They brag about it already.

It was this same elite group back in 1930, that dreamed of a "One World Government" and nothing has changed since then. It has just taken a little longer to bring it about. I don't think they're aware of the people's power." Grant added

Tim continued, "Why is there such fear of this Asteroid, Nibiru? It could be used to defend our Earth. Should there be an Asteroid threat, why don't the Soviets and Americans use this science to blast Nibiru before it even enters Earth's atmosphere? With technology, the scientists can tell exactly where this asteroid would hit. Billion Watts of laser energy used to blast this asteroid. Tesla back in 1912 knew the power of this science; now it is even more powerful.

In my opinion, it's possible to destroy Nibiru, before it even gets close to Earth. Establish H.A.A.R.P. and blast it out of the sky before it even comes into Earth's gravity. Should it strike Earth, moderate the effects of the impact? Why wouldn't these scientists attempt to do something to defend our planet? Hiding in underground bunkers is not the answer!"

Mike added, "Tesla created an earthquake in New York on July 11th 1935. Tesla's experiment nearly succeeded in flattening New York City. In his lab, he built a device to show the principle of harmonic resonance.

First, his building was shaking and then the circle grew bigger to include the neighboring buildings. He realized that he had created an earthquake with a mere rod in the ground, thirty Watts of energy, and a tapping device. Imagine! How it has evolved? This technology can protect our planet from any asteroid, including Nibiru."

New York and Japan both are on unstable ground. The slightest earthquake can collapse those areas. The East and West Coast of North America is very vulnerable to earthquakes. It is only a matter of time when the San Andreas Vault will collapse and fall into the ocean. No one is concerned, as they all believe it will happen years from now. It is such a shame that people don't realize the horror that will happen.

H.A.A.R.P. Installation

Aunt Amie stated, "Last night I had an unusual dream; that showed many earthquakes, tsunamis, volcanoes, hurricanes and extreme weather affecting the world. The Twin Towers fell after the jets blasted into them. It was horrific. However, why did the towers turn to dust? It didn't make sense that they disintegrated into dust. I'm aware of Tesla's resonance research. Will H.A.A.R.P. create this? Many people died that day. I woke up sobbing uncontrollably. I've never had a dream so overwhelming."

Tim Bears-Den consoled, "I know you have tried to warn the people of New York about this terrorist attack. Thanks to Candy's taped conversation, many people will survive. I've seen people copying the original tape and passing it from person to person. I believe that many will not go into work that day; but will be in a safe place. I believe that each of us can develop their intuition. It's important to develop our intuition; so we'll be in safe places when these events happen. Listening to the small voice that guides us and protects us is the answer."

"Wouldn't it be wise for the people to leave the coastal areas and go in land as quickly as possible? We realized that we needed to find a safe place to survive. Won't other people realize this and act quickly. Leave big cities where all hell will break loose. Surely, people realize that they would be safer in rural areas and away from the ocean?" Judy asked

Grant Stallion answered, "I believe that they are using mind control on people. We've seen what they did to Marie. She's an intelligent and aware woman. Their brain control worked on her. Imagine how vulnerable the ordinary person is. Easy victims as they struggle to feed their families. They're easily overwhelmed by these mind control energy waves.

Especially, world tragedies continue to happen. Fear overwhelms them. One does not function well in fear mode. I believe they're using H.A.A.R.P. to cripple the average citizen. Easily controlled and enslaved. Should they sell their homes, property, and investments to buy a space in a military bunker? They'll be giving up their identity just as if they were in the concentration camps of Hitler's Day. Worse this time, they are doing it readily without question."

"Hitler would be laughing in his grave at the very thought of these sheep willingly giving up their lives to make these bastards more wealthy." exclaimed Robert

"What is even more heartbreaking is that Tesla gave us electricity, radio, and technology. His goal was to have a world where all the nations would be equal. He wanted to give "Free-Energy" to everyone. He was so far ahead of his time with his 2,000 inventions

The government and the 1% drove him into bankruptcy. Their deliberate intentions of discrediting his work drove him crazy. He died penniless and homeless just like the 33 Million people living on the streets of America today. I'd like to connect to him and find solutions.

I don't believe he would want to see people destroyed by his inventions. I think that he'd give us new technology to fight H.A.A.R.P.. Today it's August 1st. 2,001. We have eleven years to develop an alternate H.A.A.R.P. program to protect our planet. We don't need to depend on the government, military or scientific elite. We can develop a way to protect our planet ourselves." Tim stated

"The Internet is our source of information and there'll be more sites that we can connect to that have our goals. It's possible to build an elaborate network that will be ready for these future events. Intuitive people will understand what is happening to the planet. I see an exodus from the coastlines. People will change their way of life. Priorities will change.

Movies like "Postman" and "Water world" with Kevin Costner shout this message loud and clear. Humanity will survive and will have new priorities. Only a matter of time and the 1% will self-destruct. They don't realize the power of Spirit World. It's intervened on behalf of nations before and it will again. Now people know their loved ones in Spirit are powerful. Remember the storm that hid England's boats so they could surprise attack. This was the turning point of WW Two. That fog was caused by Spirit World and Spirit will do it again when needed." Rosemarie stated

"Can you imagine being in a bunker with people like Harry Hall? How safe would you feel? They'll end up killing each other. Perhaps that is what Spirit intends to happen. Can you imagine people believing this lie, and selling their souls to survive in these bunkers? Only to find they are now slaves of a few Psychopaths. I remember the movie, "Logan's Run" The movie's premise was once you turned 30 years old; you were killed. I can see it now, the rich and old survivors of these bunkers killed. Karma comes full circle. I wouldn't want to live in a world like that anyway." Judy stated

Grant Stallion added, "Yes, the 1%'s goal is to limit the population to five hundred million. They believe that they can control this small population. The rest destroyed by earthquakes, tsunamis, hurricanes, weather wars, disease, and famine. My map shows where people will be safer. It is important to go inland and avoid trees and forests. There'll be fire storms. It's possible to survive. After the destruction, there'll be an opportunity to build a new world."

"If we're brave enough now to face what may come and prepare; we'll have more of a chance. Last night, we watched the Documentary, "Jerusalem in the Woods" a true story of defiance by the Bielski Brothers, during the Second World War. The people who were brave and dug a tunnel with their bare hands out of the Concentration Camp, survived to live wonderful full lives. It's better to live and fight; than to give up your freedom to hide in a bunker controlled by Psychopaths. What kind of future would you have at the hands of the Harry Halls of this "Power Group?" Tim Bears-Den stated

"Can you imagine being in this bunker and realizing that the world as we know it is no longer there. Imagine knowing that you're in a military state and at the mercy of these people. Not knowing when they's killed you. Cannibalism would be days or months away. There'd be nothing to live for. Harry Hall would have no problems cauterizing your throat. You wouldn't eat or speak. Just the very thought of that makes me realize that no way in heaven or hell would I join their underground bunkers." Mike added,

"Worse, what would stop the Soviets from launching another satellite from outside Earth's orbit? They can use H.A.A.R.P.'s energy to steer the Asteroid, Nibiru to land on the Denver Airport. With Tomography, X-Rays of the planet now available, the Soviets, and the States can see where bunkers are. There is no hiding in bunkers. Another joke played on the American people. Greater than the Banker's planned Poncy Scam. People warned about these schemes. But, how will we ever get them to believe us?" Aunt Amie sighed

Marie wrote this note and handed to Tim Bears-Den.

"My father supported Tesla. He came to our home every Saturday. I grew up listening to their talks. He talked about a "Force Field." It could protect our Earth from Asteroids, planes, and bombs. I'll find stuff on my

CD. There's a way to protect us. Westinghouse bought Tesla's 2,000 patents. They know about this "Shield." Why aren't they using it? Rich put into useless bunkers. The shield used to protect themselves. "

Tim Bears-Den agreed and pulled out Tesla's Patents Catalog. It contained the patent for the "Shield" or "Force Field" Marie had written in her note. Marie and the men looked at the patent and understood the principles of Tesla's invention. It was possible! Billion Watts of Micro-energy would prevent Asteroid X or Nibiru from entering Earth's Atmosphere. Destroyed before it even enters Earth's gravitational field.

The Brain Snap Team continued their study of Tesla's patents. They built the "Free-Energy" Generator, which gave them all the power they needed. Yes, they were off the hydro grid. Their vehicles used the Tesla energy. Even Tim Bears-Den's four-seat plane flew with "Free-Energy." They had time to sell this invention on the Internet. The settlement grew quickly and to all the neighbors it looked like any other Huderite community. Their greenhouse supplied with "Free-Energy" was the envy of the other Huderite community. It was a mystery how their food was growing in the winter. Secrecy was still important and they continued to play their hiding game.

Candy and Sam remained with the Brain Snap Team at their Lake Isle Community. Aunt Amie, Rachel and Sophie went back to New York after Sept 11th attack. They sold their businesses and homes. They had more than enough money to build their Tesla Transmitter and produce their Internet Broadcast for the world to receive their knowledge. Marie recovered and joined Tim Bears-Den and Grant Stallion in their lecture tours and forming "Brain Snap Teams" throughout the Stated and Canada.

Chapter 36

Twelve years went by quickly, now it is 2012. The visions that Aunt Amie had in her dream years ago had happened.

The terrorists had succeeded with their attack on the Twin Towers on Sept., 2001, Candy devastated by the loss; took comfort in the fact that many people didn't go to work that day due to her courage. She may have saved 4,000 Jewish people's lives. She had wanted so much more; but it just wasn't possible. The terrorists had won that battle.

The Brain Snap Team realized that the Twin Towers had disintegrated into dust because of the Bioenergetics sent to the towers; not the planes hitting the top floors. It seemed surreal watching the TV newscast when it happened. Not being able to tell anyone what had really happened was harder still. The War in Afghanistan began. It extracted the finest American and Canadian young men and women. Bush had convinced everyone that the Middle East Terrorists had "Weapons of Mass Destruction" The team knew who really had the weapons of mass destruction. Bush's smirk on National Television was sickening, as they knew who the real terrorists were.

Merryl Streep, Hollywood actress put her life on the line to play the part of the Journalist in "Lions for Lambs". That movie relates the real intention for the Middle East; intention to remove the finest young people from our the country. They wouldn't be home to understand what was going on with the corrupt Banking Institutions and the H.A.A.R.P. technology. The media would be concentrating on the war. Little to no coverage exposed for the corrupt banking situation in America.

The Brain Snap Team knew the truth. They were determined to educate the world. They continued to build their generators. Their determination increased with each hit like Katrina in New Orléans on August 29th ,2005. Bush disregarded the people in that hurricane. The Team wondered had this science create this hurricane? Total disregard for life! Even now, no real construction efforts made to restore the area. The team realized that it wasn't Nature, but the terrorists using the weather control that only it could create.

How could they prove what was happening when the government continued to lie and say that the program was a mere research project and again no one connected the dots The terrorists got braver yet and then the earthquakes began with the Tsunami that hit Indonesia and Thailand on Dec 26th 2005.

This time the Brain Snap Team knew there was proof as 30 minutes before the Tsunami hit. There were the **H.A.A.R.P. Rainbow Clouds in the sky. Since then the following earthquakes:**

Mexico City in September 2007, Sichuan, China in May 2008, Haiti in January 2010, Chili in February 2010, and Japan in March 2011. All had the Rainbow Clouds in the sky minutes before the earthquakes hit.

It's Billion Watts of Energy hits the upper ionosphere, heats it, and then, directs this energy to any place on the earth. One understands where these earthquakes are coming from. It's only a matter of time and the other countries will fight back with the same technology. World destruction is the result of this pissing contest.

Mike stated, "Enough is enough!"

The Brain Snap Team created their Internet Radio Broadcast Station.

"The Forth Dimension."

Their intention was to expose H.A.A.R.P.

Robert stated, "Tesla with a mere 30 Watts of power back in 1935 came close to destroying New York with his earthquake experiment. He stopped the earthquake vibration as soon as he realized what he had created.

Imagine the **"Force of a Billion Watts of Microwave Energy"** aimed anywhere in the world. Compare that to 30 Watts! At this time, there exists other similar Research Projects around the world. Infact, there are 17 known Installations on our earth at this time." He continued,

"Canada has one in the North and the Gas and Oil Corporations could easily be using it to open gas deposits deep in the Earth. Not caring, what the consequences are of these blasts. Like a rubber ball, they bounce the energy into the upper Ionosphere and it comes down to Earth where they need the gas deposit opened.

Only problems then is it bounces to wherever and creates an earthquake somewhere else on the planet. The energy produced is uncontrollable. Presently, Oil and Gas Corporations are looking at the Interior of Northern British Columbia which sits near the "Ring of Fire" which includes the entire west coast of America."

Mike interrupted, "In my opinion, if they begin opening these gas deposits with this technology, it will affect the entire west coast creating earthquakes that will send this land area to the bottom of the ocean. The Military already use "The New Earth Map" as a reference. It's a real possibility! **800 Billion Watts of Power or more can create these super earthquakes as easily as sneezing and it can stop earthquakes too. "**

"It can also stop earthquakes and asteroids if this tremendous power is used constructively. It can protect our Earth from the

Asteroid that the Mayans predicted for 2012.

Moreover, there's no need for fossil fuel or Nuclear Power. **H.A.A.R.P. is a source of energy of its own,** which could supply all the energy needed to sustain our planet. We could use this Tesla power and restore our environment and our world to a safe and sane place in the Universe. "Robert added

"Tesla created over 2,000 patents. He wanted our Earth a safer and better place for everyone. The American government stole them from him. They have misused his genius in their greedy attempt to destroy this planet. Maybe, we can stop it." Mike added

Mike and Robert had a large audience on the Internet. They helped Tim Bears-Den and Grant Stallion set up the Brain Snap Teams. They had them on the show often. Their audience grew.

In fact, it had gone crazy with each day the listeners doubling in size. Within three months, they had enough listeners to have a real Political Party. They were outnumbering the lobbyists, who had for so long controlled the government.

On today's show Robert was interviewing Tim Bears-Den

Tim stated, "This same government rewarded the Giant Lending Institutions of JP Morgan, KKR, Black Rock Financial, AIG, Politician Reagan, Glen Hubbard and Martin Feldstein. There is a new Documentary, "Inside Job" released yesterday, which exposes the Poncy Scheme that has defrauded billions of dollars from the unsuspecting American Public.

You, the taxpayer have bailed out these lending institutions so the States wouldn't go bankrupt. This Documentary, "Inside Job" proves these financial criminals deliberately created this Scam. It shows how the Obama Administration rewarded these criminals with government positions. This documentary, "Inside Job" was produced by Charles Ferguson."

INTERRUPTING PROGRAM! NEWS FLASH!

Important news flash! Giant Icebergs off Goose Cove at Northern Newfoundland. Our phone in listener has overheard some mining officials from FJoeisher Bay talking about H.A.A.R.P.'s billion watts of laser energy creating giant icebergs. They are opening a year round ocean for shipping above Northern Canada.

Our government has secretly used and is using H.A.A.R.P. to melt the ice in the Arctic Shield. Their priority is to create a year round open ocean shipping lane. It is why there has been extreme flooding in Manitoba and Saskatchewan.

Moreover, this caused the flooding of the Mississippi, and US' breadbasket. Photographers are taking pictures off Goose Cove. We'll confirm this latest news flash.

It was Rosemarie's turn for an interview on the show.

"Our government is totally corrupt. They've proved that fact, this is just one more time. The last thing our planet needs is to speed up Climate Change. This'll increase the heat of the planet. This ocean rise destroys coastal areas. Something has to stop this. Maybe Jesse Ventura can bring awareness to this latest attempt to destroy our planet.

Only congressman who's confronted the 1% is Jesse Ventura, the former Minnesota Governor. He did four years, from 1999 to 2003. A Navy Seal, Actor, Professional Wrestler, and TV Host and Activist Would you like to know what is really going on in your country; go to his site for the real news. His Youtube video on H.A.A.R.P.'s investigation is mind blowing. Take the time to view it. Awareness is power." Rosemarie stated

"The rest of our elected government officials say nothing at all. This is true for Canadian politics too. The lying and stealing by the members of Parliament in Canada is criminal. No Prime Minister or government official has gone to jail for their proven crimes. We don't even demand that they pay back the money they've defrauded. Millions of dollars stolen from us, the taxpayers! It is outrageous; but nothing happens. We pay our taxes to support our governments. You fought for freedom before and now you have to do it again. It is our tax money that pays for our Military and H.A.A.R.P." Mike added,

Now it was Judy's part of the Internet Broadcast, The Forth Dimension.

"I hear the song, "Dancing in the Streets" the day when the 1% and their established power system are over. At present, it doesn't matter who's elected as they all belong to this same group determined to destroy the middle class. Answer for why there is such a poor electoral vote. People already know this and feel it is hopeless. However, that is exactly what they want you to do. They want you apathetic so you won't vote.

Apathy is what they are hoping for in all elections. Your vote matters! An alternative party is growing. The Conservatives hijacked our last election with illegal tricks to make sure they won the election. A wake up call! A new party is forming; a political alternative." Judy added

The show went back to Robert and he gave the listeners the email address to send money to support their new Party. None of the 1% supported them.

"The Internet can educate all of us. Other countries like Japan and Poland do not want "One World Government" Was that why Poland's political officials and royalty killed when their plane crashed? We're they defiant to the One World Government? Didn't you think it was strange that all of the officials were on one plane? That normally doesn't happen for security sake. Didn't it make you wonder what was really going on?

As for the Japanese, Tsunami and resulting earthquake this was another travesty. They too were defiant of One World Government. Could this be the result of not going along with their mandate?

The people in these and third world countries know what's happening. They want change too. We're not alone in our wish to change things. What lessened the earthquake's power this summer in New York? Was it H.A.A.R.P.? Was it spirit world protecting the city? My insight is

3,000 souls lost in 2001 may be on guard and protecting New York. Hurricane Irene seemed to be gentled too. Was it billion watts of laser energy? There are 17 H.A.A.R.P. installations on Earth now. I wonder which country protected them. Or did Spirit world take care of the city. Only time will tell.

Yes, "Dancing in the Streets" is a real possibility. As a nation, you felt the power of this with Obama's win as President; but now the Americans need to create a new party capable of a true President not bought by the established"1 % Power Group". Robert continued

Rosemarie came back on and added, "When one hears unpleasant news we react at first with ridicule; then with opposition and finally with acceptance. Sometimes we go into denial, bargaining, and finally acceptance. No time to lose. We need to confront this "Power Group" that wish to destroy the middle class and eliminate 80% of the population. We can win when we join each other in our effort. The other nations know what is happening too. We're not alone.

We can win by uniting with other countries via the internet. The Internet gives us, the 99% a voice. We are able to see what is going on all over the world. They won't have an easy win for their "New World Order" which means "One World Government" Power in their hands of one government means Totalitarianism. "

"Communism look like the Garden of Eden. All nations needed for a healthy planet. "Free-Energy" for all Nations needed now. It's time for all Nations to become equal. Yes, Tesla's dream consisted of abundance for all. Enough food for all! Disease and birth disorders healed! Good weather. Hurricanes and earthquakes stopped! H.A.A.R.P. can create all of this. Abundance for all the Nations is a reality." Judy added,

"We can make Tesla's vision of a healed world our own. Our minds believe this concept; it is accomplished. Earth's collective thought overcomes the thoughts of this minority, a mere 1% of the population. It is possible now." Rosemarie continued

"Listen in tomorrow for our interview with Psychic Marie Goldman from Manhattan as she discusses her Predictions of 2012. Her predictions include the discovery of a hidden Mayan Temple and Giza Temple. New technology changes travel. The Healing Blanket now released to heal the Japanese survivors of the 2011 Earthquake. Aunt Amie Goldman predicts a new age in science that will revolutionize our world. Join us tomorrow at the same time and same place." Robert stated

Robert closed the Broadcast of The Forth Dimension for today.

ABOUT THE AUTHOR

Georgia Love discovered at the age of three, that she was clairvoyant and Psychic. Since then she has experienced many spiritual events. She has researched the paranormal for more than 40 years to understand her experiences. To add to her spiritual talents, she has studied the concepts of Modern Astrology, Numerology, Dowsing, and Synchronicity. Georgia has worked with other Psychics and has given readings to hundreds of people over the years in psychic events, radio and television shows.

Her intention in her book, "Escape from Manhattan" is to bring Psychics and Scientists together to understand that they are working with the same energy, Fourth Dimension and Quantum Physics. We are more than meat computers, but divine Spiritual beings.

Georgia offers you clear explanations for your Psychic talents, whether it is dreams, hunches, precognition, or synchronicity. One of her goals is to assist you in developing your intuition.

Moreover, help you to realize that your loved ones in Spirit world protect you. Your loved ones area a breath away and they are ready to help you in all areas of your life; but especially when you are in danger.

Georgia's creative non-fiction, "Escape from Manhattan" shows how the Spirit World created coincidences to guide and protect her characters in difficult circumstances. They were never alone!

www.escapefrommanhattan.com & **www.georgialovepsychic.com**. Georgia welcomes your letters and emails. She is presently working on her next book, The Canadian Mentalist.

Georgia Love; Author, Psychic, Astrologer, and Environmentalist wishes you Blessings from Spirit World and our Infinite Universe.

New found friends are great to Sean Wipfli!

Author Georgia Stre

georgia.love @ live.ca

12006529R00158

Made in the USA
Charleston, SC
04 April 2012